Other Books in print by:
Nik C. Colyer

Channeling Biker Bob 1 Heart of a Warrior
Channeling Biker Bob 2 Lover's Embrace
Channeling Biker Bob 3 Magician's Spell
Channeling Biker Bob 4 Wisdom of the King
Maranther's Deception
Trillian Rising
Kicking Ass and Taking Names
Poetry Through The Eyes of a Tough Guy

All books avaliable through:
Singing Reed Press
P.O. Box 1395
Nevada City, CA 95959
530 265-3566
www.nikcolyer.com

To those souls who stepped in
and out of my twisted youth,
and may you have found peace.

Colyer, Nik C.
    Flamenco Flood / by Nik C. Colyer. — 1st ed.
    p. cm.
    LCCN pending
    ISBN 978-0-9708163-7-5

    1. Fiction. 2. Comedy- fiction. I. Title.

1. goofball tragity. 2.adventure- underbelly-liars-theives-fiction. 3. breaking moral decency-sexual misconduct-Flamanco dancing. 4.romance-love-fiction.

This novel is a work of fiction. It does not intend to represent any person, living or dead.

Printed in the United States of America
10 9 8 7 6 5 4 3 2 1

Flamenco

Flood

Nik C. Colyer

Singing Reed Press
Nevada City, CA

Authors Note

This book represents my 4th completed novel began in the year 1996 and completed in spring of 1997.

Having spent my youth and early adulthood among a more seedy layer of society, I wrote this comedy as a window into the phyche of some of the people I knew during my wild early adult years in the San Francisco Bay area.

My observation from those early experiances is that it doesn't matter what level of society one lives in, we are all surrounded by twisted and disconnected people of all ages who can not see beyond themselves. At the same time, we are also surrounded by caring human beings ready and more than willing to be heros at whatever level is presented to them.

It's an odd world we live in filled with opposing thoughts and modes of living. I do hope you enjoy these pages as much as I enjoyed writing them.

CHAPTER 1

CHICKEN HAVEN

I glared through the bay window of my grandmother's house, combed my long, black hair and wished I had the guts to drop a bomb on my idiot neighbors.

The sad remnants of my expansive view left little for me to enjoy since the Tenican Heights housing development popped up, surrounding my little property like mushrooms after a spring rain.

It was only ten years ago when I wandered the open meadows and lush fields that stretched for miles around grandma's house. It was a home where I'd grown up. With the Sierra Nevada Mountains to the west and a huge California sky, the land seemed endless.

One day in what seemed like a blink, except for the ten-acre parcel grandma Stikes so stubbornly held onto, there were tractors and building crews, lumber and asphalt trucks. By the end of that traumatic summer there stood, not regular single-story houses, which would have left me in sight of my beloved mountains, but massive, high-priced, two and three story structures that blocked any possibility of a view.

Good Housekeeping had done a six-page spread raving about the ultramodern homes with their sculptured lots, each with its own eighteen-inch tall white picket fence. I saw the trimmed lawns, perfectly edged sidewalks and stupid little white fences as a hideous affront to good taste.

What galled me the most, what stuck deep in my craw, what made me want to erect a thirty-foot steel sculpture of a hand flipping off the neighborhood, was the street names of that despicable housing tract.

The endless entangled ribbons of asphalt, the miles of twisting concrete sidewalks and gutters were named after the very animals the development deposed. Horned Owl Lane, Silver Fox Road, Coyote Trail, Mule Deer Street and Raccoon Court were but a few of the sacrilegious designations given to the streets.

Grandma Stikes had been the only holdout when the developers whirl-winded through, buying properties like junk dealers buy dead cars; for pennies on the dollar. It all started exactly ten horrible years ago and I never forgot the day the first representative of Barney, Bowman and Whalde drove onto the property. I was celebrating my twenty-sixth birthday.

The following three months grandma Stikes countered every offer Barney, Bowman and Whalde presented in an attempt to purchase her land. Their first offer was for extra money. When that didn't work, they made thinly disguised threats. Although no one could prove it, we knew who had poisoned our well, killed the animals, broke windows, slashed tires on both cars, tried twice to burn the house to the ground, then finally sent the county to condemn the property.

Louise Renee Stilwalsky, though I called her grandma Stikes, was a skinny eighty-year-old who stood not a bit taller than four feet six. She didn't care how much money was offered or how many thugs they sent over, she wasn't selling.

One day, for the first time in my life, Grandma yelled at me. "Marylou Stalworth, load your grandpa's shotgun, we got another intruder at our door." She pulled back the hammer, poked the gun out an open side window and let loose with both barrels into a dirt pile. "I'm not selling." She yelled through the closed door, and that was the end of it. . . until court.

"This house was built by my father," she told me a hundred times. "This land's been in our family for three generations," she'd told the developers, "and it stays in our family."

"See that front door," she explained to the sheriff when he served her with the summons. "My mother brought that door all the way across the country in a nineteen twenty-two Ford pickup. That door has been in our family for eighty-seven years."

There was a lot of back room maneuvering. I heard pockets had been lined and many favors called in. When old Grandma Stikes was forced to go in front of the county judge, neither Barney, Bowman, or Whalde, nor the board of supervisors knew that she also had a few cards to play, a few back room shenanigans, as she called them. Two of her aces-in-the-hole included her friends Mayor, Bill Herfer and his honor, Stanley Shaine, the presiding judge in the case. Both were heavy hitters in the little Northern California town of Marysville. Both had long-standing allegiances with my grandma. Without anyone knowing what was really going on, the two men pulled a string or two leaving Grandma Stikes as original owner and resident of what was to be slated as the fifth fairway of the nationally famous Tenican Heights.

After every threat they could muster and all the dirty tricks, including a long protracted court battle, the corporation Barney, Bowman and Whalde and the name would forever stick in my craw, were forced to give up.

The developers built the ultramodern, upper-income, security-gated community of Tenican Heights around us. They surrounded our land with a manicured member-only golf course and full service clubhouse. The right side of our little ramshackle house faced a small upscale strip mall that included a first run, surround-sound theater.

I wasn't sure what happened. Was it the long protracted fight with the developers? Maybe it was the heartbreak of watching her little ten acres enclosed by upper-middle-class suburbia. As the first of what proved to be a wave of faceless, unfriendly, fence-building, idiot lawn-mowing, leaf-blowing, noisy neighbors moved in, my grandmother fell ill and died.

Once the development was finished, I noticed there were no streets with chicken species names like Road Island Red Road or Bantee' Court. I supposed the developers had not planned on displacing chickens.

Not long after grandma's death, I bought my first batch of chickens and let them roam the property. Soon after, oh darn, my chickens reproduced. And oops, chickens are an unruly lot, not inclined to stay on my property. They roamed the neighborhoods, cackling, crowing, scratching up manicured lawns and digging gaping holes in flowerbeds.

I hadn't realized until later, but, though the hundreds of ever-excavating chickens were so dear to my angry heart, it was the roosters that became my most prized possessions. My ever growing army of fifty-seven roosters became my favorite 'fuck you' to all my up-tight, upper-middle-class, suburbanite neighbors. I had Bantam roosters, Araucana roosters and Silver Lake Wyandottes. I had every kind of rooster known in the rooster kingdom. Through the wonderful world of unchecked procreation, I also had some new and unknown breeds.

Every day, long before my idiot neighbors were awake, my chorus of roosters began their morning ritual. To my delight, they often crowed through the entire day. Every time a rooster sounded, a small smile rose on my irate lips.

Try as they might, and the residents of Tenican Heights used every method they could, my so called neighbors were unable to rid themselves of my chickens. They used poisons and traps. They got together and put pressure on me. Some lobbed angry shouts across the fence, while others searched out old laws and sent the police to my home. Although, I was ticketed and fined many times, the concerns of my neighborhood fell on delightedly deaf ears.

And so, there it was, a good old Mexican standoff. On one side was me, Marylou Stalworth and my hundreds of ever-reproducing chickens. On the other side, the "too-bad-so-sad" residents of the nationally famous, written-up-in-Good Housekeeping, Tenican goddamn Heights.

Every morning for the last ten years, while combing my long, wavy black hair, I glared out the window at my tight-assed neighbors.

Unlike grandma Stikes, I grew tall and some say pleasingly slender, but I was never pretty in the classic American cosmopolitan manner. I'd long since given up on any attempts at hiding the growing spider web crow's feet sprouting at the outer limits of my blue eyes. I had a secret beauty only apparent after spending time with me. And so, as it goes with most American males not willing to give a second glance, I'd long forgotten what it was like to have a man attracted to me. I'd gone so long without a date I wasn't sure if I could remember how to act.

Although there was no real need, I still went out on grandma's acreage every day and tilled the soil. I grew vegetables and herbs, always careful to hedge the parameter closest to the surrounding neighborhood with the most vile smelling crop I could find.

Other than crowing roosters, only one thing brought a smile to my tired, over-stressed face and let my vindictive angry lips relax. One thing lit my fire, made me tingle and gave my otherwise barren life meaning. That one thing I'd kept secret from the world for five years. It was something I didn't want anyone to know about until I was ready.

On Wednesday and Saturday nights, I drove to the Veterans Hall next to the new mall on the north end of town. With six other townspeople and our teacher, I put on striking red lipstick, a bright gypsy patterned dancing skirt and magically transformed myself from plain old Marylou Stalworth into the dancing gypsy, Cassandra Liltkey. For those special evenings of the week, I turned up the Spanish guitar recordings, got out my castanets, moved to the middle of the floor and swirled for a precious few hours dancing the Flamenco.

Dancing was not only the thing my alter ego, Cassandra Liltkey liked to do, Flamenco dancing was Cassandra Liltkey. It was my new life. It was where I, in a drab mundane world, came fully alive. Every time I danced, I felt wild and sexy, free and light as a feather. I leapt and spun with or without a partner I didn't care. I snapped my castanets and turned into a feral, uninhibited feline.

On the evenings I didn't go to the Veterans Hall, I practiced diligently at home. My lifelong dream was to dance on stage in New York or San Francisco. My vision was to do the Flamenco at the Metropolitan or Albert's Hall in England. Madison Square Garden wouldn't be bad. Hell, I'd take an engagement at the Saturday Night Grange Hall in neighboring Woodland, it didn't matter. After all these years, I wanted to dance in front of people. I wanted to perform for someone other than my fellow Flamenco enthusiasts.

Did my dream come true? I was dancing professionally all right. Fully costumed, rose in my teeth, fire-engine-red fingernails with lipstick to match, I danced in another of a long list of wild gypsy serenades.

Performing on stage was the realization of my dream. A minor feat, albeit, but an achievement just the same.

The music, a flowing Flamenco guitarist's CD I'd picked up in Sacramento, piped out onto the street. I was in the middle of the sixth of eleven scheduled dances, which, it turned out, I would never finish.

That evening was a first step in my budding Flamenco career. Dancing on the dinky stage behind the display window was a humble beginning, but I didn't mind. Cassandra was going to be a gypsy star and I was ready to do whatever it took to attain that goal.

As I twirled and stomped my heals, clicked castanets in perfect rhythm to the guitarist, I locked my attention on a couple under a large umbrella who stopped on the sidewalk to watch me. They were my first audience. I got so excited I almost stumbled and fell. In the middle of a half spin, I caught myself by putting a hand against the plate glass separating me from my coveted fans. The balance problem was momentary and I righted myself with little hesitation.

Both castanets rattling, high-heel shoes stomping the wooden display floor, I twirled my heart out.

Finally, much to my utter disappointment, the couple's interest waned. Holding hands, the two continued down the sidewalk, away from Dickerman's drugstore display window, away from the soon-to-be-famous Flamenco dancer, Cassandra Liltkey.

William Dickerman was using me to attract customers back from the new mall on the north end of town. He billed me as, Cassandra Liltkey, Flamenco dancer extraordinaire.

Once my two fans walked away, my intensity waned. They were my first and once they were gone my first let down. I was determined to attract more, even in the middle of Marysville's month-long downpour. I wanted more onlookers and a bigger audience.

Spectators or not, I was determined to complete my contracted two hours of dancing in the display window of Dickerman's drug. This was my first gig, in what I hoped would be a long Flamenco career. How would I know that my all-important first performance would, even from inside of the drugstore, get flooded out?

* * *

Last week, of all things, I, the great Casanova of the North Valley, Billy F. Marlin, oh so quietly turned thirty-six. The big three-six was too close to over the hill. That birthday forced me to notice my long, straight, surfer-blond hair was thinning. Last month, holy shit, I found three strands of gray in my silky blonde mustache and one in my goatee. Unnoticed during the last year, my skin had turned from the healthy tan of my youth to a humbling pallid gray. My jet-black eyes were glazed and dull, probably from smoking too much pot. My good life was catching up with me. My devil-may-care lifestyle was tapping me on the shoulder and saying I was getting older, no longer a spring chicken."

All week I'd ignored that naggy little voice. I'm only as old as I feel. I'm in my prime. I looked at myself in my cracked wall mirror and flexed. As a result of working out every day at the Marysville Fitness Center, I admired my perfectly formed biceps and patted my rippled, flat stomach. My first fitness objective was to keep my body looking good, but mostly the fitness center, along with Clancy's Bar and Grill, was my place to find what me and the boys called babes.

One week after my pivotal, I'm-getting-older birthday I sat mesmerized on my avocado green, poly-vinyl couch. I held a cold beer in one hand, while my other hand fondled one of the budding breasts of my latest score, Tammy Fae Ballinger. In front of me in living color, though only thirteen inches of color, on a matching green plastic milk crate I'd borrowed from Safeway, I watched my number-one entertainment; daytime television.

Next to the couch sat an empty cardboard box on which to set my beer. The box, TV, couch and milk crate were the only pieces of furniture in my dinky living room. My two-room cabin was nestled in a quiet little out-of-the-way corner of town, backed up within yards of busy interstate seventy. What else could a red-blooded American guy want?

The television story of the never-ending rain sparked my interest. The newscaster's dire predictions of flooding gave me hope for the future, but what really caught my attention, what had me staring with open mouth wonder, was the television news anchor's, what me and the boys at

Clancy's so fondly called hooters.

I saved that special term for only the most perfectly chested women. The news anchor, Yamelda Keating, was at the front of the line on my short list of perfect babes.

She yelled over the pounding rain, "water level at the Yuba and Feather River junction is nine feet above normal." The camera panned the river. It was a stretch we'd all seen too many times in the last eight years.

In the late afternoon, with the help of glaring lights on the chocolate waters, the camera showed that the river was a delighted three feet from the top of the levee.

The news anchor leaned forward and pointed at the churning muck. "I'm standing across from the exact spot where three years ago a hundred-year flood undermined the levee. It sent half of the town of Marysville under ten feet of water for the entire month of February."

I didn't hear a word. Between shots of the river and a weakening levee, I waited for the camera to pan back to her chest, especially since she was leaning over with that low cut blouse. I wondered just how it would feel to latch onto the Keating babe's lip-smackin' tits. Ya-melt-a has tits to die for. It was a nickname I'd given her last year during intermission of a Raiders game and it stuck.

"Billy," squeaked Tammy. "Don't squeeze so hard, you're hurting my nipple."

"Sorry." I released her little nib.

I longed for the full body of a mature woman. I was tired of the little teenagers, the only women I seemed to score. I'd been told I was good looking, but that dark brown birthmark the shape and size of Poland stretching up my neck and lower right jaw was more than troublesome. It left me with a huge handicap when it came to babes. The goatee covered some of the birthmark, but not enough.

My one missing front tooth in a dentist's nightmare of a mouth didn't help.

Hell, I'm thirty-six, got an iron body, I can press two-eighty. I got money. What more could a good lookin' babe like Ya-melt-a want?

I liked sex with Tammy as I'd liked sex with every other little twit I'd been with in the past fifteen years. But, somewhere deep inside I was not satisfied. Something was not being taken care of and I was sure Ya-melt-a would be just the woman to fill in that hole in my life. If I could have her for just one night things would be so different. Maybe only an hour. Hell, fifteen minutes is all I'd really need to get straight.

* * *

I stood military straight in a fully vested, dress-for-success Armani navy blue suit. The three gold nuggets attached to my tie clasp had been found in the very river I was looking at. The clasp gripped my solid light blue tie exactly twelve inches from the top button of my blue and white striped silk shirt. My dark blue slacks were precisely creased and cut to fall exactly in the center of my spit-shined wingtip shoes.

With professionally manicured hands folded behind me, fingers nervously twirling a pencil, I look through my window with twelve-inch tall gold lettering that spelled out my name for all to see; Harry S. Trunk. Through the glass, I saw the rising waters of the mighty Yuba. I stood four stories up in the tallest building in Marysville, directly over the very levee that had given the south side so much trouble three years ago, three years earlier and two years before that.

The north side of the levee had been reinforced and strengthened with concrete fifty years earlier. The mighty Yuba never flooded the more affluent side of town, but the Yuba inundated the first floor of my building and my sixty slum houses many times.

Floods and threats of floods happened many times over my fifty-seven years. I'd seen much come and go in my little town of Marysville, but I could take to the bank the certainty that the river would flood. The only pressing question was, would it flood this year? I needed the flood.

The only thing out of place in a vision of corporate perfection was my cue-ball bald head, a flattened nose I'd acquired in grammar school and one glass eye which never quite pointed in the right direction. The glass eye was the very thing I blamed whenever I failed in negotiations with fellow businessmen. Everyone seemed so distracted by its wanderings.

I chewed a toothpick that twirled and flipped between my lips more rapidly with every inch of rising water. I gauged the nervousness of my day with the number of toothpicks I'd shredded. That day I'd chewed twenty-two to a pulp.

I wasn't afraid that the thirty days of a solid downpour would cause the levee to flood. I wasn't nervous because all sixty of my slum tenements were on the weak side of the levee. I was more afraid that the river might not flood.

* * *

I sprinted across the parking lot trying my best to miss the deeper puddles. I wasn't going to soak my new socks and be forced to work another shift in wet feet. I was about as tired of the rain as anyone in or around Marysville could be, but I had to get to work and my boss forbade his employees from parking close to the restaurant.

The torrents of rain decided to get stronger as I reached midpoint of the Lyndon B. Johnson municipal parking lot. Only Marysville would dedicate the crappy back street lot to our forty-third president.

While I strained to see more than ten feet beyond my Day-Glow umbrella, the rain turned to a wall of water.

Three quarters of the way across the lot, I felt wetness under my sneakers and gave up any hope of dry feet. At the very same moment, a gust of wind whipped my umbrella inside out. With a shift in resolve, I made a beeline sprint for the stark single light of the back door. I yanked on the rotting wood door and leapt inside. A warm blast of air hit my wet face.

"Hey Bunny," called Sandy, my gum-popping co-worker as she picked up and balanced a huge platter of food in each hand. She bound into the chaos of the restaurant.

Jack, my boss, yelled from the kitchen, "Get your butt in gear, Ollinski, we've got a full house."

I pulled my destroyed new umbrella closed and hung it and my rain slicker on the row of spikes nailed to the wall. I took a quick glance at the clock and read four-forty-seven. Sandy rushed back from the main floor. "I need help, Marie. See what you can do with that disaster you call hair and get out here."

I stepped inside the closet-sized employee bathroom and looked in the mirror at my limp bleach-blond hair. I almost cried. I'd worked more than two hours on my new style. All that was left of it and my creative two hours were three bobby pins and a limp yellow ribbon.

The hair dryer came out in a flash. I worked frantically, if not to revive the new style at least to salvage what was left in my remaining twelve minutes.

While teasing my drying hair, I glanced at the small amount of makeup around my eyes and grimaced at the smeared mess the manufacturer had guaranteed was waterproof.

Still drying my hair with one hand, I pulled some of the stiff institutional toilet paper out and wiped away the color.

At that very second, for the first time in my life, I saw them.

"Oh my god," I gasped. Horror struck, I set the drier and toilet paper in the sink. My right hand came up. I traced their horrible, ugly path. "I've got crow's feet," I murmured with a whine into the mirror. "I've got wrinkles."

It hadn't exactly been a great day. I'd felt like crying since I woke up, but wrinkles? It was my first lines in an almost perfect, you-could-be-in-the-movies face. I was looking at my first marks of age. I glanced at the clock and had only five minutes to consider the implications. Crying about getting old would have to wait. Whining about going over the hill was not an option. I had to earn a living and feed my two kids. There was no one else out there who would, including that sleaze of an ex-husband, Jake-the-snake.

At one minute to five, still soggy shoed, I stepped out of the bathroom, unbuttoned the top button of my blouse and walked onto the floor of the locally famous, Torez family Mexican Restaurant. The fifty-table room was packed and the crowd looked agitated. That fact never entered my conscious mind, but later I remembered something was awry.

CHAPTER 2

YA-MELT-A

I knew nothing of Billy Marlin's odd fascination with my stunning body parts. If I had, I probably would've taken that job in Fresno last September. Fact is, I knew nothing of the hundreds of Billy Marlins' out there in television land drooling over my famous, though secretly enhanced, orbs. I didn't go under the knife for all of those salivating pubescent wonders to ogle me. I did it for my goddamn career. Look where it got me, stuck in this fucking jerkwater town, in a dead-end job. All the networks could offer me was Fresno? God, I hated Fresno even more than this piece of crap little dipshit town.

For the second time that day, I stood under the roll-out canopy, next to the network motor home, atop the Yuba River levee, waiting for the crew to put the finishing touches on the setup. I looked across the river at greater downtown Marysville and the tallest building in town. Back lit by the only light shining on the top floor of the building, I saw the shadow of a man. Was he looking at me? I wanted to flip him off. He was inside his warm, dry office, while I was forced to stand in the downpour. I knew who he was. I knew all too well about Harry Trunk and I didn't like anything about the slippery bastard.

"Okay, Yamelda," yelled Buster Klouse, my producer.

I turned toward the crew. "Okay, what?"

"We're ready."

"Somebody give me a goddamn umbrella."

I stepped into the downpour and walked twenty feet to the inside edge of the levee. The floodlights came on and I looked over at the camera, microphone in hand.

Buster rocked to the rhythm of the countdown as he held one finger up. All I could hear was the thundering rain, so I waited for him to make a last rocking motion and point.

The second the little red camera light flicked on, I shifted from my, get-me-out-of-this-fucking-downpour grimace to that famous Yamelda Keating worried television smile. I did what I knew how to do best.

"We're standing across from the very section of the levee that gave way and flooded our fair city three years ago." I turned and pointed at the opposite bank, then down at the boiling water less than a foot from the top of the levee. I dutifully read the prompter so smoothly it sounded like the sentences were coming from my own thoughts. I reported about the levee, the water, the weather conditions and possible damages if the levee decided to give way again. My last sentence on the prompter before the live broadcast was over and I could get out of that goddamn downpour, was, "We've had two levee breaks in the last six years. This may be a third. We've suffered without the protection of a flood dam because our neighbor's upstream want to preserve a silly little waterfowl area. Come on fellow Sacramento Valley residents, let's get busy and build ourselves a flood dam so this problem won't plague our fair city of Marysville ever again."

The camera and lights went dead. I ran twenty-five feet, ducked under the RV canopy, handed the umbrella to Buster and raced up the three steps into the warm, dry motor home. Sylvia handed me a towel. I patted my face and hair carefully so as not to mess my makeup. "Jesus, no one should be out in this rain and no one should be forced to do an on-site newscast on a day like this."

"Eits yer job," Sylvia said in her heavy south of the border accent. I had no idea what part of Mexico Sylvia came from nor did I care.

"I resent doing the news in this little shit-kickin' town."

"Some days yous gets breaks."

"Some kind of national news story would give me a shot at the bigs. Something juicy. I need something hot."

"Yous needs breaks."

"No shit, but there are no mass murders or spectacular plane crashes. There are no drive-by gang shootings or riots. There are definitely no earthquakes or even any big fires. There is nothing in this crappy little town except for a car crash now and then and not even a multiple car crash. We have petty thieves and their opposites, the cops and this never-ending, goddamn downpour. I'm so tired of the rain."

"Me's too."

I watched the crew break down getting soaked in the process. Suddenly, the water surged and crested the top of the levee. When it spilled over it covered the crew's feet.

I pointed out the window at the rising water and screamed, "The camera should be on this." I swung the door open, stepped down into the muddy syrup and made sure the camera was rolling. Never one to shirk any possibility of breaking news, I hefted my umbrella and stepped away from the van. The lights followed me.

"The water has swelled, again" I shouted with horrified excitement. I pointed at the ground. "The water is pouring over the levee." I sloshed sideways making sure I was still in view of the camera. To hell with my hair and screw the makeup, this was where I felt alive. I wasn't reporting the news, I was the news."

I paced a ten-foot arc, splashing through the muddy water, continuing a constant monologue about what happened, speculating on what might happen, while the five-man crew scrambled to pack the gear. My arms swung. My face aglow. I watched Buster for any indication of when he'd had enough. I could go for as long as he wanted. There was an endless amount of verbiage I could throw at the camera.

A bright flash of lightning struck. A deep-throated rolling thump lifted me four inches into the air. Was it a quake? I braced myself for the tremble. I prepared to drop to my knees. I looked at the camera. No matter what, I was going to continue the monologue. I would dance with the tremor and shift to the subject of earthquakes. I wanted to be the first to report the quake. This broadcast was going to be a doozy.

When I landed, I was off balance. I felt my feet sink into the living earth and I screamed. I looked down and tried to lift a foot. One of my favorite high-heels slipped off. With fear in my expression I looked at the camera and it was still running.

"Buster," I yelled as the loose mud gripped me. The water rose. It forced me further off balance. I put my hands out to break the fall. I fell to my knees in a foot of freezing water.

"Buster." I yelled.

When I looked up there was nothing. The huge motor home was gone. The scrambling crew had gone with it. Worst of all, the camera and lights had disappeared. There was the dark silhouette of the four-story building with that single light. Before the water washed me over the edge, I saw the silhouette in the window. It was that sleaze-ball bastard Harry Trunk.

* * *

I was tired of waiting out the rain. I was fed up with sitting around watching TV and drinking beer. Breast fondling was the only thing I wasn't tired of, but I was even tired of Tammy's tits. I'd been inside the house for the better part of the day. Tammy and me had spent most of the morning practicing Billy inspired sex positions. I only drank two six-packs so far, but I felt thickheaded and numb.

I picked up the phone and pushed the re-dial button. The number rang my best bud, Sundog Anderson. He was the only person I ever called.

As the phone rang, I thought for the hundredth time that no mom would ever name a guy Sundog. In the five years I'd known him, I never weaseled any other name out of him.

I re-dialed twice and let the phone ring four times each call. It was The Dog Man's secret code.

He answered with his normal gruff voice. "What the fuck you want?"

I tried to match him. "Hey Dog, what the fuck you up to?"

My voice always shifted when I talked with The Dog Man. As much as I tried not to, I spoke with a nervous titter. Whenever Sundog was around, I felt uneasy. I was awed by him. He was three years older, much smarter and decades more street savvy.

Being Sundog's bud gave me extra points with the guys and babes at Clancy's. Best of all, being Dog's friend gave me suction with our boss, Harry Trunk.

Hangin' with The Dog Man wasn't being buds with just

anyone. It was a privilege to be around someone so cool.

"It's time we got going," I said, then let out that involuntary titter.

"Get fucking goin' for what?"

Dog was in rare form. It must have been the rain. The rain got to everyone.

I took a deep breath and tried to speak in my regular voice. "The Yuba's ready to flood. It's time to get out there and save some souls." It was our secret code.

His voice changed. "Yeah, let's save some souls. I'll meet you at the storage in ten minutes."

Our storage garage was kind of a hideout. No one knew about it but Dog and me. We rented it under assumed names. It was a place to store extra tools; old car parts; some drugs and any guns we happened to come across. We also stored what was left of the blasting caps and the remains of what was once a full box of dynamite. Included in the inventory of tools, were two of the best canoes left from last summer's forays to the Russian River. The used canoe and fishing boat business blossomed after a spring jaunt to the coast, where we found miles of unlocked boats along the river. Most were simply tied to stumps.

On warm, moonlit summer nights, we'd float downstream plucking boats like picking flowers. When we reached the rental truck parked on a quiet side road, we spent the rest of those long night hours loading the truck. Each truckload of boats, a single night's work, netted us thousands.

Once the Russian River locals caught on, Dog Man and me expanded to other rivers and lakes. We brought into town three truckloads of boats a week and sold them on Craig's List. It was a profitable summer.

It wasn't easy work, though. I finally called it quits when I hurt my back one evening trying to lift a ski boat four feet into the back of the freaking truck.

"Hey, Dog," I said while playing darts at Clancy's that next night. "We gotta' find a better way to make an honest living."

Sundog had his arm around a blonde in her late teens. "Yeah, this hauling heavy shit is for the birds. We gotta' find something easier."

With plenty of money in our pockets to get us through the winter, we kept two of the best canoes in storage and the next week worked out a plan for the rainy season. It was a good plan that called for waiting patiently for the right moment and that time had come.

I dressed, put on my rain slicker and told Tammy in my most manly tone, "I'll be back tomorrow."

She looked up from the television. "Where are you going?"

"Never mind. I'll be out all night."

She stood and put one hand on her hip. "Tell me where you're going, Billy Marlin or I won't be here when you get back."

"Never you fucking mind where I'm going."

Her voice got louder as I opened the front door. "You asshole. How can I have a relationship with you?"

I cringed at the "R" word, but kept moving. I had business to take care of and no twit from Clancy's was going to stop me by screaming, which she did loud enough that I could hear over the pounding rain until I got into my truck and slammed the door.

Once I managed to get my engine running, I feathered the gas and sat in the cold cab listening to distant thunder.

Maybe I'll make enough to rid myself of this old wreck and get a new Toyota four-by-four. I turned and grimaced out the back window at the half-crushed truck bed. Last winter it had been a nice truck for a sixty-two Chevy. The only tree in our entire neighborhood decided to fall across the driveway and put two semicircular dents the size of a bowling ball down both rear panels. Nothing else was hurt, but the blow to my restoration plans left me with a barely drivable bucket of bolts. With a new Toyota, I could cruise the streets with my head held high again. I'm sure a new truck would help the babe factor and I could get rid of Tammy.

Under a darkening sky, my truck lumbered toward town. Because of the downpour, three miles to the storage locker seemed like thirty.

Dog yelled, "what the fuck took you so long?"

I rushed from the truck to the open shed door. "Got caught in a flood on Seventh. Water was so deep it came up through the holes in my floor."

Dog grinned. "More water the better."

It was going to be a very cool night working with The Dog Man and netting a boat full of goodies.

We loaded two canoes and the black box into my truck, then drove toward the setting sun that peeked through a thin split in the black clouds. It was the only sun anyone had seen in a week. A moment later the light was gone leaving only the threat of a stormy night. It was exactly what we wanted.

* * *

I stood, nervously twiddling my twenty-second toothpick, glaring through the foot high gold leaf letters that spelled out my name.

For the second time that day the huge, silver RV was parked on the opposite bank of the levee and the news crew was setting equipment up. Yamelda, pain-in-the-ass, Keating was pacing under the awning.

When the camera lights flooded the river, I smiled. The water had risen another foot. My lifesaving flood was coming, it was only a matter of waiting.

Because of certain persons I didn't want to think about, I was in way over my financial head. It started ten years ago when I got in a little too deep with the Tenican Heights development clowns. Everything was fine until that old bitty on the fifth fairway balked and we were forced to go to court. During the eight-month legal battle construction was put on hold. I'd thrown every extra penny at that development and my finances didn't have eight months for legal battles. All my bills came due long before the groundbreaking ceremonies.

Had I'd thought it through, I probably would have been more cautious, but it was a chance to throw in with the shakers and movers of the land development crowd. The project was supposed to be well toward completion before my first in a long series of payments was due. If that old Stikes bitch hadn't put up a fight, we would have begun in the early spring instead of late fall and things would have turned out a whole lot different.

I glared out the window while I remembered that the only glitch, the only proverbial fly in the ol' ointment, was old Stilwalsky. When she stalled the project, I was left holding nothing but my dick.

At the end of the first year, with not one shovel of ground turned, in what would become Tenican Heights, the most famous housing development in history, my loan balloons came due. With all my political connections, everyone I had in my back pocket, and all the favors called in, I was only able to hold the banks off for a few months. Unfortunately, a few months wasn't long enough.

Less than two months before the housing development lost the court battle, less than three months before the first ground was broken and sales from lots began rolling in, I was forced to sell out to those bastards, Barney, Bowman and

Whalde. The worst part was, I sold for a dime on the dollar.

I lost my house and twenty years of work in one single day. I walked away with my loans covered and one medium-sized lot overlooking the third fairway. I rented a small apartment on the East Side of town and was left with a very large chip on my shoulder. Of course, Barney, Bowman and Whalde were well protected. Anything short of out-and-out vandalism, which I frequently considered, left me with no recourse. I was out in the rain while those shystering thieves raked in the money.

When Louise Stilwalsky died a few months later, my anger would not be avenged. I raged at that stubborn Romanian granddaughter. Every opportunity I got, I went out of my way to disrupt, disturb or discombobulate her life.

With the help of that butt-ugly Sundog and his little buddy Billy Marlin, during the next few years, I made Marylou Stalworth's existence a living hell.

I had the boys tear up her garden. They muddied her hanging laundry. Repeatedly, they poisoned her well. They broke windows. Twice the bumbling idiots tried to burn the house down and didn't succeed.

After the second year I tired of harassing Stalworth, but I was left harboring deep resentment that grew through the following decade.

It took three stressful, hard-working years to land solidly back on my feet. When I bought my first slum rental house in the flood zone and collected the insurance that next winter to repair it, I was able to buy four more buildings. In the aftermath of the next year's flood, I purchased sixteen houses. Ten years later I had sixty units and another a financial base. Again, I was in the driver's seat.

Last year the stock market plummeted. When pork bellies and metal futures took a steep dive, I dove for the phone. By the time I got through to my broker, it was too late.

I'd done plenty of shouting on that fateful day. I shouted at my secretary. She quit. I shouted at Henning, my biggest insurance client. Henning had another agent the next day.

When I got home that night, for the first time in fifteen years, I shouted at my wife. She packed her bags and spent the night at her girlfriend's. She hasn't been back since. A week ago she filed for divorce, claiming half of my hard-earned assets. Why can my wife claim half of everything? She never worked a lick in her entire life. How could the judge possibly give her half?

Through all of those events, on that fateful day in April when pork bellies puked their guts out, when metals took a flying leap, came the most devastating blow of all. A few minutes after my wife left, I yelled at my bulldog Sherman. Sherman hasn't spoken to me since.

I lost my proverbial shirt on that day and I'd been sliding downhill ever since. The flooding of my tenements will give me income to recoup like it had three years ago. I heavily padded the accounts during reconstruction and paid some bills with the proceeds. Because I was the insurance agent handling my own accounts, no one was the wiser.

I wished for the days when investments were a thing to play with like Monopoly. Mostly, I wished for a night when Sherman wanted to crawl on my lap again.

I watched Yamelda Keating face the camera as the water surged and overflowed its banks. I saw those crazy news people continue to shoot footage of the overflow. I saw the flash of lightning and heard the thunder. The building shook. The windows rattled. My false plate fell loose and banged against my bottom teeth. I clamped down as the massive motor home slipped over the edge, out of sight, as if it were being lowered down an express elevator. I saw that damn

Yamelda Keating fall to her knees and crawl away in a foot of water. I stood mesmerized while a sixty-foot section of the levee, the disastrous opposite side, the affluent, well-protected, concrete-reinforced north side opened and gushed water. For the first time in fifty years, the north barrier peeled back like a carton of milk and released a gigantic wall of chocolate floodwaters. The muddy Yuba gushed into the streets. It flowed into neighborhoods. It went first to the extremely wealthy, then the rich and finally, far out past the well-off neighborhoods to the upper middle class.

My face dropped. My ridged body drooped while my hopes plummeted. Once again, my whole life was in ruin. I was washed up. I didn't know if I had the energy to start again.

There was one flyspeck of a positive twist in the whole affair of my ravaged life. My wife will get half my assets all right, she'll get half of nothing.

CHAPTER 3

LEVEE PUDDING

"Well, shit," Sundog screamed at the windshield as we pulled up to the spot we'd so carefully prepared last autumn. "There's a motor home sitting right on top of our section of the levee."

I looked through the wall of water pounding my truck. "What'll we do, Dog?"

He slammed my dash. "Their tough luck. We go with the program. If they're lucky, they'll move before we put our little plan into action. If not. . ."

I pulled off the highway and down a back road that ran parallel with the levee. I parked under the old oak tree and switched my lights off. In the dark, I turned to Dog. "I'm worried about that motor home."

"Look here, pansy, they want to sit on a levee during a flood, it's their business, not ours. What, you gunna' go warn 'em?"

I wanted to say yes, but the tone in Dogs voice told me a warning wasn't an option.

The Dog Man opened his door, pulled his slicker over his head and got out of the truck. I followed his lead and met him around front.

He pointed forward along the levee. "We got to find the boulder we painted yellow last September. Let's spread out. Should be here somewhere."

It took ten minutes to spot the rock. I yelled to Dog and pointed. The rain kicked up another notch as we got to the truck and climbed in.

I looked at the RV. "Maybe I ought to warn them."

"And risk getting caught? I don't think so."

"They're probably a couple of old codgers camped out for the night. I'll slip over and let them know about the levee."

"Fuck 'em," said Dog.

I didn't like that aspect of our undertaking. I really didn't want anyone getting hurt. Since The Dog Man came up with the idea, he was the leader. I hadn't really thought much about it, but Sundog was always the leader. If I wanted in, I had to keep my mouth shut and follow along. I knew the rules of manhood and I knew how to be a team player.

I stepped out into the rain and pushed the canoes aside to get the black box. I drug the heavy box fifty yards over to the yellow rock while Sundog unearthed two wires and hooked them to the box. Both of us looked at one another. We'd spent long hours of hand auguring the holes at night so no one could see. We carefully placed the holes and more carefully inserted sticks of dynamite, then replaced the dirt. How could I forget the long hours of burying a half-mile of eighteen gage wire we got at the flea market in Woodland?

Plans had been hatched and carried through. That's

what I liked most about Sundog. He always came through.

I looked through the downpour. Sundog grinned. We rose our arms into the air and smacked hands together high over our heads. In the roar of the ceaseless rain, we yelped. I reached down and pulled the army surplus plunger up, then quickly shoved it back into the box. At that second flood lights came on all around the RV.

Nothing happened and I must have screwed up. I was ready to do the plunger again when a bolt of lightening struck the far side of the levee. Through the flash of the lightening, I saw the levee bulge then settle back into itself.

While we stood dumbfounded, mouth-dropped-open in awe, unable to tell one way or the other if the dynamite had taken effect, in the darkening sky the huge RV listed, then toppled. Once the RV was over and its lights extinguished, the night turned ink black. Other than an occasional strike of lightening to illuminate the breach, we saw little.

It wasn't until I heard the rush of water that I knew for sure the levee had opened. When the wall of water hit me at the knees, knocking me to the ground and sloshing me toward the truck I realized maybe we should have parked on top of the levee.

I found my footing and dragged myself out of the freezing water up the side of the levee. Too dark to see anything, I stumbled along, imagining water flooding my truck. It's probably finding its way through the rotted floorboard, inside the cab and destroying my new stereo system. It was a birthday present installed a week ago. I thought about the five hundred-dollar speakers. Then it came to me. I screamed for Dog. "The canoes are in the back of my pickup truck."

I looked around in the ink blackness and saw nothing.

I raced along the dike, climbed over bushes, stumbled on boulders and got to the truck in time to see one canoe rotate away. I leapt into the freezing water and grabbed at the second canoe as it swirled off into the darkness. In seconds, my swamped truck was out of sight. I was left hanging onto the side of the canoe.

When I couldn't find a way to get in without capsizing the boat, I realized I might be in serious trouble. The freezing water was quickly sapping my strength. Finally, as a last ditch effort, I leapt into the boat from one end and found myself awkwardly out of the ice water, shivering in the bottom of the twirling canoe.

It wasn't until it hit something, jarring me out of my stupor that I understood my ordeal was not over.

I had to get control of the canoe and find a way to dry land before I was really safe.

I sat up and looked out into the black boiling water to get my bearings. To my left I heard a squeak of a female cry for help. Next it came from up front. It came from the right. I felt dizzy.

If I'm to get this job done, I'd better not be helping any damsels. Instead of a knight in shining armor, saving the fair maiden, I imagined her to be some middle aged fat chick who would sink the boat. The image helped.

I found the paddle and tried to regain control until I felt something snag and pull my little watercraft down on one side. I leaned to counter balance and glared into the blackness at the problem. Two ghostly hands, a woman's hands, gripped the gunnel. A drowning, rat-like creature bobbed up from the edge and mewled, "help me."

Holding onto the side of the canoe was all she had left. She cried out those two pitiful words with her last breath. I felt sorry for the poor thing. I reached out for her hands and had a flash of apprehension. What if she's a chunker? I won't be able to get her in. Hell, I almost wasn't able to get into the boat myself.

I thought about my hero Sundog. It would be an easy thing to loosen her fingers and let her slip into the muddy swirl. No one would know. It's what The Dog would do.

I reached out to help her to her fate, but I couldn't bring myself to do it. I grabbed her wrist as the last of her strength waned and she let go. Oh Jesus, now that I've saved her she's my responsibility. She's going to screw up my plans?

"Oh fuck it," I screamed into the downpour, on the ever-spinning canoe. I pulled her up dragging her limp head over the edge. When I reached over the side to get another grip, I sighed with relief. She wasn't fat after all. I reached my hand down and grabbed her by the crotch. Like landing an oversize fish, I yanked her up and in almost capsizing the boat.

She flopped into the bottom of the canoe coughing and sputtering.

Too quickly I was faced with another dilemma as the boat slipped under a massive oak and tangled itself in the branches. By the time I untangled the mess and floated free my new passenger was sitting. I saw an inky silhouette superimposed over the black sky, but other than my intimate knowledge of her sex, I couldn't make out any features.

"What happened?" She asked with a shivering voice between coughs and sputters.

Even in the pouring rain, with only two little words said between us, me, Billy F. Marlin, Casanova-of-the-twentieth-century, Gods-everlovin'-gift-to-woman, man-among-men, a-legend-in-my-own-mind, recognized her.

Since she wasn't squeaking for help any longer, I knew that husky voice too well. I'd heard her hundreds of times, thousands of times and I couldn't believe it was her. Rather than come out and ask like any other normal person might do, me, Mr. smooth-talker, pulled out my four-battery Mag light and flashed it in her face.

"Yamelda!" I said.

"Get that fucking light out of my eyes, you idiot."

* * *

From my dry perch in the tallest building in downtown Marysville, my twenty-forth toothpick swirling, I watched with fascination as the motor home lifted slightly, listed and then disappeared behind the levee with a huge gush of water.

I watched in shock as Yamelda, goddamn, Keating got knocked to her knees and washed out of sight. I wished I could do something, but on second thought, maybe not. She'd been a thorn in my butt for years. She'd relentlessly dogged me ever since the Tenican disaster. Because of her, I'd been on the news more than the weather and she hadn't painted a pretty picture. Good riddance!

The gap in the levee widened allowing water to gush toward downtown.

I'd worked out all the details. I counted on the flood. When the rains hadn't stopped, I celebrated. With each rising foot of water I toasted to future success. When the far side of the levee, the freaking wrong side, gave way, my buildings were not going to be flooded. Never mind that the entire WASS news team was washed over the side and probably drowned. I didn't consider that most of upper class Marysville was going to be under water. It was the biggest disaster in fifty years. All I could think about was what was going to happen to my extremely overextended investments.

* * *

I signed my pharmacy check, spelling each letter in my mind as I wrote, William H. Dickerman. Having the gypsy dance in my window was certainly a business expense. It wasn't suppose to be for me that she danced, but for my customers. Who could have known that the never-ending rain would keep everyone in the new mall on the north end of town?

I admit, I'm a little enamored with gypsies. I especially like the gypsy famous dancing styles called the Flamenco. Okay, once in a while I fantasized about gypsies. More specifically, one might say, I loved watching the Gypsy, Cassandra Liltkey. When she danced the Flamenco, she was the epitome of womanhood. I appreciated the clicking castanets and watched enraptured when she spun and twirled in my store display window. Something deep inside me responded to her stomping feet. Her dance was so firm and commanding. Her entire personality, especially when she danced, brought forward her uninhibited feline. I wanted to join her, to sweep her off her feet and dance the Flamenco with her. But alas I was old. I'd squandered my youth on the drug store. I felt silly to be seventy-three and hopelessly in love with a woman so deliciously young. It was a love fraught with perilous pitfalls, but I was ever hopeful. It was a one-sided love that had flared up a few days before and was burning hot like a brush fire. It was the first time I'd felt that way since my wife of forty-two years died six years ago. I'd loved Lucille for all those years.

I had also loved my drugstore for almost as long. Other than that beautiful young woman, who danced and spun in my display window, I saw nothing else. I could hardly keep my mind focused on filling prescriptions, what few I had.

Since Lucille's death, I'd longed to buy an Air Stream trailer and live with the gypsies. I read everything I could about gypsy life. I drove all the way to San Francisco one night to attend the Romanian Gypsy Ballet. I've seen every movie even hinting about gypsies. I read Stephen Kings novel Thinner seven times. There was a secret part of me who wanted to travel with a gypsy band. I wanted to wake up every morning in an excitingly new and different place.

Since Lucille died, I longed for the freedom of not having to wait on sick and cranky people. I was tired of dolling out mood altering medications to all of the pill popping, drugged out residents of my town. It seemed the richer they got and I had many wealthy customers, the more demanding and rude they became. I was tired of being the whipping boy of every strung out housewife, every stressed out professional or depressed person who came through my door. Unfortunately, eighty percent of my business was people who needed drugs simply to cope with every new day.

I wanted to live more simply. I wanted out. It would only stand to reason that me, Mr. White-bread, Mr. Middle-America, with not the remotest possibility of joining the gypsy's, would fall in love with a flamenco dancer.

All of my longings were in place way before Cassandra Liltkey came on the scene. With my unrequited dreams, the drug king at Dickerman's drug store was destined to fall madly in love with the slender, dark-haired, Romanian woman, who, only four days ago had walked into my drugstore for lipstick. I fell head-over-heals after her purchase turned to conversation, which then shifted to Flamenco. I was a goner once Cassandra Liltkey announced that she loved dancing Flamenco. I ached with desire. If not sex, because I was old and had forgotten what sex was about, I simply wanted be in her company.

Once the doors were closed and the lights were out, I was going to ask her to dine with me. I felt like a schoolboy.

An old but familiar knot of fear arose in my stomach. I watched her from behind my prescription counter. I tried to work, but a big part of me wanted to be out in the window dancing with her. My weak heart would certainly give out if I'd ever attempted such a thing, but I still wanted to.

I looked at my watch and it was two hours before my seven-thirty closing. It would take that entire time before I could gather the courage to ask her to dinner. How would I know, I had less than ten minutes to do anything but run.

* * *

The restaurant was full. Most of the tables in my section were packed. I'd been hustling to take and deliver orders, pouring coffee, smiling, cracking jokes. I was certain every person could see my freshly sprouted wrinkles. There was an automatic tendency, now that I knew they were there, to reach up and cover the grotesque lines. Never mind that my shoes were so wet I sloshed. I was busy and though the crow's feet were still in the forefront of my thoughts, wet shoes had completely slipped my mind. Besides, I've worn wet shoes before. With the amount of walking I did in the restaurant they would be dry by the end of my shift.

There was a delighted exuberance I felt when waiting on people. I worked my crowd however I liked. Whatever mood I was in I brought out that same mood in my customers. I could see my name on some marquee. "Marie Bunny Ollinski, thespian extraordinaire". I was an actress with unmatched talents. I had a roll to play. The better I played my part of supplicant waitress, the jokester, playful temptress, dominatrix, the better the tips. It was easy.

I shifted to the demands of each table. My extra efforts often netted me two hundred a night in tips. In a conservative town such as Marysville, a hundred a night was great.

I never bragged about tips. My tables were always full. It didn't matter where in the restaurant I was stationed my customers followed me.

That night was no different. I smiled at one table, told a raunchy joke at another and was quiet and demure at another. It kept me busy, which was my main objective.

I was pouring Burgundy for two couples on table fourteen and sensed they needed to laugh. They had not been having much fun lately. My job was to be the catalyst for their laughter and lightheartedness. The first time I approached the table to get drink orders, I got them to giggle. The second contact, I left them cracking up. It was a tight-assed sort of laughter, but it was the effect I was looking for. The bottle of wine was a big help for an evening of gaiety. I'd just finished my little story about wine, good food and good friends to share it with. I was about to launch into a quick, well-versed joke, when Felicia did the big no-no in a crowded room. She let loose with a bone chilling scream and dropped a huge tray with four platters of food.

The scream automatically snapped my head around. When the tray hit the floor, I winced. The cringe caused my newly found crows feet to crinkle. My gaze quickly shifted to Felicia's pointing finger. I couldn't fully comprehend what was going on. How could water squirt from around the front door?

I knew the front door was leaky, but the inward cascade of water was ridiculous. I stared in wonderment. I had only a few seconds for everything to sink in. A woman in table thirty-eight screamed. I turned toward her pointing finger. The fake leaded glass windows bulged. I stood slack jawed. The bay window exploded inward. A massive column of chocolate liquid washed table fifty-five and catapulted its occupants across the crowded room toward me.

* * *

To describe a gathering of lions, one would call them a pride. Subsequently, wouldn't a group of wolves be called a pack? A skulk of foxes would be an apt description for those shy creatures. How about a bevy of quail? A gaggle of geese? A flock of turkeys? I love the term, a murder of crows. What about a troop of monkeys? My favorite of all is a parliament of owls. I also liked an exhalation of larks. When it came to depicting a group of Volkswagen beetles I could only describe them as a shit load of bugs.

For reasons beyond my ability to comprehend, I loved four things in life. The old Volkswagen beetle was ever first on my list. I bought one and reconditioned it whenever I had the opportunity. When I finished, my cars were cherry. I rebuilt the engine, trans-axle, new glass, new seat covers and new paint. I even replaced the rubber gaskets around the doors. I loved Volkswagens so much that each new car, no matter what condition, became my obsession.

Out of the eleven classic bugs I owned, my favorite was my 1954 fire engine red, six-window coup.

I'd been looking for a twelfth to round out the set.

I had no idea what to do with twelve cars. I couldn't drive them all, but I loved them just the same. My house was a small affair with a short driveway. It had reconditioned Volkswagens parked everywhere. Since only three could fit in my driveway and only two in the garage, I parked my pride and joys lined up on the lawn in front of the house. I know my neighborhood would rather have had someone who collected packs of wolves, prides of lions or gaggles of geese, but they had a shit load of bugs. As it went in any snooty neighborhood, they hated me and my cars. I didn't care. Volkswagens were my passion. I'd read somewhere to follow your bliss and I was following my Volkswagen bliss.

Maybe my German heritage had a lot to do with it. It could have been the simple fact that I liked the shape and simplicity of the car. Whatever it was, I knew everything about beetles there was to know. I could rebuild an entire Volkswagen in my sleep.

The second and third things I loved more than life itself was Budweiser beer and good Mexican food. I pampered myself often with both, but not to excess. I wanted to keep my trim, boyish looks. Too much Mexican food, as I round the bend on that quick road to fifty, was not good.

Although I never actually met him, like Billy Marlin, I also worked out in Marysville Fitness Center every afternoon. I was happy with the body I'd built over the years. It wasn't huge and muscular, nor was I a skinny wimp. Anyone looking at my wrinkless face, with a thick crop of blond hair might mistake me for a man in my early thirties and I liked it that way.

There was only one blemish, one little handicap keeping me from being the epitome of my German heritage. The one imperfection was not apparent to anyone but me and with whomever I shared sex. That part of my life was an issue that plagued me daily. Because of my problem, sexual partners were extremely rare. Whenever I did have sex with a woman, as consistent as the ticking of the grandfather clock in my hall, she might make lots of promises, but she would not return.

I don't tell just anyone, but my package is minuscule. My maleness is so small many house cats outsize me. If ever a small dick contest was held, I would win hands down. But, in a million years and with a prize of a bizillion dollars, I would never consider being apart of such a degrading contest. I've been degraded enough.

The forth thing I loved, though I wasn't sure if it was love or simple infatuation, was Marie Bunny Ollinski. I was able to enjoy three of my passions at once when I attended the Torez Family Mexican restaurant. It went without saying that I was one of the long lines of customers who waited, sometimes for an hour, to sit in Bunny's section.

I tried not to flash her my boyish, moon eyes. I tried not to let on that I even noticed her, but I couldn't help myself. My interest in her leaked out like oil in an old Volkswagen engine. Once it got started, it seemed to come from everywhere.

Oh, I had it all right, but not once in the six months I'd been coming to the restaurant, did she give me the time of day. Yes, she waited on me. She joked with me. She even reached out and patted my shoulder a number of times. It was exactly what I needed, but I always felt a professional distance.

This was the night I'd ask her out. It couldn't be that hard, or that devastating to have her turn me down. I knew she was going to laugh, but I had to try.

I'd been turned down many times by women. I was a

man for God sakes. I was well versed in the art of getting shot down, but Bunny Ollinski was exceptional. I couldn't bear to be rejected by her even once.

Because of her special love status, my I'll-do-it-tonight resolve, had come and gone more times than a Volkswagen blows engines.

Three times that night, I'd made the beginnings of an attempt. The first time was when she greeted me. I wanted to stand, take her in my arms and sweep her off her feet. I wanted her to swoon.

It happened again when she brought my beer. By then I only wanted to say something intelligent.

The last time, when she delivered my triple Enchilada special, I failed to say even one word.

It was no good. I didn't have the balls.

I was in the middle of eating my meal, kicking myself for being a wimp, berating myself for not being the man I knew I could be, when Bunny walked by my table for the tenth time. I wanted to tell her I loved her and would do anything for her.

I was in the middle of that particular fantasy, when a scream erupted from the far side of the restaurant. A platter shattered on the floor. I didn't want to take my eyes off Bunny, but the commotion was too much to ignore. I shifted my gaze toward the direction of the pointing waitress. At that moment, the front window bulged and shattered. A column of muddy water the size of a Volkswagen deluged the first row of tables pushing everything toward me. It was an impossible sight.

With all of my shortcomings, the least was my ability to think quickly. People were being tossed like rag dolls. I grabbed Bunny's hand. I pulled her toward the back door. She resisted for a second. I held on tight. The column of water nipped at our heals. I was the first to reach the back door. I rammed it like a linebacker. The door exploded. I stumbled through onto the hood of a maroon Thunderbird. My knee slammed the grill. I let go of Bunny's hand. Water gushed out of the splintered door. I was back on my feet. A dozen people sloshed out behind me. Bunny sprinted across the lot. She wasn't going to make it.

A flood was coming and I had one chance to save her. I sprinted through three inches of water for my Volkswagen, which was parked in the same direction Bunny was running. By the time I got to my car the water was halfway up my calves. Water splashed in as I opened the door, but when the door was closed any liquid would be forever sealed out.

Lucky for me, I was driving my Baja. If anything was going to hold in a flood, the Baja would. I'd chopped both front and back finders and added the high water breathing kit to the carburetor and exhaust. I'd sealed every possible opening in the engine and trans-axle. This car went on three Baja 1000 runs. In my second race, I'd taken home twenty-seventh place. It wasn't bad considering that ninety percent of cars never saw the finish.

Without so much as a hesitant cough, my Baja went through three rivers and skated along hundreds of miles of sandy Sea of Cortez beaches. I didn't know how much water was coming down the streets of Marysville, but I knew my car could make it in four-feet of river. I slid the key into the ignition and heard the purr of my little four-banger engine. When I slammed the shift into first, the car jumped ahead, pushing two feet of water. I turned right onto the street and drove to Bunny. She was frantically grinding her engine.

I rolled my window down. "I'll get you out of here."

She ignored me and continued to grind the starter.

I patiently waited one minute for the inevitable.

When I heard a scream, I looked over and watched Bunny's window open. In a fast second she'd climbed onto her roof.

I yelled over the pounding rain. "Come on, I'll get you home."

"Leave me alone."

"Jump from your car to mine. I'll let you in through the window on the other side."

"Leave me alone!"

I'm a patient man, so I waited. Once in while I throttled the purring engine to make sure it was still running.

It took another minute before the water got high enough to leave her no choice. She leapt over and landed flat on my rounded roof. The metal caved but I didn't mind. It was fitting that the woman of my dreams was on the roof of my car. That was all that counted. Getting her in would be another problem.

I rolled the shotgun window down and climbed across the seat. I stuck my head out and twisted around to see her.

"Come in feet first," I yelled.

She lay flat and bellied her way over to the window.

In the time it took to position her to slide in though the window, the water had risen another six inches. It might only be a moment before it poured through the opening.

As she pointed her feet toward the window, I grabbed her ankles and supported her slow progress into the car. She'd have to drop at least a foot to the edge. It was going to hurt. It might even crack her tail bone.

With a nervous reluctance, as she let go, I grabbed her upper thighs. Through the thunder of the rain, I heard a nails-on-chalkboard shriek as she kicked and struggled to climb out of the car. It was my only chance. If she got back on the roof she would never get in and we would both be sunk. Determined to be a hero, I gritted my teeth, took three or four kicks to the chest, got a better grip on those luscious thighs and plucked her off the roof, all along trying to cushion her fall. She dropped hard onto the window edge crushing my fingers against the metal.

She slid into the car swinging, yelling obscenities and pulling her hiked up skirt back down toward her knees.

"You son-of-a-bitchin' pervert," she screamed fumbling for the door handle with one hand, pummeling me with the other. "Don't ever touch me again or I'll call the police."

I held my arms up to protect myself.

A moment later, before she could find the handle, the first gush of water splashed over the open window. She stopped all movement, turned to look at the rising water, transferred her hand from the door handle to the window crank and rolled up the window. Always the opportunist, I smiled and slid the shifter into first gear.

"Sorry to grab you like that. Didn't know any other way to get you in."

Once the car pulled out of the flooded parking lot and onto Laurel Boulevard, she went silent.

Along the boulevard, my Volkswagen found three low spots in the road and left the pavement each time. It bobbed and rotated, turning into what any observer might mistake for a large toilet bowel float. Each time the car looked like it may careen out of control and smash into telephone pole or parked car, it found pavement and the back wheels gave it direction again.

I turned on the dome light. "Where can I take you?"

She sulked, sitting scrunched against the door like a drenched and trapped animal.

I turned the heater on high.

After repeating the question three times, giving a long pause between each, Bunny finally said three sharp, short words, "Third and Donaldson."

It wasn't much, but it was an in. "Is that's where you live?"

"My kids are with my mom."

Okay, she was warming up. Could I keep the talk going?

"You got kids?"

"Two."

Wow, all that and kids too! I was feeling lucky.

"If we can get to the tracks, we can slip over the trestle and find our way through the back streets."

I was in my element now. I was a born hero and I was about to save my first damsel.

The car swam along Fifth Street toward the tracks. When we found solid ground again, I climbed a side street and across a vacant lot, then we bobbed once more. The car bucked and heaved as it floated through the turbulent lake toward the railroad tracks. Once we reached the thirty-foot high embankment, I gunned the engine and pulled the car out of the boiling lake onto dry land. I climbed the burm, turned left, straddled the tracks, stopped, reached under the dash and flipped the bilge pump switch.

In a few moments, three inches of water disappeared, leaving only soggy, original equipment rubber mats.

"We can get to your mom's if we drive along the tracks for a mile and drop down on the far side."

Her eyes were big, but she said nothing.

Riding over unevenly spaced railroad ties was not the best driving I'd experienced in a Volkswagen, but ride the rails we did. After a bone-jarring mile, I turned off the tracks and pointed the car down the long slopping grade.

I wasn't sure what to expect when we reentered the dark water. With the bilge pump running, my car could float indefinitely. As I eased into the water, the front wheels left the ground. Myself, the woman of my dreams, and my little canary Baja Volkswagen floated like a turtle along the very street I lived.

We reached my house in time to follow four of my fully restored Volkswagens, also floating along the middle of the street.

CHAPTER 4

DRUGSTORE COWBOY

I performed my best dance of my first evening when another browsing couple happened to stop and look in the display window. They became the second audience for the soon to be famous Cassandra Liltkey, Flamenco dancer extraordinaire.

They would remember that night, because they'll soon read about me when my name becomes a household word. I spun, stomped my heals and clapped my castanets with an even greater fervor than before.

I was so caught up in the dream of being famous that I failed to notice the couple disappear from my display window stage. When I opened my eyes, they were running in the direction of the Torez Mexican restaurant. It's their loss.

I was so engrossed in the dance I failed to notice water seeping around the front doors.

When the doors pushed open from the pressure of a foot of water, I stopped dancing and gasped.

"Mr. Dickerman," I yelled.

* * *

"Call me Bill," I said for the tenth time that night.
"Water!"

I looked up as the Flamenco Gypsy pointed and gasped. A six-inch column of muddy liquid was turning my very tidy, well-stocked drug store into a lake.

"Are you okay Miss Liltkey?" I spoke, even voiced, like it was nothing out of the ordinary. I didn't want to frighten her.

She stood big-eyed on her twenty-four inch display platform, while an ever growing parade of chocolate liquid pushed its way through the front doors. Outside, the rising water rushed by at a frightening pace.

In the few seconds it took to have our little exchange, the drug store sat in ten inches of flood.

I walked out from behind the counter, stepped down into the freezing liquid and sloshed my way across the room to the glass front doors. I struggled to push the left door closed and snapped the latch, locking it to the floor and ceiling at the same time. By the time I began on the second door, the outside water level was up to Miss Liltkey's sweet and beautifully slender waist and she was standing on the platform. Although I tried, the incoming water pressure insisted that the right door be left unlocked.

After a moment of frustrating attempts, with the water level creeping half way up my thigh, I abandoned the effort, waded over to the gypsy woman and turned around.

"Get on. I'll ride you piggy-back to the stairs."

"Mr. Dickerman, this is highly inappropriate."

"Otherwise you'll have to wade across on your own. By

the looks of things outside, we'll need to get upstairs pretty quick before we get swamped."

"No thank you," she said. "I'll make it on my own."

I turned and watched as she hiked up her bright red Flamenco dancing dress mid-thigh, stepped down into the water and gasped.

"Cold?" I asked.

"Bitterly."

"The stairs are back there." I grabbed her sweet little hand and sloshed her across the room. For a split second she tried to pull away, but I held on tight and stepped her through a quagmire of floating Pampers boxes, bobbing greeting cards and those stupid crocheted doilies I'd been carrying because Mrs. Peters, who made the doilies, was my best customer.

I led the cute Flamenco dancer past an entire armada of floating plastic bottles of that damned dish washing detergent. I'd been forced to put the detergent on sale in a never-ending attempt to draw the public away from the despicable new mall on the north side.

Once on the stairs, out of the waist high water, to my disappointment, the Gypsy woman released not only my hand, but also her sexy dress she'd been hold up higher as the waters rose.

I'd gotten a good look at those silky milk toast thighs and a glimpse of one deliciously round buttock, red thong panties covering almost nothing. Although everything below my waist was frozen solid, it was a hot moment.

My wandering thoughts should have been on the wholesale destruction of my swamped drugstore. I was ruined. I should have been wondering if we were going to get out of the mess alive, but I wasn't. My thoughts were on one thing only. I wanted another glimpse of those strong dancer thighs and thong panties. Oh yummy.

When the gypsy stepped through my door a few days ago, my long forgotten hormones kicked up a notch. A small notch, so be it, but it had been too many years. To my delight my libido was slowing coming out of its catatonic inactivity. It had been a long, long time.

It was way before the Big Super Drug Mart had moved in on the north side. It was back in the days when Fredrick's and me were the only drug stores in the area. It was when the money flowed in like the muddy waters of the Yuba. Although Fredrick's had closed up shop some years ago and gone south by way of the wintering snow geese, it was still hard to stay afloat once the chain guys moved in.

It was long before Lucille, my loving wife of twenty-two years, suddenly fell dead on the floor of her bathroom. The doctor said it was a heart attack. A heart attack? Weren't women supposed to have the babies, leaving the heart attacks to us men? It had been a shock, not only because I loved her, but because I was suddenly alone again.

The day the gypsy woman showed up, my ever-illusive sex drive went from almost nothing to zipity-do-da.

It began long before anything started chipping away at my soul and my very livelihood. Dickerman's drug store was all I had. My entire manhood was directly connected to how well the store performed and my dwindling manhood, until earlier that week and more specifically earlier that evening, had looked more than a bit shriveled.

Since my extremely under insured store, and who could afford good insurance anymore, was three feet under rapidly rising water, one part of my entire manhood was again looking extremely shaky. But, and that was a big but, another kind of manhood in my pathetic little life was coming alive once again. Getting a good, long gander at Cassandra's silky thighs seemed to help dissipate the certainty of the immenant disaster.

After who knew how many years, good ol' one eye was climbing back into the driver's seat.

The overall situation was dangerous. I had no idea how high the water would rise. If it rose to the height of the levee my hidden upstairs apartment would be swamped. Instead of the comfortable digs I had prepared so many years ago and cleaned once again yesterday afternoon, we might be forced to spend the night on the roof.

With all of the considerations, all of the implications, so many potential dangers, did I have any of those things in mind? There was only one thing on my mind, one prevailing thought coming through my high-voltage power lines. For the first time in eleven years, since before Lucille died, I actually felt a slight tingle down there. No, it was more than a tingle.

The feeling was something I had come to accept might never occur again in what remained of my lost little life. To my delighted surprise, me, the drugstore cowboy felt the beginnings of a long forgotten erection.

"Let's go upstairs," I said, hearing a slight, but very recognizable nervous titter to my voice. I hoped the Gypsy woman hadn't noticed.

I led the way, unlocking the door at the top of the stairs.

As I flipped the switch in the storage room, the light in the room, the street lights outside the little windows at each end of the loft, every burning globe within my sight, flickered, dimmed, then dropped the whole town into a darkness I hadn't seen in years.

I wanted to grab her right then and throw a sloppy kiss on her tight little sexy lips. I wanted to take her there in the darkness, on the floor, unannounced, uninhibited, but alas, me, the ever-predictable William H. Dickerman reached into my pocket and fished out one of those cheap Bic lighters I was forced to carry in my store. The days of Zippo's were long gone.

The first strike and the space flickered into my dim shadowy storage room filled with thirty years of stacked boxes and discarded display tables.

I stepped across the room and lifted three boxes off a stack. "I think I have some candles." I dug into the fourth box and pulled out a handful of long slender dinner candles and another fist of cheap plastic holders left from a Christmas special five years ago.

One at a time I lit three candles, jabbed them into the holders and handed them to the Gypsy woman. She placed them on the floor in the middle of the room.

I sat on a box of shampoo within the circle of light while Miss Liltkey sat on a deodorant crate on the opposite side of the three minuscule flames.

"What do we do now?" she asked.

"I could kiss your entire body one little square inch at a time. We could lay right here on the floor and have wild sex." I didn't say those things, but I thought them.

In the few moments it took to get settled, my maleness had miraculously grown for the first time years. I wanted to use it quickly before it faded back into its self-imposed obscurity. I wanted to do so much with the Gypsy woman, but I hadn't a clue as to how to broach any subject, much less the one that was so much on my mind. I also wasn't sure if I could handle the almost certain rejection.

She was thirty years my junior for God sakes. What would a sexy young woman want with an old fart like me?

Instead of swooning her, taking her, having my way with her, I said with that same nervous titter, "We'll have to wait until someone comes by with a boat."

There was an exceptionally long pause then I said, "We may be here till morning."

"Oh great," she said. "Who's going to feed my cats and chickens? For that matter, who's going to save my animals?"

I nervously fiddled with a candle. "I think we're pretty well stuck here for the night. I wish there was something more I could do."

I really didn't wish I could do anything more. In fact, I liked the situation we were in just fine. My only question was, how was I going to get the Gypsy woman into the same mood I was in?

* * *

The great Yamelda Keating shouted over the pouring rain, "get that fucking light out of my eyes, you idiot."

I was beyond crushed. I'd seen her on the news so many times. I'd seen her beauty, especially her body, in particular her ever so perfect tits. I'd heard her pleasant news anchor demeanor, though I didn't really know what demeanor meant. I'd seen her in more newsworthy situations than I'd seen Tammy in bed, but I'd never seen nor heard Yamelda Keating utter one unpleasant word, much less a cussing one.

No woman had ever said anything like that before and gotten away with it. Well. . . okay, there were those two bar fly sluts over in Woodland last month. They couldn't keep their little filthy mouths shut, but they didn't count. The entire bar ended up brawling over those two. I sported a shiner for a week.

No woman, especially my ultimate babe, Ya-melt-a, tits-to-die-for, Keating, had ever talked to me like that. I was ready to backhand her. Maybe I should turn her over my knee like I'd done to Sara. Sara loved spankings. It turned me on to whack her butt. Sara couldn't get enough, but for the last year she's been in some Napa mental ward after trying to commit suicide.

When I tried spanking Tammy, I almost chased off the only decent pussy I'd gotten for eight months after Sara. I was always a quick study when it came to women. I learned spanking was only for a few, very special babes.

Just the thought of spanking Yamelda boiled my blood. It made the hairs on the back of my freezing neck stand at attention. As expected, my Johnson, though it was also freezing its butt off, rose to the occasion.

I sat at my end of the canoe wanting to say something cool to my dream woman, but not knowing what, so I said nothing.

The canoe tangled itself in another tree, knocking the flashlight out of my hand and overboard, almost pulling me into the icy water with it. While I struggled to get untangled, I watched the beam flip and spin, rotating into the depths.

Once out from under the tree the pitch darkness of the night enveloped us. Had I blown any chance with the great Yamelda?

I came back to attention when the boat slammed sideways against a house and bucked in the boiling water.

I was yanked from regret and forced to concentrate on keeping the canoe upright. It took a few minutes to slide past a series of shadowy monoliths until we came to an open area surrounded by the mansions. Holy shit, we were on the Tenican Heights fourth fairway. The richest community Marysville had to offer and I was stuck with Ya-melt-a. It was a burglars dream, just like we'd planned.

I only wished Sun Dog was there.

The boat bucked and swirled across the open lake for ten minutes until it beached itself in front of the only house not submerged in ten feet of water. It was that ramshackle Stalworth house with its small barn out back. Dog and me had been there many times.

There was no sign of life. It couldn't be a more perfect staging ground. It was centrally located and still had lots of exposed earth to bury any goods I happened to accidentally come across.

I sat silent, not forgetting about the shivering Yamelda. My all time ultimate dream had turned into a nightmare because I didn't know what to do with her.

After a minute of a complete loss for ideas, I simply ignored her and got out. I lashed the canoe to a small oak standing in three inches of water a hundred feet from the house and walked toward the front door. Half way up the walk, I realized Big Tits Keating had fallen into step behind me.

There I was, the great Ya-melt-a, babe-of-all-babes, was completely and totally mine, and I didn't know what to do? I couldn't believe myself. What would the boys at Clancy's think? I had the ultimate, numero-uno, top-of-the-heap woman in my grasp and I didn't have a thing to say. I sure as hell wouldn't tell anybody.

It never happened before. I'd always had the gift of gab with women. At Clancy's they said I had the touch.

Like any normal citizen, I knocked on the hardwood front door. After no answer, I knocked a second time, then a third, each try getting louder. When I heard no movement or saw no lights, I tried the front door. To my amazement, it was unlocked. To look good in front of Yamelda, I opened the door cautiously and yelled into the darkned room, "Anyone home?"

* * *

My little rolly-polly makeup person applied a fresh layer of foundation the next day. Although I was exhausted, I had to do the noon news and Sylvia worked double time to get me back in shape. I needed to tell someone what happened and I knew Sylvia could keep her mouth shut.

"I was sloshed over the side of the levee into the freezing water. I dog paddled for a while, but the cold was getting to me."

Sylvia let my foundation set as she pulled some knots out of my hair with a soft brush.

I looked in the mirror at her. "I was so cold I lost my ability to swim."

"Yous didn't drown so somethings must of happens?"

How long has she been with me, five years? When is she going to stop speaking that chopped Spanish and start using decent English?

"My thoughts got sluggish and my limbs froze. I was sure I was going to drown in that cursed river."

Sylvia stopped brushing and looked in the mirror at me. "Whats happens then?"

I swished my arms in front of me. "Something loomed up in the dark. At first, I thought it was a floating tree. It was better than drowning, so I took a few strokes, reached out in my last conscious moment and grabbed onto, of all things, a boat."

She pulled at a particularly stubborn knot. "Where does a boats comes from?"

"I don't know, but there it was and that's all that I cared about."

With a scissors she cut the knot. "Whats dids you do?"

"I didn't have enough strength left to reach out and grab the side of the boat, but somehow I did. It was the last thing I remember until he shined that flashlight in my eyes."

"Some guy pulls yous out of the water?"

"I guess so. There was no one else around."

"Whats does he looks like?" She was getting worked up.

I turn to her and look her in the eyes with reproach. "Let me tell my story."

She shrugged. "I was only askings."

I look at her through the mirror. "I was wet and freezing, but I was out of the water as the boat twirled through the currents. Except for that damn flashlight shining in my eyes, everything was black. He spoke my name and I snapped at him. As soon as I did, I wanted to take it back."

"What's did you says?"

"Something about getting the light out of my face."

"That's okays."

"I expected him to point the light the other way, but he didn't."

She stopped again and looked at me.

"When I put my hands up to shade my eyes, the boat tangled in a tree. The flashlight went overboard, but I did get a glimpse of him."

"Whats did hes look like?"

"Heavy muscles, like I like 'em. He had a thin goatee and a blond ponytail. The guy was a Greek god.

"Hes was cute?"

I nodded and gave her a secret smile. "At that moment I wasn't sure, but he'd saved me and that was enough."

"I's bets he was cute."

"Let me tell my story, damnit."

Sylvia got quiet.

"My teeth were chattering, my body was numb and the rain, that never ending damn rain, continued to soak me. I sat there while he battled the elements and finally got us out of the tree. We swirled around for what seemed an hour, hitting houses and trees, until, out of no where he beached us on dry land."

"It's no dry land for miles."

"I know, but when I looked around, I couldn't believe it, we were at Marylou Stalworth's house."

"Thes old farm in the middles of Tenican Heights?"

"The very one."

Sylvia combed out most of the knots and was putting on finishing touches with hair spray. "So's, what happens next?"

"He got out and tied up the canoe without even looking at me, then he walked to the house like I didn't exist. Me, Yamelda Keating didn't exist."

"The nerves."

People know who I am. Hell, most guys fall all over themselves. I couldn't believe it, he didn't say boo."

Sylvia raised one eyebrow.

"Didn't even help me out of the boat. I mean, not since I got my implants has any man turned his back."

Sylvia looked through the mirror at my chest. "They's are beautiful. What happens next?"

"It was too dark and I was too cold to stay in the boat, so I got out and followed. My knees rattled every step and once inside the warm house I wanted to jump in a hot tub."

"Did you?"

"It was pitch black in that house. I stood there shivering. He rummaged through drawers in the kitchen and found some candles. When he lit the first one, I saw him."

"He's was cute?"

"Whew, was he cute! He looked like a centaur in his mid-thirties. He was strong and silent. He had long flowing blond hair. But he paid no attention to me, what-so-ever."

"Mens!"

I said, "You might guess though, it didn't end there."

"Umm."

"He handed me one of the candles and I went to the bathroom and took along look in a mirror. I mean, something was wrong."

When I looked at myself I almost screamed. I was a mess."

"What did yous do?"

"He and I were stuck for the night. I had plenty of time to put my little plan into action."

"Plan?"

"I turned on the hot water spigot in that old claw-foot tub. Blessed be the gods, hot water steamed out and filled the tub. In a few minutes, I was immersed in life-saving hot water. My chattering teeth calmed, my toes and fingertips turned from blue to pink. All was right in my world again."

"What happened to the guy?"

"As I said, he was a mystery. That vision of Michelangelo's David, that all male, male, still hadn't said a word. He still hadn't even given me so much as the time of day. It was a mystery, and what a luscious mystery he was."

Henry knocked at the door. "One minute, Yamelda."

I looked at Sylvia. Can you get me ready in a minute?"

"Almost theres."

"The rest of the story will have to wait."

* * *

I was so nervous and cold I couldn't speak. I didn't dare do a thing for fear of doing the wrong thing. I handed her a candle and went to the kitchen to come up with some kinda' plan.

I turned on the oven and pulled up a chair, but ideas were not coming. Maybe I was too cold. Maybe thoughts of the Keating babe in the next room was too much.

After waiting a minute, I peeked through the door. Right there, not thirty feet away, through the partially opened bathroom door, the famous babe of the century was bent over with the candle as a back light, She was pealing herself from her wet clothes. When she pulled her top off, I was beside myself. When her bra dropped away, I was left with my jaw dropped to my chest. I slipped through the kitchen door and across the living room. I had to get a closer look. They were better than any of us at Clancy's had thought.

* * *

I stood behind my protective plate glass window on the top floor of the highest building in Marysville looking through my Harry S. Trunk lettering when a strike of lightening hit a telephone pole a few hundred yards beyond the levee. Although I heard the immediate report of thunder, the building shook too hard for simple lightening. I was surprised my window didn't shatter.

I watched as the white news-van, with its obnoxious telescoping antenna, its garish declaration that it was a news vehicle, listed, and floundered.

I smiled when that Yamelda, pain-in-the-ass, Keating also washed into the drink. She'd never bother me again.

But wait, the gap was on the wrong side of the levee. With every passing half second, like a sand castle at the shoreline, another ten feet of levee melted away.

By the time I picked up the phone and punched in a number I knew by heart, I measured a hundred feet of water pouring through the wrong wall.

"What is going on?" I screamed into the line. "What the hell are you fuck-ups doing down there now? Didn't we all agree you were suppose to blow the south side of the levee."

I listened to lame excuses for a moment then slammed the phone. I screamed to the glass wall. "How could they let this happen?"

It was a no-brainer. Whenever the water rose to a critical level, we'd dynamite the levee. If there was going to be a flood, it was better to control the break, rather than leave it up to nature and not know what part of the county would flood. How many years could I take to the bank the fact that the levee would always be blown on the ghetto side of the river? Samuel Tenter and myself owned substantial holdings on the south side. We both voted levee explosions somewhere around our holdings to collect flood insurance. We all profited so what was the problem?

The fourth position in our little levee committee rotated active members like Sally's lunch counter rotated the blue plate special. That person, whomever he or she might be at the time, didn't have a chance in hell in deciding where the bulging levee might be relieved. The only decision they could help make, and it was one that meant diddley to Samuel or I, was when the levee was to be blown.

The levee had collapsed and the gap, as I slammed the phone, had grown to three hundred yards. It was flooding the wrong side of the river, leaving me up the old financial, shit-creek-without-a-paddle. Since the water was pouring out of the wrong side of the levee, I was going to be left high and dry in more ways than I cared to consider. Man-about-town, me, Harry S. Trunk had not shown black since the pork belly fiasco a few years ago. Without the life saving levee, I was, figuratively speaking, washed-up and dead-in-the-water. Oh, I had land holdings all right. I had holdings up the old ying-yang, but in a soft real estate market, if I sold any property at all, I'd have to take it in the shorts. In my entire life, except for that Tenican debacle, I had not once taken anything in the shorts. I prided myself on making a profit.

Okay, my pride had been chiseled away more than once those last few years and it all started with that old Stilwalsky broad.

* * *

I knew that house. I knew Mary Stalworth. If she had money, she never showed it. The house had no secrets, no treasures, carried no family jewels to slip into a pillow case. Marylou didn't care about stuff. Her couch was ragged. The TV was an old twenty-four inch tube type. Even the big throw rug in the middle of the living room wasn't worth picking up much less carrying away. I could tell from first glance that she cared little for the possessions she did have. Everything was laying in a wherever-it-lands-is-where-it-lives, manner.

Once I'd gotten an eyeful of Tits Keating getting into the tub, I gave the house a quick once over without touching a thing. If I was going to be stuck there, I had to leave the place alone. All the two and three story houses surrounding that little farm cottage would be my focus.

I'd bring riches back. I could find a way to retrieve them later, but for the moment, the robbing-the-rich-to-feed-the-poor concept, namely Sundog and me, was the only job on my mind.

I thought about Ya-melt-a and her hot body. I thought about those great tits that gave not a hint of disappointment. Although my mind was on her chest, I had work to do and I only had one long, dark night to do it.

The next morning, in the light of day, things would be different. People in those dark houses would be more prepared for my special kind of skill.

I had twelve, maybe fourteen hours until dawn. The Dog Man and me planned that little caper to the tee. I knew what was needed.

Since Sundog was no longer in my part of the picture, and I hoped he'd found his way into a mansion or two, I was going to have to go it alone.

I went back to the front door and looked out at the canoe. It was still tied to the oak tree.

I stood at the door looking out at the never-ending rain trying to think of what The Dog would do. How could I go out there alone and do what Sundog and me had planned for the last four months? How could I complete my task, my one chance at a fortune, my only opportunity at riches and the easy life, and still get back to the little island to see if I could have an hour or so with the Keating babe. One nights work and I could afford to keep her in style for a long time. With the jewelry alone, I could live high for years without having to think about working any lick-the-boots-of-your-fucking-boss construction jobs. I liked being my own boss just fine thank you, but I had to get back to the little island. I had to put into action, my other dream. That dream had blonde hair, blue eyes, and though a much more filthy mouth than expected, wow those tits.

It was hard to decide on a chance with the woman of my dreams or the money.

It came to me like the waters of the Yuba. I went to the bathroom swung the door open and looked down on her. She was ready to scream. I wanted to say that I'd be back in five or six hours, but the words wouldn't come. After standing there for what seemed like an hour, without a word said, and what kind of dick doesn't say a word, I turned and left the house.

* * *

After noon news, I raced back to my dressing room. Sylvia was putting on lipstick. She looked at me in the mirror. I ignored the fact that she was applying my lipstick and continued the story. "He simply busted in the bathroom and scared the hell out of me, but he wasn't even looking at my naked body. He wasn't looking at me like all other men, drooling, trying to undress me with their eyes. He looked me straight in the eyes and didn't say a word. I sat in the chair next to Sylvia and spoke to her through the mirror.

"Can you imagine, me? I mean I've never met a man who had nothing to say."

Sylvia raised one eyebrow as she put the lipstick back on the shelf.

"Not one of those wimpy little weasels I'd been dating has even rated a second glance. Every goddamn one of them couldn't wait to get their grubby little hands on me. They all made me sick, but that guy didn't even look once, like he wasn't interested."

Sylvia stood, stepped behind me and gave my hair a

professional fluff. "Was hes nuts?"

"It was like, for the first time, something else was more pressing than getting into my pants. I mean, what a relief. Now, there was a man."

Sylvia turned to me and smiled. "You gots that right."

I gave her a grin. "When he turned and walked out, I was a goner. He could do what he liked and I would love every minute of it. If he ignored me, I'd have to pull out all the stops."

"Hes better watch out."

I glared at her. "Let me finish the story."

She went back to my hair.

"I had one long night to wrap myself around him. We weren't going to be rescued that evening, nor, hopefully, anytime the next day. I had time."

* * *

After I'd refilled the tub for the third time and it had certainly been way over an hour. I lifted my newly realigned mammary glands slowly out of the sudsy water. Although I was half-frozen when I got into the tub, I still felt sexy. Maybe it was the guy saving my life. Maybe it was that I was out of the loop, away from the ever-increasing pressures of work. Maybe it was simply my time of the month, I didn't know, nor did I care. For whatever reason, I felt an overwhelming desire for sex. Not just regular sex either. I wanted wild, uninhibited sex. I wanted to pull out all of the stops and I wanted that Greek God to do it to me with all of the passion I knew he had. When I, the famous Yamelda Keating had an urge, I always found some willing participant to accommodate me. When I got into the tub, I purposefully left the door ajar, hoping my savior would chance a glance in. Prior to actually getting into the tub, though I was almost blue with cold, naked as a jay, I bent over deeply with my backside facing the door and did my little tush dance to lure him in. I made sure he would be waiting. In a world of predatory humans, I, Yamelda Keating, predatory female extraordinaire, future news anchor for the nation, had graduated with honors. Wasn't it the real reason I'd gotten the boob job, with jab of silicone here and there to help round out my already amazing bottom?

I wanted the man. Like most men I desired, I wanted to consume him. I wanted to suck every bit of spirit out of him, then spit him out and leave him for the dogs to fight over. I wanted his power. I wanted him on his knees kissing my toes, begging for whatever scraps I'd throw. I would have him before the evening was out, of that I was certain. I'd turn him every way but loose. I would have my way with him over and over, then I, like I'd done so many times, would turn my back on him and watch him squirm. I wanted him to whine for more. I wanted to feel the ultimate tingle of having dominion over, yet another, in a long string of broken men. That one, though he'd saved my life, was no different than the rest. He was a man after all and didn't all men blindly and completely follow their dicks right into the mouth of the lioness. Weren't they glad to go in, but not so happy about the repercussions when my pussy trap slammed shut, metaphorically cutting dick, balls and the very soul.

Those were not thoughts I considered in a conscious way, because most of the time I ran on pure feline instinct. They were thoughts under the surface, just out of sight. Periodically, they bubbled up to haunt me, but were usually overridden by the next in a long line of assignments, or the next in my long history of shattered men. It was a good life and while I still had it, I was going to use it.

After an hour, I, the famous Yamelda Piranha Keating slowly and with much emphasis on each movement, pulled myself out of the tub. I did so with a certainty that he had been watching that whole hour. He was hard as a rock and waiting.

When I toweled I bent and twisted, giving the partially open door views of me men only dreamed of. I gave the door so much more than an eye full. It was winding my clock. With each time I bent over to dry off my foot, with each long sweep of the towel up a milky thigh, I felt tingles and a greater need for that sexy god of a man. Later he would be a whimpering fool, but for now I wanted him. With each swipe of the towel, my nipples rose.

When I finished I bent low over the tub, my backside facing the door and searched long for the plug.

I, Yamelda, the-black-widow, Keating, had reeled in my prey. There was no doubt I'd fattened him up for the kill. He was standing outside the door ready. I was certainly, after displaying every intimate little hair on my body, ready for him.

I turned, wrapped the towel around me, pulled it up high enough to reveal the beginnings of my blonde tuft and walked out of the steamy, for more reasons than simply hot water, bathroom. I expected two responses and I was ready for either. The first and most exciting was to find my victim standing, maybe even naked, ready to pounce. The second and not as exciting, but more so in the long run, was to find him sitting on the couch in embarrassed, jittery silence. The second more appealing response meant that my little dance could continue, but more blatantly, more in an attempt to draw him out, then draw him in. This second kind of man was more satisfying, because they were the one's who fell the hardest. They were the ones who sent bouquets of flowers, love notes, candy-grams. They sat at restaurant tables across the room a month later, puppy-eyed, waiting for me to throw them a scrap.

As long as I had a man like that on the string, I never had the urge for sex. I never felt like restarting the cycle.

My last fling was three months ago. He was the young, very sweet, Stewart Plumb, office manager of Prudential. He tailed me for two delicious months.

I slowly, with much anticipation, pushed open the bathroom door and prepared myself for the pounce. I was slightly disappointed when he wasn't standing naked at the door, his male explanation point at attention. I'd expected him to be the pounce and ask questions later type. Although I was seldom wrong, that time I was surprised.

I pranced down the short hall toward the living room. I made a grand entrance, but to my utter surprise, no one was there.

That was a first. Maybe he was in bed waiting for me. I sashayed to the master bedroom, made a grand, lightly clad entrance, but no one was there either.

I got more agitated with the inspection of each room. By the time I'd inspected the entire drab little house I was in a boil. Had I been home, or at a man's house, I would have broken things, but this was Stikes' granddaughter and nothing looked expensive anyhow. I restrained myself.

There was no Greek sex god waiting. There was no masculinity for me to consume. There was no one in the house at all. My swollen libido, which had been tingling for an hour, immediately shrank back into an old familiar anxiety. Since I'd left home ten years earlier, I had never spent even one evening alone. I always had people around.

I'd never been forced to face any of my demons. It was the first time in my adult life I didn't have TV, didn't have a telephone, and worst of all, didn't have any way to get out.

The house, with the electricity off for a few hours, was definitely cooling off. It felt bone chilling cold. The quiet little cottage was a prison filled with big, scary sounds, especially the scratching sounds in the walls.

Once I was certain I was truly alone, after I tried the telephone, the radio, I found myself unreasonably frightened. As quickly as I'd expected the Greek god to attack me, my scared little seven-year old jumped to the forefront. I sprinted for the queen-sized bed in the master bedroom and scooted under the covers, then pulled them up tightly over my head.

CHAPTER 5

TY-STICK SCRAMBLE

I didn't like that situation one bit. Stuck in the upper floor of the drug store with William Dickerman was not exactly my idea of where I'd like to wait out the flood. I wanted to be home caring for my cats and chickens. Although he had never once been anything but an absolute gentleman, I knew he had more in mind. I saw the hungry look in his eyes and the awkward way he moved. Hell, I could smell his intentions on his sin-sin breath.

William Dickerman was at least thirty years my senior. Although he was a sweet man, he was much too old to be more than a father.

I gave him a stern look. "If we're going to be stuck up here in your loft, then I'm going to need something to sleep on."

* * *

In a hot second, I got up and pushed around some old

cardboard boxes stacked against the wall. Once the boxes were cleared, I looked at Cassandra. "When I was younger, sometimes I worked late. I set up a room behind this wall."

There was a big chunk of my statement that was a lie. The bigger than life truth had been sitting in the drugstore loft, was it really forty years?

In the sixties, I was forced to wait on young vivacious vixens who came in for birth control pills, condoms and diaphragms. All those years ago, as my youth slipped through my fingers, I stood behind that damn counter waiting for my opportunity to join the love generation, but my moment never came.

I built my little love den especially for Mary-Jo Severson in 1963. She was more than willing. During that summer she came into my store doing everything she could to get my attention. I never once had the guts to broach the subject. Later my little plan was for Susan Forsner, then Sally Freedman. Although they all gave me so many signs, I never got the nerve.

I'd brought in bottles of cognac and Grand Marnier and sat them on the dresser next to the queen-sized bed. I'd pilfered supplies of rubbers from the store. An old console high fidelity record player with Johnny Mathis and Frank Sinatra sat ready and waiting. In sixty-seven, I'd even got three pre-rolled Marijuana cigarettes, which I never had the courage to try even one puff. I bought them during a time when smoking a joint was like taking a drink of water. Those little bombshells had been hidden under a small razor slice on the side of the mattress all that time.

I was in my mid-thirties during a time no one trusted anyone over thirty. Free love was uninhibited, untamable, wild as a storm at sea and I was too old.

I'd never been close to a love-in, nor did I have the opportunity to participate in any free love during a time when sex was being passed around like penny candies. Although I thought about it for years, I never had the courage for a one-night stand. I wanted to in the worst way, but not once did I have sex just for the fun of having sex.

I was married and happily raising two children in the sixties. Except for more than a few unscheduled stops at the corner of Height and Ashbury during business trips to the city, I was a daddy, sole provider and loving husband. I worked long hours every single day of my miserable life in my drug store. Although I dreamt of being passed around between a score of hippie chicks until my eyes bugged out, it never happened. I dreamed of many things in those days. I'm certain the ever so sexy Suzanne Wilson would have followed me up that dark staircase, past the shipping boxes and old displays.

How about Miss Flanders, the blonde bank teller from down the street. Gilda Sherman, Wanda Smith, Marylou Radclif? They had all been willing participants, I was sure, but I never had the guts to take even one of them by the hand and lead them upstairs.

Since the gypsy woman came on the scene, old failed memories haunted me again. Ms. Flanders had stopped in too many times. For months she had given me unceasing hints. She had all but asked me out loud, but I was too scared to take her up on it.

There was the widow Lisa Hesner. After her husband died, she constantly pulled at me with her short dresses and sexy perfume. She would have been more than happy to visit my den.

When it came to attractive women, the only thing that

got in my way my over bite of extreme shyness.

It was not until that night when Cassandra Liltkey and I were forced up the stairs, had I gotten the courage to ask, trick, finagle or entice even one woman into my long forgotten lair.

There was always too much to do, but now that the flood was climbing above nine feet, that sorry, well-worn excuse drew no water.

The bed was still made, the velvet cover, though faded, still glistened red. The bottles of liquor sat on the dresser next to the bed. My room had been secretly walled off with an even more secret door hidden behind some large cardboard refrigerator boxes. It was done in case Lucille accidentally sauntered upstairs.

All of the preparation, the plans and expense had been, not only for nothing, but an extreme disappointment.

Years later, far beyond the years when a man's fantasies cease to focus on that soft triangle of fluff at the upper reaches of a woman's thigh, long before those thoughts are replaced by thoughts of longevity or simply getting through another day, I quit dreaming. I stopped going up to my special room.

After many more years, I'd merely forgotten about why I'd built the room or that it even existed. How many years had it been; twenty, I couldn't remember?

It wasn't until the Gypsy woman burst upon the scene that all those old tomcat feelings came flooding back.

Once I agreed to her dancing in the drugstore display window, some ancient thing was re-awakened. After I grasped her slender hand and looked into her deep blue eyes, the neglected hidden little den took on a whole new meaning. For the first time in a decade, I'd not only returned to my virgin sex room, but also spent one entire afternoon cleaning, dusting, changing the sheets and replacing the condom supplies. Two nights before Cassandra's debut in the display window of my drug store, the room was sparkling clean, ready for whatever might happen.

Although I had plans, I was also realistic. I'd cleaned until my fingers were sore, but I knew I hadn't a chance in hell of getting her to take one step up the stairs to my lair. . . until the flood. Now that she was so close, I had a giddy flutter in my stomach.

"I'll get a pillow and you can sleep on the floor out here or you can stay in my little apartment."

"Apartment?"

I pointed at the open framed blank wall. "It's behind there." I was beside myself with anticipation. She would put a halt to my silly advances somewhere along the line, but I didn't care. I tried not to crack the grin wanting to spring onto my lips. I'd waited all my life for that moment and it didn't really matter that I wasn't going all the way. It certainly didn't matter that she was thirty years my junior.

My unstoppable grin turned up the corners of my mouth. I had to turn away so she couldn't see. What mattered most was for the first time in my silly-assed seventy years, I was going to try.

* * *

I snapped my head up and gave him a glare. "Get me a pillow. I'll sleep here."

"You might have a look. It'll be more comfortable than this floor."

"Get the pillow."

He shrugged, walked behind some boxes and returned

with a red flannel-covered pillow and a down comforter. When he handed them to me. I smelled the freshness and felt the softness.

He grabbed a broom leaning against the wall. "I'll sweep the part of the storeroom you want to sleep in." He had a nervous titter to his voice.

"No need."

"We need to get some of the spider webs and mouse dropping off the floor before you lay down."

I'd spent the last thirty years in my grandmother's spider and mouse-infested house. I'd actually come to terms with the creatures that shared my living quarters. As long as they didn't show their little faces, or leave any sign that they'd been around, I left them alone. The first sign of mice or spiders and I went into a rampage that sometimes lasted for days. I'd lay a storehouse of traps for the mice and got out the broom for the spiders, but never in my entire life was I able to sleep knowing the creatures were on my side of the wall.

I looked up with the very face that I was sure he had hoped for. It was the, I'm-not-sleeping-with-any-mice look. Not to my surprise, the room behind the wall took on a whole new meaning. "Okay, show me your room, but no funny business."

He looked at me with hurt and I immediately wanted to take my accusation back.

Without saying a word to me, he reached out his arms, took the pillow and comforter and turned on his heals. I followed as he wove his way among shipping crates and cardboard boxes to the wall that stretched across the far end of the loft.

The side door creaked as he pushed it into the room.

When I walked through the doorway, my eyes widened, nostrils flared, heart skipped a beat, which it was prone to do in the latter part of my third decade. I almost turned around and went back out to face the mice and spiders.

Before I stepped completely through the door, I looked hard at Dickerman. "Where are you sleeping?"

He pointed at a couch that took up the far end of the little room. "It folds out into a bed. I also have an aversion to sleeping with mice."

It was the only answer close to acceptable. Any other and I would have booted him out on his ear.

"Okay, but no funny business."

He crossed his heart with his index finger.

He tossed the pillow and comforter on the bed and walked over to the small window that overlooked the southern end of the Lyndon B. Johnson parking lot. He unlatched the lock, pulled the window up and peered out on a wall of rain. "Oh my, the entire parking lot is a sea of water. It's so high, only the top of Sandy Conners stupid macho truck is visible."

I walked over to the window. "The water was half way up his windshield."

Dickerman pointed. "It must easily be six feet."

"This could be a problem if it gets much higher."

"Dear lady, if the water stops rising at this moment, everyone who lives within six feet of the earth has already got big problems. I only hope no one got hurt."

Dear lady? What kind of an archaic, male chauvinistic thing to say.

We stood at the window looking down on the murky bay as it rapidly rose another foot, swamping Sandy's outrageously high truck. Once it was completely under, only telephone poles, surrounding buildings and the back section of a speedboat were left to gauge the level of the rising water.

"What happens if it reaches this loft?" I asked, though I already knew we would be on the roof.

"The levee's nineteen feet. The water will have to fill the entire valley before it could rise above this floor. I think were pretty safe. Hopefully, it'll taper off around ten feet. We might get another foot or so, but I'd be surprised if it would ever reach us."

"Let's close the window," I said. "It's cold and scary out there."

I was very worried about my animals. But, there was a deeper thought, so dark and sinister it only surfaced for fleeting seconds. That thought I would never admit, was of my lawn-mowing, ever-car-washing, manicured-yarded neighbors. It came through more as a wish. Maybe the water would wash away the entire housing tract. I wanted the buildings leveled, the lawns buried in six feet of mud. I wanted those stupid white picket fences pulled up and scattered far downstream.

Much later, I learned that I would get part of my wish. Those freaking pickets were that moment being pulled up by the force of the water and floating downstream toward Sacramento.

These and other thoughts were fighting their way to the surface. I wanted nothing to do with the ugliness of bad thoughts, but there they were welling up in my craw, bubbling from my unsatisfied belly, gurgling in my throat and almost being spoken. It took a Herculean effort to keep the words from forming, then blasting out in a profusion of cuss words.

There were too many things I had been holding back

since grandma's death. As my Grandma Stikes lay in the hospital, her last few words were, "Honey child," it was her favorite name for me. "Go get the bastards, but don't let your anger get the best of you. It ain't worth it."

It was the only cuss word I'd ever heard her utter. It was the last sentence grandma Stikes ever spoke and it stuck in my throat like dry peanut butter.

Being stuck in that room with Mr. Horneytoad, with the flood outside and not knowing what had happened to my animals, brought up my rage like a hair ball; first in spits and sputters, but too quickly with all the power and force of a freight train.

I sensed its true intensity for the first time since my Grandma died and it frightened me.

There was one thing held the rage monster at bay. I seldom needed to resort to it, but only that one substance satisfied the hunger of my anger. Unfortunately, I was more than five miles of torrential rain and eight feet of muddy Yuba water away from it. Without thinking about what I was saying, without considering the implications of my request and with whom I was requesting, I turned to the fatherly William H. Dickerman in his white smocked pharmacist uniform. "You wouldn't happen to have a joint would you?"

* * *

I pushed away from the shore, leaving the babe of my dreams behind. My little black bag of tricks was still lashed to the bottom of the canoe. In my bag was a small crowbar, two flashlights, a set of skeleton keys I'd bought at great expense from The Dog Man and a twenty-five automatic pistol with which I'd never had the opportunity to fire. The damn thing wasn't even loaded.

Since the paddles of the canoe had washed downstream, I had no way to control my progress. My plan was to float to the nearest empty mansion and find my way in. Once I relieved the building of its treasures, I'd move to the next structure. The houses were so close together, I could easily work my way upstream by pushing from building to building around the huge open space of the golf course until I was upstream from the house then I would float back to the little island. I would bury the booty then go check out my dream babe. Dog and me could retrieve the goods later.

The first part of my plan went like clockwork. I floated to the nearest house and inspected it for sign of occupancy. When I tied the canoe to the veranda railing of the second story, I simply stepped out of the canoe, sloshed my way over to a double glass door and slid my Slim Jim between the two doors. I popped the lock like a jack-in-the-box.

Dripping on the white carpet of the master bedroom, happy to be out of the downpour, I stepped over to the antique dresser, opened the top drawer and rifled silk panties and cotton bras.

I was strictly a professional at my chosen field. I knew just where to look. It took less than five minutes to find the hidden jewelry box and pour its contents into a new flannel pillowcase from the bed.

There were times when I was more thorough in my search, but I had a lot of ground to cover in one night. I had a lot of houses to visit and I didn't have much room in the canoe for stereo systems.

I did a quick search of the other rooms on the second floor, but knew I'd already gleaned the lion's share of the goodies in the one jewelry box.

Always a considerate thief, I closed the double glass doors as I left the building. No use in getting the carpets soaked. I threw my bag of goodies in the canoe and pulled it over to the far southern edge of the veranda, fifteen feet from the next building. I pushed off and the canoe shot directly for the window on the upper floor of the next house. The current grabbed me and almost capsized the boat. At the very last possible second, I latched onto the overhead telephone wires. With every ounce of my one hundred eighty pound bench-pressing strength, and not until I friction burned one hand, was I able to pull myself along the wire to building number two.

I tied the canoe off to a metal down spout and climbed along the roof to the first window, which I smashed with my crow bar. It was only my second house and already it was more work than I was used to. I was exhausted and I hadn't even really begun to stockpile the treasures. What kept me going was my ticket to Peru and all that Peruvian blow. Oh yes, and the babe of the century was waiting for me back on the island.

I went from house to house in a professional systematic order, seeking my own version of the American dream. A-chicken-in-every-basket, a-new-car-in-every-garage, wasn't exactly what I had in mind, though a new Toyota truck wouldn't be bad. Enough money to go to Peru on a whim and buy all the blow I could use was so much closer to my dream. That was the night my all-American dream might come true. I only wished The Dog Man were there. It wouldn't be bad to have Dog share in some of the work too.

By midnight I had a boatload of pillowcases filled with jewelry, gold watches, cash and rare coins. I took anything that was small and could withstand being underground for an undetermined time.

It was two-thirty when I hit my bonanza. The house had not been easy to get into. The alarm sounded the second I smashed the upstairs window, but the bell was six inches under water and the sound was so muffled it was easy to ignore. I climbed into a room me and The Dog Man had only dreamed of. Tears welled up in my eyes. Would it ever get any better? Dog would be the only other person who'd understand. He'd be the only person I could tell. I stood in the grandness where even the knickknacks were priceless. Everything I touched would bring high resell at Rightway pawn in San Francisco. All I wanted was someone to share the moment. It was the crowning jewel of my career.

While digging through some drawers, I came across Harry Trunk's checkbook. It served the bastard right to live in such richness and pay his help a pittance. I was making up for all those long nights I'd worked for Trunk without once getting paid my real worth.

It wasn't until I found the safe and after an hour opened it, that I really felt the score was even. There was a second where I actually felt sorry for the old fuck.

The goods from the Trunk house alone overfilled my canoe and I had to leave some earlier loot behind to lighten the load.

With seventeen stuffed pillowcases and a full canoe, I pulled myself through trees and along rooftops to get to what I thought was a good position to float back to the island where my real booty, or was that booby, was waiting.

It was long past three before I got myself set and let the canoe float effortlessly across a quarter mile, ten feet above the sixth fairway. I beached at the west side of the only land for miles all around.

I pulled the canoe onto shore as far as I could and tied it off on a fruit tree. It took a while to find a shovel then the second part of my job began. It was long after the break of dawn before I had a four-foot hole dug and refilled. With the treasure buried, the blisters on my hands boiling, I replaced the shovel exactly where I found it and walked up the flagstone to the front door. I felt so giddy I wanted to open the door and yell, "honey I'm home." I wanted to go inside, out of the never ending pouring rain, pull off my dripping poncho and wet clothes and climb into bed with the great Ya-melt-a Keating. Even though I wasn't exactly sure what the word meant, I wanted to ravage her. Better yet, I wanted fuck her brains out.

* * *

After climbing from the roof of the bug in through the window with my work dress embarrassingly hiked up to my waist, and worst of all being grabbed in the ass by that geek who seemed to show up every time I did a shift, I sat sullenly against the door. I knew the guy had some kind of googoly-eyed schoolboy crush. After the last experience with the jerk in the restored fifty-seven Chevy, I was having nothing to do with guys.

"I mean he's cute enough, in a scarecrow sort of way," I said to Sandy, my co-worker even last week when it was slow. I'm just not that interested in men."

"Get that jack-off Chevy guy out of your mind," Sandy said. "Not all guys are like him. Some are really okay."

I didn't believe her. All men were total dicks. Hadn't my ex-husband been a jerk. Hadn't Nathan, the boy I loved through high school, turned out to be a total weirdo? As far as I was concerned, they all were losers. Since my two kids consumed every ounce of my energy and every minute of my waking hours, didn't I have enough on my hands as it was? I wasn't about to complicate matters.

But, there I was riding down the center of the railroad tracks sitting next to Googoly-eyes.

He turned to me. "There's a towel in the back."

Without saying a word, I grabbed the rolled up towel and unfurled it to dry my hair.

He gave me an odd grin. "We're going to have to go back into the water again to get to your mothers. Don't worry, this thing floats like a duck."

"Down this road," I said, pointing out the windshield toward the bay that used to be mom's neighborhood. I just hoped mom and the kids were okay. At that end of town the windows of parked cars were still visible. The tops of fences shown and in some places even fire hydrants poked their mushroom redness out of the water.

The uncomfortable little car lurched over the steel rails and down one side of the hill at an angle I'd not been prepared for.

Once at the bottom and back into the dark water, the unstoppable little Volkswagen slowly pushed its way through three feet of liquid. When it came to Walker Street, the car lost its footing and floated down the middle of the street, nudging against parked cars as it went.

Through the entire frightening mess, the little engine kept chugging along.

We made our fifth dizzying rotation when I noticed, not only were we floating down the center of the street, but we were following a whole line of bobbing Volkswagens just like the one we were in.

I came out of my huddle next to the door. "Where did all the Bugs come from?"

"Well," he said with a worried voice. "There mine."

For the first time I looked at him, illuminated by the meager dash lights of his car.

"They're all my cars." He pointed to the left. "I live there and I guess every thing is floating away."

"Where did you get so many Volkswagens?"

"I. . . well, I collect them."

Except for his little ass-grabbing incident back in the parking lot, he seemed a nice enough kind of guy, but he collected Volkswagens? All my warning buzzers screamed. My danger, nut-case lights flashed. Red emergency flares went off in my head. I'd have jumped out of the car that very moment if it had been a regular kind of day. It was not a regular day. We were floating down the center of Walker Street, one block from mom's, for God sakes. We were bouncing off parked cars like a pinball machine. Each of those stupid little Volkswagens ahead of us was doing the same. For some reason, they all managed to stay in the center of the road, crossing through the darkened stoplights on second street and continuing down Walker toward the park.

I wanted to jump out, swim to my kids and make sure they were all right. Most of all I needed to get far away from Mr. Volkswagen collecting, Googoly-eyes.

We passed mom's house one block to the south. I hoped my kids and mom found their way to the upper floor. There was a moment where, though I knew it would most certainly swamp his car, I snaked my hand down to the door handle and actually pulled it. I heard the click of the latch. I felt the door let go. I pushed with my right shoulder but it wouldn't budge.

"Hang in here," he said. "We'll get you home soon."

He'd heard the click of the door too.

"I'm worried about my kids."

"As soon as we find solid ground, I'll see if we can get back around to my house and grab my fishing boat. This thing floats like a cork, but a boat would be so much better."

"How long will it take to get around to your house?"

He shrugs. "Soon as we find solid ground."

As it turned out finding solid ground would be next to impossible.

The little Volkswagen bobbed along the middle of the street, now and again careening off a car, a tree, the top of a street signpost. It lazily rotated as it floated toward the park.

* * *

I looked at Bunny, then reached down and flipped the bilge switch again. When I heard the whir of the little motor at my feet, I smiled. We would be safe.

In Baja, I was forced to drive up the center of a creek bed for a half-hour and got soaked in the process. Last spring I installed the bilge. Bobbing in a long pan of seeming never-ending water, the pump was coming in handy.

I wanted to assure Bunny that all we had to do was wait it out and the Volkswagen would find its footing somewhere. What I couldn't have known was the flood level had risen another foot and a half since we re-entered the water. The extra eighteen inches meant that we wouldn't touch ground for a long, long time. The car was sealed well enough to forever bob in the freezing water, but I knew which way the car was floating. Once we reached the Feather River, we would no longer be a bobbing cork in turbid water. We would be dashed and sloshed, banged and crashed, against every other floating object in a fast moving river toward only God knew where we might end up. Although we were headed straight for the river, at the speed we were traveling, it would take the better part of the night to reach it. There were many buildings, trees and bridges we could come to rest against first. I was worried, but there was plenty of time to pick and chose a spot to land my epitome of German engineering.

CHAPTER 6

TRUNK CARD

I continued a faster pace in front of the wall of windows overlooking the one spot along miles of levee least likely to break. I glanced down at my side of the embankment. It was the side that was supposed to be ten feet deep under water and if not save my financial empire, it would have held the wolves at bay for another year.

At the end of each pace, I looked out the window, shook my head, took another twirl of my toothpick, turned and traversed the window path again.

I was scared. I hadn't been that scared since I was a young man. I'd bet my last ten dollars on a sure to win horse in Berkeley and lost. There was no place for me to go then and there's no place for me to go now. The only difference was, standing in the top floor of the tallest building in Marysville, the stakes were so much higher.

In Berkeley, all those years ago, getting another ten dollars took me all day to dig a five-foot trench across the back yard for that nice old woman.

Sure, the bank and I owned properties all over Yuba County. It was an economy where interest rates were high and properties weren't selling. Banks were foreclosing on private investors left and right. Me, Mr. Shrude investor, finger-on-the-pulse-of-the-economy, had not been able to make payments on most of my properties for the last three months. I was counting on that flood to save my butt.

My pacing continued for another hour. The masticated toothpicks piled on the floor along my path. My brain was looking for a solution, or was it another solution than the obvious.

"How could those water board bastards be so stupid," I screamed aloud a hundred times during the hour.

Who can I call for help?

Lately, all of the high finance, politically connected friends I thought were in my back pocket, simply had their hands in my back pocket. Now that the chips were down, those ever-needy friends were nowhere to be found.

I was more than desperate. I was on my way over the edge. Had I been homicidal, I would have long ago blamed my troubles on the world, procured a shotgun and finished off those so-called friends I'd been cultivating. Three times last week, I thought seriously about my ridiculously huge three-fifty-seven pistol hidden under a stack of manila envelopes in my desk drawer. Three times last week, when I thought things were bad, the only thing that kept me from taking the pistol out was the heavy rains and a certainty that the levee would fail. The only thing that kept me from that particular corner of my desk was I and the other board members had already decided where and when the levee would be set with dynamite and blown to save the town. The only thing that kept me from reaching into my desk, pulling out that pistol and putting the business end in my mouth, was the certainty that the levee was going to flood. When it did, I could take to the bank that it would flood on my side of the river. Other than a wall of rain pattering on the sidewalks below, no water was on my side of the river.

Dreamlike, I walked away from the window and sat at the desk. I put another toothpick in my mouth, bit down hard and opened the drawer. When my hand found the cold metal, I pulled it out as quickly as possible and put it on my spotless desk. By the time the gun was on the desk, my toothpick was shredded. I grabbed for another. It was the first time in a long time that the gun had been out for anything except a cleaning and oiling. I looked at its true potential.

With a single digit, I reached over and touched the barrel. As if playing spin the bottle, the gun spun around easily and stopped with the business end facing me.

"You're it," the gun said, or maybe, "you're next."

I was as close to picking it up as I could get. Once the gun was up, nothing short of winning the lottery would stop me. I sat mesmerized.

Maybe an hour passed. I looked alternately at the gun, then out the window at the flooding opposite bank of the levee.

Dreamlike, a dozen toothpicks later, I picked up the pistol for what I knew would be the last time.

* * *

"Yes, Ms. Liltkey, I do believe I have a joint."

Dickerman stepped over to the bed, lifted the covers and slid his finger into an almost non-existent slit in the side of the mattress. "I don't know how fresh they are. I put them here a long time ago."

I bounced on the bed to feel its springiness. "This flood

thing has me on edge. An attitude adjustment is more than called for, don't you think?"

By his look, Bill didn't have a clue what I meant. He pulled out a slender rolled paper and a wad of batting. He dusted off the cotton and held it up triumphantly. "Here's one."

"God, Mr. Dickerman, I've never seen one so skinny. Are you sure there's anything in it."

"Call me Bill," he said with a smile.

"Gees, these look positively mummified."

He handed it to me. "If they don't work—"

"Any joint is a good joint. You got a match?"

He found a book of matches in the dresser, pulled one off and struck it. When it finished flaring, he carefully held it to the end of the pathetic little spiff. I pulled a long drag, turning half of the mostly paper joint to instant ash. I inhaled and held the smoke for as long as possible.

"It doesn't look that difficult," he said as I handed the dubie to him.

As I slowly released my smoke, Bill began a five-minute jag of coughing. By the time he'd calmed, the joint had turned to a roach. We both giggled and guffawed every time he started another jag of coughs.

I pointed at the leftover roach. "This is good. Was that the only one?"

Between giggles he said, "I think there's one more in there somewhere."

While he dug out another pound of cotton, I asked, "What kind is this?"

He laughed. "It's a Marijuana kind, what else."

"No silly, where did it come from?"

He looked at me quizzically.

"You know, is it Colombian, or Mexican, or some local stuff? I pointed through the window toward the mountains.

"They grow some pretty good stuff up in those hills."

"I don't know exactly where it's from. A friend brought a bag of it back from Viet Nam when he returned from the war in sixty-nine."

"You've had these since sixty-nine?"

He handed the second one over to me and struck a match. "I guess so."

I took a long pull and handed it over. While holding my breath I said, "Don't smoke much, do you?"

"Never smoked anything till now."

"Hold it in as long as you can."

I couldn't believe it, after the second joint, the druggist William Dickerman took off his shoes, climbed up and bounced on the bed like it was a trampoline.

* * *

For the first time since I could remember, I felt like little Billy Dickerman again. I remembered how long it had been and all the suffering in those sixty odd years. The misery didn't get me down though. At that moment nothing could get little Billy Dickerman down. Sure, it was a huge black hole in a major portion of my life, but I was having such a good time, I wouldn't consider it. If I even approached the darkness of my pathetic existence I was sure to go into a pit so deep I might never recover. I wanted to romp and play, to catch up on sixty years of missed frolicking.

A minor piece of me wanted to, but unfortunately I was no longer interested. Sex was the last thing on my mind. What I really wanted to do was wrestle.

I turned to her with a giggle on my lips. "Can you teach me to dance the Flamenco?"

"What?"

"Teach me to dance."

"Here?"

"Yes, right here."

"We don't have any music."

I giggled. "I'll hum a tune."

When I finished a rough rendition of a musical score, I said, "Teach me to dance."

* * *

Mr. Dickerman could have said or done anything else and I'd have easily pitied him, then looked on him with a superior attitude. But, he asked to dance the Flamenco and with the better part of two Thai-stick joints under my belt I was a goner. "Sure," I said in a stoned muddle, then pulled myself to my feet. I took the castanets from a hidden pocket in my wet red skirt, clicked them a few times to warm up, then motioned him to join me on the little square of carpet in front of the window.

I was amazed at how quickly he caught on and intrigued by his smooth transitions from one step to the next. Although it was the last thing on my mind, when we stopped a half-hour later and I lit the remains of the joint, I was tingly with excitement. It wasn't exactly the ferment of the dance, nor finding that old William could be a future Flamenco partner. It wasn't even the delight of finding a new friend in a town where anyone who could possibly understand had turned their backs. I was, for the first time since I could remember, in the early throws of a sexual awakening.

The last couple of puffs from the Thai-stick clinched any possibility of counteracting my budding sexual desire. My uninhibited mind soared. I let my body do the dance of the Flamenco, sex personified. Bill, I thought, though still not fully conscious of where I was going. What a sweet name.

Oh yes, me, Cassandra Liltkey, modern Flamenco dancer extraordinaire, fighter of the powers that be, chicken and more pointedly, "fuck you" rooster farmer, woman who stands alone in her rag-tag little farm in a world who wants white picket fences, was a goner.

* * *

If I had more worldly experience I would have recognized the look in her eye. Had I not just smoked a few puffs from my first ever Marijuana cigarette, I might have seen the signs. Had my mind not been floating somewhere between Saturn and Jupiter, I might have spotted her look.

After both of us fell exhausted on the bed and took another drag from the little cigarette, it caught me off guard when she reached across the bed, pulled me to her and planted a wet, juicy and very sweaty kiss on my lips. Not once in all my years had even one woman ever been so bold as to simply plant a wet one. I didn't know how to act. The marijuana cigarette only helped to confuse matters.

At first contact, I choked like a baseball batter with an unsuspecting pitch, a steady three hundred bowler throwing a gutter ball, an under par golf champion digging a divot and dropping the ball in the lake. My entire body went ridged. My brain locked. I would need to reboot. The only thing responding in the critical first seconds was my maleness. It immediately, having not had the opportunity in more months than I could count, sprang unabashedly to full attention.

Cassandra pulled back and looked at me in surprise. "I'm, I'm sorry," she said. "I. . . I didn't really mean to do that."

"It's okay." Although I was more nervous than I'd ever been, I was able to squeak out, "I rather liked it."

Without saying another word, she laid her sweaty body against mine, touched her lips to mine and pressed firmly as she explored my tongue with hers.

The rain stepped up. The sound of distant thunder hid the noise inside my little passion room. The floodwaters had reached the highest mark in fifty years, eleven feet three and one half inches, but at that moment I didn't care.

* * *

I, Billy F. Marlin, babe-magnet, God's-gift-to-women, best lay this side of Colorado, stepped into the house and wanted to say the words, "Honey I'm home". Why am I nervous? She's just another babe with hooters, but for some reason I'd have given half of my nights haul to yell those words and have her come running.

I was no movie star or even partially famous. . .well, okay maybe in Clancy's I had a little fame, but in reality I'm just some guy, able to bench press 280 and think on my feet. Hadn't I come up with the idea of blowing the levee? I was the leader of the pack with the canoe caper last summer. I was just me, but I already knew it wouldn't be enough for the Keating babe, a woman who'd hung with the famous. I just wasn't going to cut the mustard when it came to the babe of all babes. My dream had come true. She was around. How was I going make her see I was an okay Joe? I knew how to lay my cards on the table when it came to the dipshit boppers. I knew what girls wanted and it was easy to go into my dance. She was the great Yamelda Keating, number one on Clancy's babe charts. She was anchor of WASS news, a real woman, not some twit in a bar.

I had to get rid of a nights grit. A shower was first on my list. After the shower, I'd figure what to do with Keating.

* * *

I'd slept fitfully. The sound of the downpour, that damn scratching in the walls and the threat of the flood swamping my bed didn't help matters. I was scared and exhausted and I'd just spent the night alone, without even late night television. It was my first. Although there were many blankets on the bed, I was still an icicle.

When I awoke to the sound of the front door I froze. It took a few moments for me to remember where I was and how I'd gotten there. It wasn't until I actually got out of bed, peaked through a partially opened door and saw him, that I remembered the Greek God pulled me out of the freezing water and saved my life.

While peeking through the door, I watched him undress as he walked toward the bathroom. Each mud soaked layer revealed more of his delightful masculinity. By the time he closed the door behind him, he was stripped to his jockeys. I saw every muscle, especially the ones in his forearms. It was the bulge under a man's sleeve that lit my fire and he had bulges that wouldn't quit.

While I waited for him to finish showering, I combed my hair, brushed my teeth with a finger load of toothpaste from the master bath then borrowed a touch of perfume. When he turned off the shower, I was tucked back into bed, covers up, wet and waiting.

Ten minutes later, I realized he wasn't coming. No man had ever acted that way. No man had simply left me alone. Even the shy ones always knocked and tried to be nice. He simply ignored me. I, the great Yamelda Keating was not used to that kind of treatment.

It had been an hour since my savior had returned. I

was beside myself. Out of sheer frustration and unbending curiosity, I got out of bed, applied a dab of makeup, re-combed my hair, and wrapped the very towel around me that I'd worn when I was dancing around earlier.

When I stepped out of the bedroom and strolled across the living room in front of him, I was the epitome of Marilyn Monroe.

I gave a quick glance at him on the couch pretending to be asleep. I purposefully knocked over a water glass sitting on the coffee table. When it fell, it rang like the liberty bell. I bent, as if not noticing that he was there, picked the glass up, looked at his open eyes and coyly reached up to cover my bursting store-bought bosoms.

I gave him an expression of surprise, pulled the skimpy little towel up to cover my breasts and purposely exposed my slightly siliconed butt. When I sashayed to the bathroom, I turned at the door and glanced back. The goddamn idiot had not moved a muscle.

Some moments later, and I wasn't about to stand in the freezing house naked for more than a minute or two, I promenaded back across the living room. The second time his eyes were closed. I cracked a satisfied smiled as I passed, then turned as I got to the bedroom door. He was watching, I knew it, but I'd done everything, short of actually inviting him and he'd done nothing.

* * *

I couldn't believe myself. I'm a man's man and I didn't know what to do. Truth be told, I'd never had a real woman, especially one so famous. And there she was, traipsing by me with no clothes. She seemed so comfortable, I figured she must belong to a nudist colony or something.

Women were all overly embarrassed about their bodies. They're downright squeamish about being naked anywhere except in the bedroom and mostly only in pitch dark. Women are weird, but this woman was the weirdest of 'em all.

I didn't have a clue in hell as to what to do. Of course I wanted to jump her, but how?

Her first pass she knocked over the glass and woke me. I coulda' died right there because staring me right in the face was those zowie Hooters. It was all I could do to look her in the eyes. I'd read in Hustler, women didn't want men looking 'em up and down. 'Till then, I'd never put it to practice. I never really cared what women wanted. There was a steady stream of boppers at Clancy's and I didn't give a damn whether they liked me or not. Ya-melt-a was different. I'd give my eyeteeth to do the wild thing with her.

On her second pass, I pretended to keep my eyes closed, leaving slits to get a gander of that blonde tuft between her legs.

When she turned, I snapped my eyes closed. I shoulda' leaped to my feet right then, ran into the bedroom and pounce her. I wanted to more than anything, but I, Billy F. Marlin, the greatest heart breaker in the history of Clancy's Bar and Grill, didn't know what to do. In complete and total confusion, I stayed on the couch. I did reach down and give my Johnson a little squeeze and boy was he ready.

* * *

What was it with that idiot? Didn't he get it? I was the great Yamelda, always-got-what-she-wanted, Keating. I wasn't about to let the moment pass. I had to have him. I needed another notch. The more he resisted, the more I wanted him. I had little tolerance for his disinterest. He would get the best he ever had, then I'd throw him away like yesterdays news. The longer he resisted, the better I was going to make it for him and the further I was going to throw, but he wasn't cooperating. Damnit, I was tired of pussy footing around. Who knew when Stalworth would return? Me, take-the-moment, Keating was not the kind to let any opportunity pass.

For the second time, I jumped out of bed, glanced out the window at the morning light. I was so intent on my conquest, I didn't notice the sea of water starting a few yards from the house.

Again, I wrapped the towel around me and stomped through the door he was supposed to have burst through long ago. Barefoot, heals thumping, I took long strides across the room. Without any preliminaries, I shook him. "Well, you want to do it or not?"

I spun, tramped across the room, turned at the last second before going back into the bedroom. I expected him to be tight on my heals, but he hadn't moved.

I turned fully around, put my hand on my hip, gave him a scowl and shouted with enraged abandon. "Are you coming?"

* * *

I was getting back to sleep. It was hard after the eyeful of Keating's luscious body. I was dropping into a sexy dream about her and me when I heard stomping feet come across the floor. Had the Stalworth woman returned? I never met her, but I knew her. Hadn't Sundog and me been paid to poison her wells, break her windows and kill her chickens? We'd been to the Stalworth property so many times I knew the place and Marylou like the back of my hand. The stomping feet blew my single chance with the Keating babe. My one and only chance to prance around Clancy's and brag, though no one would ever believe me.

During the night, I'd run a hundred stories in my head. I had plenty, but a believable one was a whole other ball game. No point in telling the truth. Truth had never gotten me anywhere. In fact, too many times truth had landed me in jail. Truth was a black shadow to be avoided at all cost.

I was ready to tell about abduction and abandonment on Stalworth's little island. I was ready to place all the blame on a vague someone who'd disappeared during the night, leaving us stranded.

I was sitting up to tell my story to a pissed Stalworth, but Yamelda came at me like a freight train and she didn't look friendly. With a scowl on her face, she spit out a sentence I didn't understand. "Well, do you want it or not?"

Do I want it or not? What did that mean? She was the great Yamelda Keating. She was a woman from a whole other planet. Do I want to make breakfast or not? Do I want to get my lazy ass of the couch and get her off the island or not? Do I want to build a fire and get her warm or not? What she meant I didn't have a clue, but I wasn't going to fuck this one up. If I made a wrong move I'd blow any chance of getting next to my dream woman, so I sat still.

Making the wrong move would be a bigger mistake than getting busted for that jewelry heist three years ago. The Dog Man had gotten away with the goods and was able to get me a good lawyer. I still had to do a year in county.

Blowing a chance of getting next to the great Yamelda Keating was much, much bigger.

I sat pondering the "Do you want it or not," statement. She stomped back across the room, stopped at the door, then turned. She said something, but the ringing in my head muffled the sound. Did I hear it wrong?

"Are you coming to bed or not?"

I was sure I heard, "are you turning red or not? Are you coming to a head or not? Are you turning to lead or not? Are you wetting your bed or not? Is it something you said or not? My mind was reaching for anything that made sense, something other than "Are you coming to bed or not?" The great Yamelda Keating would never say such a thing. She'd never think those thoughts.

More confused than I'd ever been, and I'd spent more than my share of time being confused around women, I, Casanova-of-Clancy's-Bar-and-Grill, Don-Juan-of-the-south-side, a man all men aspired to when it came to handling women, looked over the back of the couch at the Medusa. She was enraged, half-draped in that skimpy towel, standing in the doorway of the bedroom.

I asked, "what do you want from me?"

She shifted nervously, throwing all of her weight from her left leg to her right. Her wildly exciting hip thrust into the air, pulling the towel open. She jabbed her other hand onto her raised hip and sneered. "What part of 'are you coming to bed or not' don't you understand? I'm standing in this cold room with nothing on, freezing my ass off and you're pussy footing around with semantics?"

I didn't know what semantics meant, but I knew what she meant.

She stopped for a moment. I was so confused I couldn't move.

After what seemed like an hour, she snorted, then shouted, "Why, you bastard. Not enough of a man to get it up, huh?"

That got me moving. I'd had more than one woman throw that atom bomb at me and there had been times it'd actually been true, but not that night. In fact, I'd been up and rarin' to go since I'd watched her get into the tub.

In one sudden leap, like a giant spring, I was on my feet and rushing her. Yamelda turned on her heals and sprinted through the door slamming it behind her.

I reached for the handle, missed and shattered the door into a million splintering pieces.

She squealed and ran for the bed as her towel dropped to the floor. I was two steps behind her.

She didn't throw herself on the bed, but jumped over. She grabbed a lamp and gave it a long sweeping arc an inch from my face. The cord caught. It pulled out of the wall. It was the only thing that saved me. The lamp flew past and shattered against the wall. She leapt off the far side of the bed and pulled the second desk lamp back for another swing. It shattered over my back as I came in low to tackle her. Cat quick, she leapt into the air, rolled over me and back onto the bed. She grabbed a pillow and swung it into my upturned face. Feathers went everywhere.

She bounced off the bed and leapt across the room. She grabbed an aluminum TV tray.

I stopped as she swung it dangerously close to my nose. The second it passed, I rushed her and pushed her to the floor. She rolled out and was back on her feet. She slammed me with a full swung gut chop, shattering the tray.

I looked down at a trickle of blood.

She seriously wanted to maim me. I'd had this kind of sex before, but it had always been playful. This woman was serious. I'd have to get to her before she killed me. The thought drove me on. She ran to the far side of the room and grabbed a small wooden chair. Before I could get up, she smashed it across my back.

So far, there had not been one word, only grunts, banshee wailing and animal sounds of a life or death fight. I broke the silence with a deep growl. "When I get you, you're mine."

107

She gave me another yowling cougar wail. "If you're man enough."

I pulled my pants off. My Johnson, under tight shorts was at full attention. I tore my shirt off. I bounced on the bed as I leapt at her. She sidestepped and karate chopped me on my right kidney. I crumpled to the floor.

The death dance played for fifteen minutes, turning neat little, Marylou Stalworth bedroom into a dump site. I was getting the worst of the beating. I had claw marks and bruises I'd sport for weeks. I had cuts and a bloody nose. The wounds would be proof at Clancy's. No one would believe me, but I'd tell the story anyhow.

I was getting winded when, and just by chance, I was able to grab one of her wrists. She came at me like a buzz saw. She kicked and gouged, but I had her and the game was soon to end. When I could, I wrapped her arm behind her and grabbed the other hand. Mostly out of self-preservation, I pushed her face down on the bed. She kicked and screamed. She bit my hand, but I had her and the enviable was going to happen.

An hour later we lay in each others arms sound asleep. Three hours later she awoke me with scrambled eggs and toast. By noon, I awoke again with the great Yamelda Keating asleep lying next to me.

I slipped a hand under the covers and stroked her long legs, her thighs, her butt and up to those enormous hooters. She came fully awake. This time she took me, not with the wild abandon of the early hours, but with force, with intent, with the strength of her mounting me for her pleasure, not caring about me at all.

* * *

I felt different after the romping with the Greek God. Something inside shifted. I had, in one fell swoop, in a single night, maybe in a nanosecond, fallen head over heals in love with the centaur and at that point I still didn't know his name.

It took the week and another sixteen assignments before I put my finger on it. I talked to no one except Sylvia about what happened and even her I didn't tell about the love part. I was embarrassed to be longing after a man because I had for so long been Yamelda the-ice-queen Keating, walker in only the highest circles, talker to only the shakers and movers. I'd been sought after from Saint Louis to the San Francisco, but in my eyes they'd all been wimps. I was a virgin to love and the Greek God was my first.

Oh, I had it big time and it all started with the wild morning after the flood when I gave him that black eye and cracked one of his ribs.

After two more amazing couplings, I awoke at two-thirty with the sound of the front door. My eyes flew open as I heard footsteps and voices.

I nudged him. "Someone's here."

"I'll take care of it."

He did it again. He couldn't have said a more perfect, more masculine sentence. He was taking over. In a world where everyone looked to me to lead, this man was taking over.

He got up, found his clothes in the rubble, put them on and stepped out of the room.

I was in Yamelda heaven. All of my life I'd been forced to take the helm. After mom died when I was thirteen, I did the shopping, cooked the food, changed the diapers on my sister and took care of my eight-year-old brother. On the farm there was no one for miles. Instead of joining Job's daughters or 4-H, I was designated chief cook and bottle washer.

It wasn't until a year after mom's death when I was forced

to take the one final roll of lover to that asshole. After he made his moves, the next morning I left and I never looked back. After a lot of therapy, I realized that it left me with the intense desire to devastate all men.

Once I came to that, I wanted nothing to do with any old memories. The present was my friend. The future was mentor and, up until the other night when everything shifted, it had remained steadfast and consistent.

I heard some frantic, loud talking and a woman getting hysterical. When it came to women and hysterics, few men could hold their own. I got up, found my clothes and dressed.

The volume got louder when I looked around at the trashed room, turned on my heals and stepped out into the living room to face Marylou Stalworth and an older gentleman. He looked like her father.

As usual, when I walked into the room, every head turned. I gave Stalworth my up-to-the-minute news worthy smile and walked over to The God. What was his name? I stood shoulder to shoulder facing the opposition. The Tammy Whynette song, "Stand by your man" came to me. I couldn't believe I was thinking in those terms.

The centaur was finishing up the tail end of his story as I cut in. "Sorry for the mess. I'm afraid it couldn't be helped." I fished into my vest pocket and pulled a soggy business card. Please call me when you have an inventory and I'll be happy to reimburse you."

Marylou looked around and shrugged. "Reimburse?"

I pointed back. "The bedroom."

She walked past me and stepped into the trashed room, made a gasp then a short little scream.

Stalworth came back in pale faced. While looking at the card, she said, "How did the intruders get off the island?"

I looked at Billy who had his back to Stalworth. He

winked and said, "I don't know."

I reached out and did something I'd never considered and it surprised me. I found his hand and curled mine into it. He pulled away, stepped a nervous two paces back and put his hands in his pockets. I was stunned. I was the great Yamelda, every-man's-dream, Keating. For the first time in my entire life I had a man pull away? He was acting like he didn't want to be seen with me. He certainly didn't want to hold my hand. The tragedy was, it just so happened to be the only man I wanted to hold hands with. Although I wasn't calling it infatuation, because very soon after we got back to dry land and went our separate ways, soon after the last time I saw him, I jumped right over infatuation. I called it L... O... V... E... Love, love, love. I had it bad. Me, the very woman who'd shattered so many, the ice queen who couldn't be touched, had it so bad I was willing to back any story he told without even knowing the story.

Tammy Wynette's voice kept repeating itself in my head.

* * *

After a nights sleep in the passion bed I'd created so many years ago and never used, I awoke with a start when I touched the flowing hair of Cassandra Liltkey. When the entire nights experience replayed, I felt embarrassed and anxious. Once we'd taken puffs from those anemic cigarettes, I felt giddy and playful.

The moment she'd pressed her lips against mine, I froze. I felt like a child and her very adult act took me by surprise. I returned the kiss all right, but I knew where the kiss was leading. Although I'd dreamed of that moment so many times, all I could think of was playing Yatzi or pin-the-tail-on-the-donkey, maybe breaking a piñata and scrambling for the candy. I did give it the old College try, but all I could think of was Lincoln Logs and Monopoly. Sex was the last thing on my mind and yet she was beside herself with the thought.

I awoke with the humiliating truth of my failed romantic interlude. I was ashamed that I'd forced Cassandra Liltkey into a Scrabble game, and more than one. It was more like a symphony of Scrabble games. I was so self-conscious, I quietly slipped out of bed and got dressed. I stepped over and looked out on the Lyndon B. Johnson parking lot. It was under ten feet of muddy water. The day was dark gray, but it had finally stopped raining.

On first glance, I thought it must have been some kind of marijuana after effect. There was a single bright red object bobbing out of the turbid water at such an odd angle I had to blink and rub my eyes. It wasn't until the lazy currents of the lake nudged it around that I saw it was a boat and Sandy Franklin's red ski boat to be exact. Sandy and his wife walked by the store last night just before the flood.

Its nose was deep in the water, but it was a boat and wasn't that exactly what we needed. While Cassandra was still asleep, I went out to the warehouse, opened the door leading downstairs and looked at the two dry steps that led into a blackness of the muddy water.

I looked back toward the hidden room. Its window was the only portal of escape. I searched the upper story warehouse for an old truck tube I'd stashed in the far corner. In the back of the stacks, I found the half rotted inner tube, stabbed a kitchen match in the stem to open the valve, and began the long breathless process of blowing it up

* * *

When I awoke, I heard a steady hiss and huff in the next

room. I leisurely got out of bed and dressed. After a long gaze out the window then primping in front of the dresser mirror, I got out of those stupid pajamas, put on last night's dress and walked out into the warehouse to investigate the incessant swishing sound. I found William pale and out of breath.

"Hi," I said.

He nodded, gave me cursory grunt and kept blowing.

"Let me help."

He shook his head while still blowing.

"Come on damnit, you look spent."

He shook his head.

"Mr. Dickerman," I demanded.

I grabbed the tube and playfully pushed him aside. "I'm taking over."

I took a deep lung full and blew into the tube. On the second breath of air I asked, "Why are we blowing this up?"

He pointed toward the back lot. "There's a boat in the parking lot. I thought I could retrieve it and take you back to your house."

"Boat?"

"I think it's Sandy Franklin's. Its nose is buried in the water maybe attached to a trailer. Either way, I can dive down, cut it loose and we'll have transportation."

"You're going to dive into that water?"

"We have to get out of here and I don't know any other way?"

"Don't you think you're a little too old to be diving into melted snow?"

His face dropped. "Hadn't thought of that."

"If anyone should get the boat, it would be me."

"I couldn't let you—"

"Mr. Dickerman, you can't stop me. If there's a boat to retrieve, I'll get it. Plus, do you know how to hot-wire a boat?"

I filled my lungs, took the stem in my mouth and blew a trickle of air in the valve.

Fifteen minutes of concentrated puffing and the tube was full. It wasn't the tight donut balloon I'd seen during the summer months when rafters floated down the river, but serviceable enough to drift forty yards over to the boat without getting too wet.

I pulled open the window, hiked up my dress and stepped out onto a foot wide ledge six inches above the water.

William wrestled the inner tube through the window, then handed me a kitchen knife. I cautiously sat, holding my legs out of the freezing water and paddled across the placid lake toward the boat.

I reached the sleek ski boat, pushed my arm deep in the water and cut the rope. The boat popped like a cork, raced backward across the water and slowly floated downstream.

I paddled frantically for a few minutes and finally caught it nudged against a telephone pole.

I pulled myself into the boat, turned on my back and popped my head under the dash.

It took a freezing fifteen minutes to get the right wires connected and the engine started. My teeth were chattering as I idled back to the building, pulled up to the window and threw William a rope.

"Tie me off," I said.

He grabbed the line. "Your dress."

I looked down and shrugged. "I'll get it cleaned."

I leapt from the boat to the window ledge and Bill helped me in. I was shaking. "It's freezing out there."

He pulled the crumpled comforter from the bed and wrapped me in its warmth.

"Once I get warm, we'll see if my animals are all right."

It took a half-hour and two candy bars to warm up, but

the moment I did, with William's extra pair of sweat pants, a plaid shirt and a thick scarf, the two of us boarded the boat. I pulled away from the building.

Piloting the boat up Main Street was strange enough, but when I saw people trying to wave us down, the scene became surreal.

"We need to stop and help those people," William said.

"We'll come back later and help people. "Right now I want to make sure my animals are okay."

* * *

Last nights puffs from that Marijuana cigarette helped bring the scene into focus. If I'd not taken those puffs, I might have had a pleasant memory of Cassandra Liltkey to take to my grave rather than Scrabble, a game I never liked in the first place.

My floundering masculinity had not come close being fulfilled. My fantasy about Cassandra Liltkey had not been realized, but a sliver of a smile crossed my lips anyhow. Of all things, Scrabble.

While she idled past a hail of waving arms and screaming voices, my smile widened. Although I'd blown my one chance of being her lover, I had a better time than I could remember. Even the years before Lucille's death. Had it been the little cigarette or maybe it was the circumstances? Either way, I finally christened the den of sin, though it was nothing close to the sin I had in mind.

The boat pulled through the hailing crowds and down Laurel Boulevard filled with single story, pitched roofed houses. People and animals were huddled on roofs and in upper stories. I saw the top half of the McDonald's sign on the corner. It pleased me to no end that the big conglomerate drug store in the fancy new mall was also ten feet under water. If I was going to have to bite-the-bullet, I was glad to see they would also be hobbled, at least temporarily. Of course, they had the fancy insurance.

We passed drowned gas stations, bookstores and grocery stores. Even the first floor of the county library was floating books instead of loaning them.

Cassandra ignored all who attempted to wave her down as she sped away from town. She was a woman on a mission.

Maybe later she'd take me home. My house was probably drowned in ten feet of water like all the rest. For now, I was with her and with her I would stay until she'd done what she was so determined to do.

Up one street, down another, across an intersection, through another, we wound our way through neighborhood after drowned neighborhood until Cassandra surprised me by turning into Tenican Heights.

I pointed at the security shack. "You live here?"

"It's not what you think."

"What do you mean? This is Tenican Heights. If you live here, you've arrived."

"You were around when my poor grandmother fought the developers. You must remember what happened?"

"I don't read the papers."

"Hell for months it was on everyone's lips. Where were you?"

I gulped, "Working, I guess. I work a lot."

"Gees, William, get a life. Things go on outside of your little drug store."

"So what happened?"

Cassandra filled me in on the details as she piloted to her place. I quickly got the picture, but didn't say a word. She wasn't going to one of the three story fancy houses in the development. She wasn't even going to a lower class two story ones. She was going to the farm on the fifth fairway. She was Marylou Stalworth! She lived in that rag-tag farmhouse and decomposing barn sitting in the way of an easy birdie to the sixth tee. I'd golfed past that house more times than I could remember and I always wondered what kind of stupidity it took to keep a farm in the middle of the nationally known Tenican Heights, exclusive neighborhood of exclusive neighborhoods. Cassandra was the chicken woman. She was the granddaughter of Stikes who had bucked the powerful development corporation Barney, Bowman and Whalde and won. I was at the same time impressed and mortified.

We got out of the boat as three cats pranced over to greet us. Cassandra knelt and picked each one up, held them for a moment, then I followed her to the run down house. I wanted to ask her a battery of questions, but I said nothing. Maybe someday I could ask, but for now, I was simply following her, right smack dab in the middle of the fifth fairway.

What I hadn't realized until the moment Cassandra put the key in the lock was hers was the only house in a ten miles radius not under water.

I followed her inside and she started moving around like a cat looking for a mouse. She sniffed the air. "Something's not right."

"Hi."

I snapped my head toward the single masculine word.

"Who do you think you are?" Cassandra demanded.

"Billy Marlin. I got stranded on your island last night. Hope you don't—"

"I know who you are, asshole. Where'd you come from and why are you here?"

"Me and Yamelda was forced here by some kidnappers on a boat and dropped—"

"Why are you in my house?"

She was getting worked up and if there was a problem, I would be no match with the buff guy in the skimpy tee shirt.

I quickly interceded. "You got stranded? We'll take you back to town as soon as we get the animals taken care of."

"What the hell do you think you're doing here?" Cassandra barked at the young man.

"We were kidnapped and dropped here."

His one missing eyetooth gave him a goofy look. The dark birthmark on his neck didn't help.

"What do you mean you got. . ." Cassandra dropped her last words when the anchor from WASS news stepped out of the bedroom. Her hair was tousled and dress wrinkled. What used to be a white blouse was blood stained and half-buttoned. I'd never seen her such a mess, but it was Yamelda Keating all right.

She stood next to the young man and snaked her fingers through his. He yanked back, then stepped sideways. The movement was clear, the message precise. She liked him, but he wasn't so sure.

"What, wha. . ." Cassandra stammered.

Ms. Keating pointed at the young man. "He saved my life last night and we had to spend the night here. I hope it wasn't a bother?" I'd heard her throaty voice many times on the eleven o'clock news. I liked her voice and she was easy to look at on TV.

"Well. . . well," Cassandra tried for a coherent answer.

"I'm afraid your room got a little messed up." She dug into her pocket and pulled a soggy business card. "Please call me when you figure out the cost to replace the broken things. I'll promptly send you a check."

Cassandra took the card.

Keating said. "Did you get here in a motorboat?"

I nodded.

"Would you be so kind as to give us a lift to dry land?"

Cassandra walked past the two strangers, ran her fingers along the shattered door, then gasped when she looked in the bedroom.

"What happened to my fucking room?" It was the first full sentence Cassandra spoke since Keating appeared.

"There was a fight," the young man said. "The kidnappers trashed the room on their way out the back door."

Keating took a single step sideways to the young man and put a hand on his shoulder. He noticeably winced then went silent.

Keating smiled. "Can't we just say things got out of hand last night?"

The story seemed plausible, but her smile was smug. It might have been the same kind of getting out of hand I'd had in mind for Cassandra. Unfortunately my getting out of hand took the form of too many Scrabble games. God, I'm such a loser.

Cassandra was silent when she tried to close the splintered door behind her.

"Mr. Dickerman, can you take these two where they want to go and come back for me later."

I smiled. "Sure."

* * *

Geek-boy nodded toward the windshield. "I'd say it's out of the question."

"Let me out at the next corner." Although I didn't want to, my voice had telltale nervousness to it.

He pointed out the window of our bobbing Volkswagen. "There is no next corner. It's only water."

"Just let me out."

He shrugged. "Where would you like to be let out?"

"Right here. I can't be in this car any longer."

I wanted to get out for the entire time the two of us had been bumping along from housetop to telephone pole. What had it been ten hours? I wanted to remove myself from the floating coffin in the first ten minutes.

I'd not been used to being in such close proximity to any man for more than thirty-second intervals for longer than I could remember. I certainly had not been forced to sit in the same car with one since my ex kidnapped me just after little Tammy was born. What was it, two years ago? There I was, stuck in another car with another geek. The only difference was, the car was not even close to a Camero. I was worried sick about my kids. I couldn't hold back another second.

"I've got to get out of here." I reached for the door handle.

Geek-boy pleaded, "please don't. If you open the window, the water will swamp us."

"I can't stay in here."

"If you open the window the water will flood this little floating bubble and we'll rudely drop out of sight."

"I can't stand it in here any longer."

"Wouldn't it be better to float out this flood high and dry than try to swim for it in the freezing water?"

"But. . ."

The engine on Geek-boy's little bug had long since died. He reached down and turned on the radio. "Why don't you find a station you like?"

I felt another rip in my fabric of guardedness, another strand loosened from my reality. It wouldn't take too much more of what was left of my sanity before I opened the window. Who cared about the cold water? Who cared about swimming? I needed, no I had to get out.

I was at the end of my rope and the radio reminded me of Frank, that bastard, and what he did the last night I saw him. Just before he forced himself on me, he suggested I listen to the radio.

I reached for the window crank and tugged at the handle. In less than one half turn, after five gallons of the freezing Yuba River dumped onto my lap, my frantic, I've-got-to-get-out-of-this-car, turned more reasonable.

I rolled the window up. Geek pulled his feet off the floor, leaned to the back seat and handed me a blanket.

While I scrambled to get the window all the way up, there was a moment of clarity. He could've stopped me. He could have fought me, but he didn't. He was willing to swim rather than force me to stay.

Adding to the uncomfortable feeling of being stuck in a car with a strange man, I was soaking wet and freezing. The same few gallons of water that dumped on my lap sloshed around on the floor as the little car jostled from house to light pole. I pulled my feet up, but in a minute the water was gone.

"I'm sorry," I said.

"It's okay. I felt like doing the same thing a dozen times."

"Why didn't you stop me?"

"I would never stop you. You chose to do what you want."

"Even if I swamped your car?"

"I can swim."

"What do we do now?"

"Wait it out. Hope for some high ground."

"Doesn't look like high ground is anywhere in sight."

"I know."

Something in me shifted. Some basic feeling of uncertainty and being trapped had been replaced with something else. I couldn't put my finger on it, but I wasn't as frantic.

The car nudged up against a house and scrapped along

one wall, shattering some windows. The crunching glass unnerved me. "I can't stand the sound of breaking glass."

He looked at me with a reassuring smile. "As long as it isn't Volkswagen glass, I'm fine with the sound for now."

His little joke made me snigger. Now that I was sure he wasn't going to take advantage of me, I felt calm. I managed a small smile and looked over into the darkness.

"Are we going to get through this?"

"So far we're doing pretty good. This car can probably float for hours, maybe days, that is if no one opens the windows."

I giggled. "Thanks for saving me in the parking lot." I hold out my hand, "I'm Marie."

He griped my hand for a second. "Sam."

"I guess I waited on you for months, but I never knew you by any other name than table forty-two."

"Is that the table I sat in?"

"Every time you came in to eat you sat at the same table. Sometimes you'd wait for an hour to get that table."

"Creature of habit I guess. I felt more comfortable there."

He paused for a moment then stammered getting the next sentence out. "It. . . it. . . well. . . it was in your section."

Thank God it was still dark because I felt myself flush. I'd known his story ever since he started coming in the restaurant. I saw his puppy dog looks. I'd heard it in his nervous voice when he ordered. I felt him watching me.

He had it all right, but I was not in any position, nor was I in any mood to reciprocate. As far as I was concerned, romance belonged in the movies. There was no room in my life, except for my kids of course, for the word that rhymed with dove.

He didn't sound the same in the car. His voice didn't have that lost quality to it. His acceptance for whatever I wanted made me feel more comfortable than I've ever felt with a man. The fact that he, except for the embarrassing moment when I got into the car, kept his hands to himself was in itself a miracle. He might be the first man in my entire life who didn't try to maul my breast the moment he had me alone.

When I reached puberty and my chest swelled beyond anyone's expectations, men couldn't keep their eyes or hands off me.

Even my father, damn his dead and restless soul, had tried once. If it hadn't been for my screams that woke mom, he would've succeeded. I never told mom, but I made sure never to be alone in a room with him. I was never alone with any man.

Frank was the only exception. With Frank —ten years my senior— I was in the state of mind and heart rhyming with dove.

Mom tried to help me make some clear-headed choices around Frank, but I didn't trust her. Since that night dad tried, all I wanted was out from under his peering eyes and oppressive attempts to corner me. I wanted away from my dingbat mom who couldn't see what was going on.

Frank was the answer, at least for two years. For that first year I was swimming in it and I found myself trusting again. We were like two inseparable peas in a pod, except for Wednesday nights when he went bowling with the boys.

It was just past the second year and our second child when I found out. For over a year, Frank had been using his Wednesday nights to visit that damn Selma Franklin slut on the south side. Why he wasted his time on trash like Selma, I never could figure out. He had more than he could handle with his own little Bunny at home. Why he needed her was beyond my comprehension.

Once I found out, except for the night in the Camero six months later, I was never with Frank again. With that one stupid move, he joined the other three billion men on the planet. Frank confirmed once again that all men were complete and total scumbags.

Ten hours and this guy had not tried a thing. He hadn't even looked at my breasts.

Once I was assured that Sam wasn't going to try anything, the question of where the little floating coffin was taking us was foremost in my thoughts. As dense as she was, I was sure mom had enough savvy to get the kids safely upstairs.

We bobbed along, floating past housetops and telephone poles. The rain thundered on the roof. I sat in uncomfortable silence, getting warm under the blanket, feeling safe in more ways than one.

Okay, maybe there were only two billion, nine hundred ninety-nine million, nine hundred ninety-nine thousand, nine hundred and ninety-nine, men on this planet who are total jerks. Maybe there was one nice guy. Maybe, just maybe, the one and only nice guy in the entire world was sitting right next to me.

In the early pre-dawn hours, I awoke sobbing and felt a consoling hand touch my shoulder. The hand didn't try to grope me anticipating inching down to my troublesome bosoms, but just a hand reaching out in support.

"You okay," his soothing voice said in the dark.

I'd been dreaming of the one good man on the planet. He had not been Jimmy Stewart or Robert Redford, what I thought a good man might look like. He had been plainer, more like the guy down the block. He had been a well-meaning man with heart and integrity. When I awoke, I realized where I was and who was sitting next to me. When the hand of concern touched my shoulder, I broke into a fresh round of sobs.

* * *

It was pitch black. The car had been bumping along for most of the night. Although I'd been able to sleep some, my long legs were cramped, my arms had nowhere to rest and I was a bit cranky. I'd been awake for over an hour, when the woman of my dreams awoke in the darkness with a start. I touched her shoulder as an automatic response and asked if she was okay. When she opened up into a full blown wail, I had no idea what to do. I left my hand on her shoulder and simply waited it out.

When she calmed she said, "I've never been so long in the company of any man without him trying to grope me." She went into another short bout of tears.

Putting my hand on her shoulder took extreme boldness. Keeping it there took acts of heroic proportions. Not that I didn't want to grope her, I was much too shy to be so overt. Thank the gods for my shyness.

I needed to say something to assure her, but I didn't have anything to say, so I just sat quiet.

The rains had stopped. Dawn was tracing the outlines of buildings and trees as we floated past. I could almost see Marie Ollinski's tear streaked face.

By the time I was able to think of one thing to say, her milky white, movie star face, was easily recognizable.

"When we hit dry land I'll get you back to your mother and kids." It wasn't much, but so much time had gone by, I felt obligated to say something.

We sat in awkward silence, pitching and bumping along, now and then recognizing landmarks and speaking about where we were.

I sensed a shift in Marie's demeanor. After her cry she seemed friendlier, more willing to interact. It was so much easier when she wasn't speaking. It was simpler when I knew she wanted out of the car. It was more feasible for me to feel the familiarity of rejection by yet another woman. It was so much harder to face a woman who wanted conversation. I'm only a guy. All I know about is Volkswagens. I can talk Volkswagens a blue streak. I could give an hour dissertation about brake systems alone. I had a keen sense of the sound of the engine and what might be wrong. I could recite the history of Volkswagens, but I'd never met one woman who gave a damn. Why would I assume this lovely dream girl would be any different?

At that moment, like no other, I wished I knew more about other things than Volkswagens. I wished I'd taken that art appreciation course at the junior collage last autumn. With that class under my belt I'd have something to say. I could talk about Monet or Picasso. I could remunerate about the works of current artists, and talk the talk of the centuries. At that moment, I could, if I was able to get my cramped leg out from under the dash, kick myself for not taking the class and having something intelligent to say.

If only that little blue bug hadn't shown up the first night of the class. I was so excited about working on it, I forgot to go to the collage. When the next class came around the following week, I was elbow's deep in another restoration and happy as a bug in a rug, or was it a bug in a bug.

The day was well on its way before I came out of the depths of my regrets and up for air. Marie's smooth face was easy to see and I loved looking at her. In the few inches of space between the line of the water and top of the window glass I saw the gray of another day, yet thank the heavens, no rain.

After an entire night of leg cramping, woman crying, bilge pumping, the little Volkswagen jerked, bumped and without warning, came to a halt.

I looked through the side windows, then turned fully around to the back. There, in the middle of the biggest lake I'd ever seen, was a small island about twenty yards off to our stern. A crumbling cottage sat at the very pinnacle of the island, which couldn't have been more than a foot or two out of the water itself.

I turned to Marie. "I think we've arrived."

I reached for the ignition and turned the engine over. After hours of being under water, even though my special attention to sealing every possible crack, the water had swamped the engine. It turned over all right but so sluggishly I was left with putting the car in reverse and using the starter to back up. The starter gave up after a ten yards, but the car had pulled out of the water enough that we could open the windows without getting swamped.

I turn to Marie. "If we climb out the windows, we can wade to shore and see if anyone's home."

Marie looked at me. "I won't need any help this time."

I got an embarrassed look. "I'm really sorry for what happened, but there wasn't any other way."

She pointed at my window. "You climb out first."

Getting my scarecrow body from under the steering wheel and out the open window was another thing altogether. My right knee locked up under the wheel and Marie had to jiggle the steering until it slipped free.

After a few minutes, I stood crotch deep in ice water.

Marie made a swirling motion with her index finger. "Turn your back and I'll get out."

"The water is cold. If you want, I'll ride you piggy-back to shore."

With a cautionary voice, she said, "I can make it."

I obeyed and stood for another minute in the water. My

legs began to go numb before I heard Marie gasp for air. "It's cold."

I turned, reached inside my window and rolled it up as far as I could.

I sloshed around to the other side, rolled Marie's window up, then followed her to shore.

A light shower began as we stepped onto dry land. I led the way to the house. I couldn't help but noticed a profusion of chickens and roosters posted on tree branches and pecking on bare spots of earth. We waded through the flock and reached the door. I knocked.

* * *

I couldn't do it. I'd put that pistol in my mouth how many times, but I wasn't able to pull the trigger. Hadn't I bought the gun for that express purpose? What was it, ten years ago when everything looked so bleak and the IRS had ol' Harry by the balls? Hadn't I kept it in my desk for just that reason? I certainly didn't need it for protection. My buddies in the state senate and congress needed protection. My idiot associates on the city council needed protection, mostly from me when I got a hold of them. I was connected in more places then anyone could ever imagine, but it was all behind the scenes. I was so incognito, no one would even consider I was behind every dirty deal I could get my hands on. No one could point at me and say I needed taking down. Only a select few knew the real Harry S. Trunk.

Hadn't I been the one who had bought up all of that property out on the north side of town then talked the county supervisors into cutting a wide four lane past my land. It was me, with my political connections, with Barney, Bowman and Whalde who built Tenican Heights. Weren't we written up in good housekeeping and didn't they write that scathing article about Stikes, the last holdout? Just my luck, because of that article that old woman went national. Every newspaper in the country printed a blow-by-blow report about her grass roots resistance. She became a fold hero. The day the courts made their decision and the fifth fairway was lost forever was the very day I'd purchased the gun. I wasn't sure if it was to do myself in or finish off the old woman. The loss was such a blow, I almost went to the old woman's house that very night. Was it ten years ago?

I'd put that gun in my mouth more times than I can count. I'd also taken it out to finish off that Stalworth bitch, but I didn't have the guts to do either.

I was angry, mostly with myself, for not being man enough to end it all right there in my office. I was rabid at the idiots who blew the wrong side of the levee. I was enraged with the old woman on the fifth fairway, who'd had the audacity to die a few days after the court battle. I was furious at the daughter who continued to contaminate my neighborhood with her fowl crops and those crowing roosters. Marylou Stalworth was the real cause of my troubles. She was the original sin that brought my house of cards tumbling.

I put the chrome pistol in the pocket of my slacks, got a supply of toothpicks out of the right drawer, took a quick glance in the mirror and walked down the stairs of my building.

When I rounded the last turn, looked down the stairs and saw no water, not even a hint of a dribble of water, a knot rose in my throat, but this time my rage focused on Stalworth. I was going to do it.

I stepped outside. The streets were heavy with rain, but not a hint of a flood. Even the sewer drains were clear.

I walked around the building under the private covered

parking lot, pulled off my raincoat and got into my gold Mercedes.

With the engine warming up, I took a small hand towel from the glove box and dried off my bald head. Once I was settled, I pulled my car out onto Baker Street and drove west along the levee, following its contour.

Once on top of the levee, I drove to the breach and sat enraged for the remainder of the night, periodically turning on my headlights to watch millions of gallons of water pouring through the wrong side. Several times I felt for my gun.

Many hours later, for the first time in weeks, the rain stopped. As dawn broke, I came out of my depressed mental wanderings and started my car for the sixth time that night. I wasn't simply going to warm up, I was going home. I wanted to see what was left of the kitchen, the living room and my den. I'd be able to collect some insurance money, but it would be for personal possessions. There's little profit in replacing personal stuff.

On the way to Tenican Heights, I'd make a visit that bitch Stalworth. On a day like that, I could do my deed without ever being noticed. If I killed all of her chickens too, the entire neighborhood would cheer.

I drove to my storage garage and entered the code. The gate slid back. I pulled the garage door open and dug through a pile of discarded junk, old clothes, a dead lawn mower, an upright piano, one entire row of stacked milk crates filled with what, I couldn't remember, three bicycles, one each from a different era. A three-speed from the sixties, a ten-speed narrow tire racing bike from the seventies, and an eighteen-speed mountain bike bought in the eighties. All were, except for rotting tires, in perfect condition.

I waded through IRS boxes, outdated furniture, paintings my ex-wife left behind, too ugly to look at, but too expensive to throw away. In the very back of the shed, behind an avocado green refrigerator, under a carefully folded water bed mattress, I found what I was looking for. Getting it out was an entirely different matter. Sweat was rolling down my forehead and I was gasping for breath by the time I dragged the inflatable four-man dinghy out to the driveway.

Before I attempted to find the motor for the little raft, I unfurled and inspected it for rubber rot. It had been years since I'd looked at it. Once I bought the ski boat, the raft went into storage. My poor ski boat was either grinding its windshield on the roof of my garage or sitting on the floor under ten feet of water. Either way it was useless.

The little raft I thought I'd never use again was still in reasonable shape. I folded it and wrestled it into the trunk of my car.

The little gas engine was leaning against the opposite wall behind an old kitchen table turned on its side. Compared to pushing and pulling a hundred pounds of loose rubber out from behind all that junk, the engine was easy.

Once I found the fuel tank and some paddles, I slammed the garage door, locked it and drove to the Ecco station next to the levee. It cost me seven dollars, fifty cents at a time to blow up the raft, then another thirteen dollars for gas.

I turned to the station attendant, some punk kid with tattoos and a rings in his nose. "Give you five bucks to help me drag this to the top of the levee."

The kid grinned. "Fifty."

"Fuck you."

He laughed. "Have it your way."

He walked to the office and sat with his girlfriend who was watching television.

I stood for ten minutes waiting for someone to drive in. At five-thirty in the morning the day after a flood, the likelihood of someone getting gas was slim. I finally walked to the office and opened the door. "I'll give you ten."

"Thirty."

"Thirty dollars to drag this raft up a twenty foot incline?"

The kid shrugged. "Buck and a half a foot."

"Twenty and that's it. Hell freezes over before I give you a penny more."

The kid's smirk broke into a wide smile. He held out his hand. "Up front."

Small patterings of rain hit my yellow slicker as I pulled the rope of the little engine who knew how many times. I was in a sweat for the second time that day, the first time in a year. Every time I pulled the cord the little engine coughed and sputtered like it wanted to start, but it wouldn't engage.

I wasn't going to give up. I'd paddle the entire goddamn ten miles to Tenican Heights if that's what it took. The engine was going to start if I had to pull on the rope until it broke, which was exactly what happened.

It took five minutes of ranting before I calmed enough to come to the one conclusion I'd been trying so hard to ignore. I'd seen grease under the kid's nails. I recognized the look in his eyes. He had the logical eyes of a mechanic.

I knew how to maneuver a hostile takeover and how to create a tax base to save me from ever paying a penny in taxes. Because they owed me favors, I had a half dozen officials in my pocket. I knew what it would take to build an empire, which I'd done three times in my life, but I knew nothing about paddling a raft in a fast moving river, nor did I know how to replace a pull rope on a cheap Sears and Roebuck motor.

Reluctantly, I removed the little motor and walked it back down the incline of the levee into the Ecco Station.

The kid grinned. "Now I'll take that fifty."

He had me over a barrel. It was something I'd been so happy to do many times in my illustrious career, so I should have understood.

I glared at the kid then pulled out two twenties and a ten.

He pointed. "Put the engine on the bench."

"I just paid you fifty bucks to get this thing running. The least you could do is put it on the bench."

The kid turned his back, flipped open his roll around toolbox, pulled out some wrenches, a screwdriver and a new piece of rope. "Put it up there and I'll throw in a new rope."

Exasperated, I grabbed the little motor and flipped it harshly onto the bench.

"Careful. Sears doesn't open till ten, then who knows how long to order any broken part."

I glared. "Fix the goddamn motor."

"It's an engine."

"Who gives a flying fuck?"

"A motor is powered with electricity."

"Well, thank you very much, Einstein. Just fix the fucking thing."

Within a minute, the kid replaced the rope and pulled it. The engine coughed as before.

While concentrating on the repair, he asked, "how long has it been since you started this thing?"

"Coupla' years, I guess, maybe three."

"Carb's clogged with old fuel."

"The kid smirked and pulled out another handful of tools. In a minute he pulled out a carburetor the size of my thumb and disassembled.

He pointed with his screwdriver. "There it is."

I wasn't interested.

The kid opened a penknife and scraped something, then took a thin piece of wire and jammed it into a little brass part. In another minute, he had the engine back together and pulled on the rope.

I broke into a smile when the familiar putt-putt sounded from the exhaust.

The kid grinned, turned the engine off and wiped his tools. "Should get you where you want to go, but soon I'd take it in and have it looked at."

I wasn't listening to the little twerp. I was half way out of the station before he finished his sentence. I made a silent vow to call his boss later that very day and get him fired for pocketing the money.

I mounted, then started the motor. I put another toothpick in my mouth and launched the boat. With the little motor put-putting away, I stepped into the middle of the boat and sat on the wooden crossbar. I grabbed the throttle handle and gave it a twist. The put-put sound instantly turned into a leaf blower whine. The little boat reluctantly pulled away from shore.

The current was so much stronger than I'd realized. The boat was pulled into the middle of the torrent, spinning me around before the motor could correct my course. It would be another mile before I reached the breach. I'd have to be careful running through the gap, but beyond that it would be smooth sailing. Watch out, Stalworth, here I come.

The rain started again. Within minutes the bottom of the raft was an inch deep. To bail, I scooped water with my hands. It would stay afloat, but the freezing water was already too cold for my feet, which were soaked before I got into the boat. I wasn't about to sit waist deep in muddy ice cubes.

I was so engrossed in bailing, the breach in the levee snuck up on me. Like a vacuum, it sucked me in, tossed me from side to side, pulled my boat under then threw it into the air. For a moment I thought I was going overboard. Maybe I'd get my end-it-all wish after all.

Once through the breach, over the twisting white water rapids of the opening, the water spread out and calmed. My little leaf blower engine chugged me down Main Street. I passed the new mini-mart, Molly's dress shop, Dickerman's drug, Marysville auto parts and swung around the bend toward fast food row.

What was left of the businesses were under ten feet of water. Product floated out front doors and broken windows to join other floatables. The place was a mess.

I steered my raft past people sitting on roofs and looking out from upper story windows. I wanted out of that disaster as quickly as possible. I wanted to put the devastation behind me and get to my house.

I bailed more and more water the further I floated down the boulevard. Steering got sluggish.

It wasn't until I piloted down the highway and turned right into Tenican Heights that I realized the boat was loosing air.

If I went through the fifth fairway, I could cut out a number of turns and maybe make it home before the raft sank.

I made it a hundred yards up the fourth fairway. I'd long since given up on not sitting in freezing water.

All I wanted was to get home where I could get warm, get my ski boat and deal with Stalworth.

As much as I tried to keep the nose out of the water, the boat took its final plunge into the drink. The minuscule motor plugged on. It was pushing an airless inner tube when lawnmower sound that permeated the silence, coughed, sputtered and stopped.

I pulled out the aluminum paddle and tried desperately to hand pull myself down what was supposed to be the fifth fairway. In the distance stood high-and-dry the eyesore, the pain in my ass, that chicken loving Stalworth property and that rag-tag house, and it sat on the only patch of dry land for miles. It galled me when I realized that if I didn't head for that land I'd be up to my chest in muddy ice water.

I paddled for the only piece of earth I'd openly sworn I would never set foot on until Barney, Bowman and Whalde owned it. I'd never even look at it until the bulldozers leveled the house, tore up that stupid garden and every damned crowing rooster and flower-digging chicken was eradicated.

There I was seeking refuge on the last place on earth.

The boat gave up any semblance of being the thing it was designed to be as the last of the air bubbled out of a three-inch rent in the rotted fabric. The weight of the motor pulled it under.

I'd been sitting waist deep in the muddiness, but suddenly found myself up to my neck. I let go of the useless paddle.

Although I knew nothing about swimming, I dog paddled toward the shore. Lucky for me, and not a second too late, on my third dip under water, my last try to coherently swim, my foot touched land. I kicked off the ground and breached the murky depths for another breath. Each time I dropped under, I found the ground closer. Each time, my footing got firmer. As my strength gave out, I could stand and breathe at the same time.

I'd have to get out of the water quickly or I was going to freeze.

Once my feet found the earth, I pushed fast through the freezing water toward the shore until I stood dripping on solid ground.

I trudged up the path to the front door. My entire body was shaking so much I almost couldn't knock. It was a reoccurring nightmare I'd had since the old woman died.

The door opened and there she was. My damn teeth were

chattering. I almost couldn't talk.

Although I was never on the forefront of any court battles, never had my name or picture in any newspapers, my dream was always the same, Stalworth would recognize me and turn me away at the door and it was always a matter of life and death.

She grabbed my hand, pulled me into the house and over to the fire.

"Hey boss."

I looked to my left and sitting on the couch was that sleeze, Billy Marlin. Oh god, nightmare number two. Billy called me boss in public.

"Hi Trunk," Yamelda said sitting on the far end of the same couch. Nightmare number three. Yamelda, that squealing, tell-all-whore, Keating was there.

"Hello, Harry." The druggist, William Dickerman was standing by the picture window at the opposite end of the room.

I was so cold I couldn't respond, nor did I want to.

Stalworth said, "go in the bathroom and take off these wet clothes. I'll get you a robe."

Marlin asked, "how'd you get here, Mr. Tee?"

I could do nothing except shiver.

Stalworth led me to the bathroom door. I stepped in and stripped down to my underwear. Immediately I felt warmer. Through the door, Stalworth handed me a robe. "The tub'll be full in a minute. Get your body temperature back up before you die on me."

I took the robe and closed the door.

She hadn't recognized me. Wasn't it just a few years ago that someone killed all her chickens? Only a year ago all her windows were broken for the fifth time. Only last month her hanging laundry was ripped from the line and stomped into the ground? She blamed it on neighborhood kids, but the two people responsible were sitting in her house. Billy and that sleaze ball Sundog did the dirty work. I paid them to do it.

* * *

Ms. Keating got up, walked over to me and whispered. "That's Harry Trunk."

"Yes?"

"He's one of the biggies in this county."

"Oh really," I said. "Well, he's about to go into hypothermia."

Keating said, "when Harry lost his shirt a few years back, everyone in the news room cheered. He's a sleaze from the get-go.

William dropped his voice to a whisper. "He's been in my drugstore many times. Kinda snooty, if you ask me."

"Please," I said while hanging his clothes from hooks over the wood stove. "I don't want to hear another word."

Keating shrugged. "Just saying."

Dickerman opened his mouth, then decided against it.

I was warming to my little group of stragglers. I hadn't had so many house guests at one time in years. The least I could do, considering the circumstances, was treat them as guests.

I turned to William. "As soon as Mr. Trunk is warmed up and dressed, can you take everyone back to dry land?"

William nodded.

In the mean time, I have an extra egg or two in the frig. Anyone like something to eat?"

I was kidding, of course. I had more eggs than I could ever want. Once a week, I took my extra ten dozen eggs to the food bank.

My whole motley group went into the kitchen. I pulled

out frying pans and cooking oil.

By the time Trunk sheepishly stepped into the kitchen, I'd fed half my guests.

I wiped my hands on my apron and put one hand out. "I don't think we've been formally introduced. I'm Marylou Stalworth."

The idiot just stood there like he didn't know what I was talking about.

I retracted my hand. "Want some eggs and toast? I'm afraid I don't have anything to go on the toast, shopping day was tomorrow." I waived him to the empty chair. "How do you like your eggs?"

* * *

On the dry end of town, inside Clancy's Bar and Grill, in my own unique way, The Dog Man was grieving his friend. Dog saw Billy run for the truck, then disappear into the wall of rain. By the time Dog arrived the truck was half-submerged and Billy was gone. Following our plan, Dog went for the canoes, but they were gone too.

How could that dick have been so stupid to park in the path the flood? All that money lost because of fucking Billy Marlin.

Dog Man was working on a sixth beer —but who was counting— quietly giving thought to the loss of a fortune. Mostly, The Dog missed the balls-out adventure of stripping all the houses in Tenican Heights, the wealthiest digs in the county. Dog also thought about the lost canoes, oh yes, and by the way, that fucking stupid-assed Billy Marlin's dead.

Dog wanted to buy a round of drinks for the bar and honor the lost money, but like Billy, Dog'd been counting on that big-assed caper to pull Dog through the rest of the year.

Dog and Billy counted on it so much, money was spent like fucking no body's business. Dog Man had enough for three beers, a burger, which was on the griddle and a fifty cent tip for Cindy, the hooter babe waiting tables.

Dog wasn't cheap. He knew when to tip and how much. The way to a waitress's heart and maybe a chance to get into her pants, was big tips. Dog Man wasn't about to pass any chance to get closer to Cindy with that hot ass, but fifty cents wasn't gunna cut it.

The Raiders game on the big screen flipped to some dick in a suit. "We interrupt this broadcast to bring you an update on the levee break in Marysville."

Dog shouted, "would you get on with the fucking game."

Of the seven people in the bar, only one turned toward The Dog for a second. They all were listening to the Middle-aged asshole on the screen.

"What the fuck you want?"

"Nutin, Dog." He snapped his head back to the TV.

Oh yes, Dog Man was in a fowl mood all right. He'd just lost a boatload of money and his buddy drowned, but he couldn't tell a soul about it.

The Dog wasn't looking forward to going into Clancy's back room and hustling pool to make beer money.

Sundog just watched all his dreams float down Shit-creek and he definitely didn't have a paddle.

Clancy, with his beer gut gait, his six-inch long handlebar mustache, stepped over and dropped the burger and fries on the table.

"You okay?"

"Dog's always okay, motherfucker. What the fucks it to you?"

Clancy's mustache perked up followed with a smile. "I don't know, you're looking kinda' down."

"Well, shit. Dog guesses he is. This major job he had lined up fell through."

"Make you feel any better, I can run you a tab for a week or so."

"Money's not the bummer."

Clancy leaned one arm on the bar, reached up and twirled his mustache.

"Billy's drowned in the flood."

"No kidding? How do you know?"

"Dog and Billy were on the levee fishing when it let go fifty yards upstream. Dog watched Billy sprint for the truck, but Billy and the truck was gone when Dog got there."

"What the hell did you do?"

"Stood there. Dog Man was hoping Billy was just fucking with him. He's good at that kind of thing, you know."

"Anyhow, Dog Man waited ten minutes and Billy never showed, so Dog came here."

"Maybe you should call the cops."

"Dog Man sits this one out. If Billy's okay, he'll show up. If he's not, there's nothing the cops can do."

"You got a point. Want another beer, it's on the house."

"Yeah, sure. Hey Clancy, front The Man a five for Cindy."

Clancy shook his head, pulled a five and grinned. "You never give up, do you?"

The Sun Dog took the first bite of a burger he couldn't taste. The Dog took another sip of a beer that didn't satisfy. Dog Man wanted to tell someone the rest of the story. Billy's disappearance was a blow, but the money, the jewelry, the guns and knives, the antiques, but most of all the adventure. The Dog missed it all. The cool-assed charge of searching for goodies, and most of all checking out women's underwear was the real loss. It always left Dog breathless.

Dog Man stalked the house first and only raided houses

with babes. Along with everything else, Dog always took a piece of underwear. The Dog's collection was in a refrigerator-shipping crate in the storage unit. Sometimes Dog would crawl into the mound of silkiness.

The next beer came, then the next and the next. By the end of the night, Dog was plastered.

* * *

When Sundog's head dropped to the bar, he stayed in that position until Cindy and I closed.

I shook him. "Come on Dog, we're closing. You gotta' go home."

Cindy put her hands on her hips. "I don't think he's moving, boss."

"Let's lower him to the floor where he can sleep it off. When he wakes he'll find his way out."

Cindy helped me lay him out on the floor. "You know, when he's out like this, he's kinda' cute. If he just wouldn't open his racist and sexist mouth, a girl like me could fall for someone as cute as he is."

I put a towel under his head. "There's a bunch of cute jerks out there, Cindy. They're usually the most exciting ones. If you want to live a normal life, find one not so exciting. This guy is trouble with a capitol Tee."

"How can I tell?"

"Each one's different. Each one is a jerk to some degree. Look for one who's jerkiness matches yours."

"You don't seem like a jerk."

I walked over and flip the six electrical switches. "I got my shit too. It's just well hidden in my fifty-three years."

The room went dark and Cindy and I walked into the parking lot. I locked the front door.

"I'd like to find someone like you, Clancy."

I knew Cindy was infatuated with me. What, was she twenty-two? I didn't need the trouble. Back when I first opened the bar, I'd taken advantage of situations like that, but I learned my lesson and I wasn't about to make the same mistake.

I walked her to her car. "Keep your eyes open. Some great guy is going to walk into your life."

"I'd like to know what he looks like so I don't tell him to get lost."

"Think about it this way. The exciting ones are just that, exciting. Most of them don't have the wherewithal or the stamina to stick something out for the long run. The ones who are more predictable might have the ability to stick around and work through the stuff that comes up in a relationship."

"The exciting ones are so much fun."

"Just my point. Wouldn't it be easier to choose one less thrilling and try to figure out how to have fun with him, than constantly being abandoned or abused by the likes of guys like Sundog."

"You might have a point."

We got into our cars and drove in opposite directions.

The next morning, when I opened the bar, Sundog was still in a fetal position.

"What?" Sundog demanded when I nudged him with my foot. "What the hell you want?"

"You gotta' get up, Dog. I'm opening in a while and you can't sleep on the floor."

"Okay, okay!"

A minute later, I nudged him again and we went through another round.

The fifth time Sundog opened his eye. "Things'll be much better with a cold Bloody Mary."

I mixed the drink, then penciled the four dollars under a long list he'd drank the night before.

I held the drink over his head. "I got your drink, but you gotta' sit at the bar to drink it."

He pulled himself to his knees, then to one foot. He held onto the closest barstool and drew himself to a standing position. When he found a seat at the bar, I slid the Mary in front of him. "Hey man, you look like shit."

"What the fuck's it to you."

"Don't you think you ought to go home and sleep this off?"

"You go home and sleep it off. It's my nest egg that just flew the coop. It's my buddy out there drown in the big muddy."

"Well, at the very least, why don't you go into the bathroom and wash up. I got customers—."

"Fuck off, asshole."

* * *

The old guy gave us all a ride back to dry land. He dropped Billy off first. I wanted to give Billy a juicy good by kiss, but he had something on his mind. I wanted to give him much more than a kiss. Pulling him to the bottom of the boat and having my way with him again was more of what I had in mind.

He got out of the boat without as much as a glance in my direction. No man ever brushed me off and walked away. I'm Yamelda Keating for God sakes. I'd never been so humiliated.

We pulled away from shore. I sat in shock. I couldn't help look at his cute butt and his sexy, Marlboro-man, stride. God, I wanted him. There was little in my life I didn't get when I set my mind to it. Billy goddamn Marlin wouldn't be an exception.

A voice brought me out of my thoughts.

"You got it bad."

I shot a look at the pertinent little bitch sitting across from me. "What did you say?"

She held out her hand. "I'm Bunny Ollinski. I waited on you at—"

"So?"

"You must really like him. I mean, I don't blame you, but honey, you've got it bad."

"I don't have anything bad, sister." While I'm responding to the little twit in the waitress outfit, I have to pull myself away from the last sight of his sexy backside. "He's only a man. There are many more where he came from."

The bitch gave me an all-knowing smile.

After a stare down, of which I won she glanced away and I went back to my thoughts.

Why'd he walk away? No man's ever done that before. Is my beauty slipping? Is my sexual magnetism failing? The only time my seduction doesn't work on a man is when he's gay. Even then sometimes it works, but it didn't work on Billy? After a night of the best sex in years, he simply walked.

The boat wound its way through town and stopped by my office. I'd resolved not to think about that bit of fluff called Billy Marlin. I mean, hell he was only a man after all. No man ever meant more than a roll in the hay to me. Truth be told, it's all that happened, a roll in the hay.

I walked into the building, not exactly fresh and prime for the noon news, but ready for work. Sylvia could fix anything.

"What happened to you?" the waif of a receptionist asked.

I stormed past the desk without saying a word. She's not a main player, so there's no reason to respond.

I stomped upstairs and burst into the newsroom.

I heard a bunch of, "what's happened and where you been's", but it didn't slow me down. I was headed for Sylvia and straight for the telephone to find Billy Marlin's number. Why couldn't I get him off my mind?

I walked into my change room and some fat, dizzy blonde was standing with a comb.

"Where's Sylvia?"

"Who's Sylvia?"

"My makeup girl."

"I don't know. I'm a temp for the next few days."

"I want Sylvia."

The door burst open and my producer, Harlin stepped in. "What the hell happened last night?"

"You're not going to believe me."

"I already got the story about the mobile unit. Two of the guys and Sylvia are missing. The other two are in the hospital."

"Sylvia's missing? Well who the hell is going to get me in shape for the noon?"

Harlin points at the blonde. "This is Anne."

I put my hand on one hip and glared at him. "I don't want some dipshit blonde, I want Sylvia."

He takes a breath. She's missing. . . and presumed dead."

"Dead?"

He nods. "It was pretty crazy last night. Till you showed up, we thought you were a gonner too."

I sat on my chair. "Sylvia's dead?"

"Anne will have to do for now." Harlin turned and left the room.

I submitted to the course treatment of the blonde who eventually brought me back to something suitable for noon news as I fingered the white pages.

"No Marlin. I can't believe it, there's no Billy Marlin in Yuba County."

Anne teased my hair back to life. "Call information."

I picked up the phone and actually punched the nine of

911 before I caught myself. Well hell, it was an emergency. I'm Yamelda Keating, 911 would understand."

After getting the information, I hung up the phone and looked at Anne through the mirror. "No one by that name in the Sacramento valley."

"Maybe Billy Marlin doesn't exist."

"I just spent the night with him."

"Maybe he gave you the wrong name."

"Think so?"

"I do it all the time."

I stood as Blondie put on the finishing touches. "I'm Yamelda Keating. No one does that to me."

I left the room headed for the news set.

"Good morning," I said, "In late breaking news about the flood in the Marysville Valley."

CHAPTER 7

CLANCYS BAR AND GRILL

I was dropped by that old pharmacy guy, then walked down the side of the levee, across the two-lane and through the doors into Clancy's. I was hoping Dog was waiting, because I had a story to tell and only The Dog Man would believe me.

He was nursing the last bit of color from a third Bloody Mary. He liked to line the glasses. He looked at me and his face lit. "What the fuck, I thought you were dead."

"Shit, Dog, can't get rid of me that easy."

I told Dog Man what happened. I told him about rescuing the ultimate Babe, but I saved the best for last.

"Shit, I couldn't get away from her fast enough. I mean, don't get me wrong, she was a great lay, especially when she turned up the heat, and I don't mean room temperature, if you get my drift."

Dog grinned.

"The destruction of the bedroom was totally out there. When she and I came together, I mean the sky opened up. But after she turned into what they all turn into, a clingy, never-get-enough babe."

"I get you man," Dog said and sipped at the ice. "But shit, Dog can't believe you banged Ya-melt-a."

"Believe it, pal."

I dug into my watch pocket and pulled out a broach. Ya-melt-a wore it every broadcast. It was the size of a quarter, the general shape of two bananas and made of platinum.

For Sundog, it was the clincher. "Where the hell'd you get that?"

"Took it from her coat."

"Is it the very one?" Sundog examined it like a jeweler.

"Let's watch the news to see if she's wearing it."

I point. "Hey Clanc, turn on channel seven news."

"Sure as shit, buddy," Sundog whispered. "You banged the great Yamelda Keating." The Dog Man held the pin up once again. "You fucking well did it."

I scowled. "Wasn't as good as I thought it would be."

"What do you mean?"

"I mean hell, all us been dreaming about doing it to her for how long? When she and I got down to it, she was a little better than most but much more demanding. I held my own until the third time, but after I wanted out. I would have run, but we were stranded, so I fell asleep."

"You fell asleep?"

All I know is she wanted more and I was all washed up. Am I gettin' old?"

"Shit man. When you were done, you should've given ol' Dog a call. He would have come over in a second."

The Dog Man, prowler-of-the-night, wild-man-of-the-south-side, professed unequaled lover in three western states, forgot he'd spent the night passed out on Clancy's floor. Had the flood reached Clancy's, Sundog would've floated away with the wooden bar stools and all those half-empty bottles of booze. The only reason why Sundog was alive at all was because of his fourth Bloody Mary.

He pointed at the screen. "You're right, she's not wearing the pin."

I smiled.

"She-it man, if you'd just given Dog a call."

I looked at the TV as Yamelda was rounding out the day's news. "Now that I've had her, she doesn't turn me on any more. I kinda' wish last night never happened."

Sundog had a gleam in his eye. He had a catch to his voice. I'd seen it too many times and lately with Cindy. The Dog's blood was up. Nothing short of a woman in his bed was going to satisfy him. Maybe I could distract his one tract mind for a moment.

I lowered my voice and pulled up close to Sundog. "I did get into Tenican Heights."

"You what?"

"You know."

"Are you serious?"

"Got a pile of goodies."

"No shit."

"Coulda' gotten lots more if you were along, but I got enough to get us a good chunk of some of that Peruvian blow, I mean first hand. We'll have enough to keep us in good coke for a few winters."

"Where's it at?"

"I couldn't fight the currents. I had to stash it on the only dry ground in ten miles. Never guess where."

Dog shrugged.

"Stalworth property."

"After all Billy and Dog done to her."

"Far as I could get. Buried it in the garden."

"In the middle a Tenican Heights."

"Well, yeah."

Sundog's expression drooped. "The middle of Tenican?"

"Far as I could get."

"How's Billy and Dog supposed to get it? That place is a bank vault."

"We put our heads together, we'll figure a way. I mean we got in all those times to fuck Stalworth's property up. We could figure out how to get in one more time."

"Got in with Trunk's pass, you dick."

Sundog put his elbows on the bar and rested his head on his hands. "Probably got the place surrounded by now. Getting in won't be easy. Back out with a bunch of goods, it'll be impossible."

We sat with our dilemma until noon, pulling on Bloody Mary's and beer shooters. I used a gold coin I'd found the night before to pay Dog's and my tab. Clancy was happy. By one that afternoon, I slammed my last Mary and turned to Dog. "I'm going home and get some shut eye."

"Dog'll be working on an answer."

I stumbled out of Clancy's, around the corner and up the block to my little duplex. My bed hit me in the face and I saw or heard nothing until later that night when Cindy called. "Billy, Sundog's causing trouble."

"What else is new?"

"Maybe you could come get him or we're going to call the cops."

"Why would you call the cops?"

"I don't want to call anyone, but if you don't get over here quick, I'll be forced to. He's busting things up."

"I'll be over in a minute."

"Make it quick. Clancy isn't here and I don't think I can handle him."

"I'll be there."

I hung up the phone, pulled on yesterday's jeans, a plaid shirt, then sprinted out the door. I knew from experience, Cindy wouldn't call unless things were really out of hand. There wasn't much time.

The night was cold and soggy. Fog hung over Marysville like a wool blanket. The streets were wet, but the rain had finally stopped.

I sprinted through the front door as Sundog raised a chair over his head to slam it into the back of the bar. "Gimme' another Russian or I'll. . ."

The chair was beginning its arc as I caught it and yanked it from Dog's grip. I carefully set it on the floor and prepared to fend off his attack.

With a grimace, Sundog spun, almost lost his balance, then his face relaxed. "Billy."

"Let's get out of here."

"Cindy won't give The Dog Man another Russian."

I looked at Cindy with phone in hand. She gave me a nervous smile and hung it up.

I slipped my head under one of Sundog's armpits and turned him around. When I got my charge pointed in the right direction, I moved toward the door.

* * *

I'd completed the twelve o'clock, six o'clock and finally the eleven o'clock news before Steven Hammer and Frank Johns, the two office messengers, got a bead on Billy.

Frank pulled on his little gray goatee. "All we know about Marlin is sometimes he hangs out in Clancy's Bar and Grill on the south side."

Steven sat on the edge of one of the secretary's desks. I was surprised he didn't crush the desk. "Marlin's pretty secretive. What do you want him for anyhow?"

"He might know something about the flood." I lied of course. I'm Yamelda Keating. I never need to find a man. There was always a long line of 'em waiting. Searching out a man was a first for me. It was my one, and I hoped only, but I was determined.

"Keep on this, boys."

Steven stood like he was ready to race out of the office that very second. "Yes mame."

I went into my dressing room and allowed the new girl to remove my makeup, then I kicked her out and tore through my wardrobe for something appropriate.

The station shuttled me three hundred yards across the lake. Since my car was under ten feet of water, the station rented me a Lexus. It wasn't as nice as my Mercedes, but it sufficed in a pinch. I climbed in the car with my appropriately broken-in, faded designer Levies, pointy-toed cowboy boots, and silver tipped collars on a cream colored western blouse. I was dressed to kill and I had my sights on one man. My entire focus was all for Billy F. Marlin. I got the middle initial from Steven.

I found myself getting more nervous the closer I drove to Clancy's. It was only five miles, but it seemed like it took an hour. I parked as far from the pickup trucks, beat-up cars, and rag-tag motorcycles as possible. I sat in my car getting up the courage to go in. I'd never been inside a bar like Clancy's. I'd never been inside anything except for the uptown nightclubs. Clancy's had a dirt parking lot, faded paint and neon sign with two letters burnt out. The outside was enough to make me drive home, but I would never be dissuaded from anything I set my mind to and that bar was no different.

I turned my idling engine off, had a last look in the rear

view mirror, got out and walked across the muddy lot to the paint chipped front door. Under the glare of the low watt bulb I halted, took a deep breath, then grabbed the filthy door handle.

* * *

I was bent low from the added weight of my plastered buddy. When I opened the door all I saw was polished cowboy boots and faded Levi's. Was it a female? I didn't look too hard in case it was some guy.

Sundog was so out of it, his head flopped in front of my face as I tried to get a better view. I wanted one single look at the rest of the leggy view in case it was some new babe. Just one glance before I took Dog back to my place. I could come back once I got him on the couch.

I shifted my load, flipping The Dog over my right shoulder fireman style and rose to face the last person I wanted to see.

Dog Man slurred in a loud, singsong voice. "It's Ya-melt-a."

"Hi, Billy."

"Oh, hi." I slipped around her.

"Wait, Billy," Sundog yelled, arms flailing as we passed through the front door. "Dog Man wants his chance at her."

When I got to the corner, I looked back to see if she'd followed. She was half way across the parking lot coming my way.

With Sundog as baggage, I couldn't move so fast, but I picked up my pace, trying to get around the corner and to my front door before Yamelda could get a bead on me.

I reached the door, pushed it open with my foot, carried Dog in and dropped him hard on my avocado couch. Once I unloaded my cargo, I raced for the switches, turned off the inside lights, sprinted to the door, closed it, and turned off the porch light. I stepped over to the window and looked out at her silhouette standing with one hand on her hip.

I waited in the dark until Sundog moaned on the couch and rolled onto the floor with a thump.

At the same time I turned to help The Dog Man back to the couch, the heavy sound of intent knuckles rapped my door.

"Yes?" I answered through the closed door after the third knock.

"Are you going to open this door?"

I reached for the handle, but I really wanted to snap the dead bolt. I cracked the door.

"I want to talk to you."

I slipped from the house onto the dark concrete porch. "What?"

"This isn't exactly the welcome I had in mind. Can't you at least invite me in?"

"Place is a mess. Let's go for a walk."

"In this neighborhood, t night?"

"I'm known. Nobody will bothers us."

* * *

That damn Billy and I walked around a block with no sidewalks, few working streetlights filled with shanty one-room houses. Except for an occasional jaunt into these neighborhoods with my entourage, I'd never visited this part of town.

While I tried to get stuck-up Billy to talk, my thoughts kept finding media stories. First, there was the dirt-poor-getting-the-short-end-of-the-stick, angle. There was the who-really-owns-the-ghettos story? What about why the city ignores the needs of this part of the community?

With my brain jumping from story to story, I said, "Thanks for pulling me out of the drink last night."

"It was nothing."

"At first I simply wanted to give you a gift for your trouble, but it's turned into something more for me."

"Humm."

"I thought we had something real nice."

"Hurmph."

"Didn't you think it was a little more than a roll in the hay?"

"Well, umm, sure."

I turned to him. "Damnit, Billy, are you going to talk to me or do I have to. . ." I didn't want to say it. I didn't want to turn and walk away like I'd done so many times. For some reason, I wanted to stay and work it out. It was a Yamelda Keating milestone.

"I, I don't know what to say, Ms. Keating,"

"Ms. Keating. . . Ms. Keating? Why you bastard. After last night, that's all you have to say?"

"Okay, Yamelda."

I was fuming. "Your turn to say something."

"I don't know what to say, Yamelda. I guess it wasn't as good for me as it was for you."

"What?" I screamed. My little fist from hell unleashed its spring-steel coil and came out of nowhere. Even I didn't know it was coming. I was surprised when it connected with Billy's lower jaw.

In the darkness of the unlit street, his knees unhinged. When he crumpled toward the ground, I registered what I'd done, but I was so mad I didn't care. I spun on my high-heeled cowgirl boots, rubbed the sting in my right fist and stomped away. I hadn't taken three steps when Billy's body hit the pavement. I didn't even think about turning.

157

No one treated me like that. No one used Yamelda Keating then threw her away like yesterdays garbage.

By the time I got in my car, I'd calmed. The drive back to the dock, then getting ferried across the flood to my third story apartment was in a bleakness I'd never before experienced. No one ever turned me down. No one!

* * *

I'm Samuel W. Trainer, ex-football star, now simply an old black man. I happened to be sitting on my front porch with a lit pipe as I watched Billy The Kid and some fancy dressed woman have their little altercation. I sat outside because Wilma no longer allowed me to smoke inside my own home. She'd laid down the law some years back when two things happened on the very same day. The first was the heart and lung association's study about second hand tobacco. Sheeit man, someone doctored that test.

The second thing that came down the pike in my sixty-nine years, twenty-three years of being married to the same wonderful woman, though she was eighteen years my junior, was menopause. Wilma turned from a loving, demure, selfless woman, overnight into what I could only describe to my pals down at Clancy's as a screaming me-me.

I'd been sitting on the porch for over an hour when my beer-drinking pal, Billy, walked by with that good lookin' blonde. Billy with a good-looking woman was not an odd sight. Most every night he had some female on his arm. The odd thing was, she was no teenager. It was just not Billy's style.

The two of them were in a discussion that'd come to a standoff. The air smelled of anger. Many times I'd seen Billy in that situation. It was always interested to see how Lover Boy handled himself.

When the woman cold-cocked him, my pipe dropped from my mouth and thudded on the rotted wood porch.

When she stomped away angry and Billy crumpled to the pavement, I leapt to my feet.

I reached Billy as the woman disappeared.

I slapped his cheek. "Hey boy, you got to find yourself another kind'a woman."

Billy was out. I wrestled the kid to his feet and carried him fireman style to his house. I staggered onto the porch, opened the door and since the couch was full, I walked him into the bedroom and dropped him on the swayback bed.

After I got him into a position where his breathing was clear, I looked around. I expected some exotic sex den with red lights, mirrors and soft velvety couches. At the very least, I expected a nice bed, but it was just a dirty bachelor pad.

* * *

Being the helpful and conscientious man I am, I spent most of the rest of the day ferrying people back and forth from the roofs of their flooded homes to dry land. Maybe I drummed up some new customers for my drugstore. Not that I did it for that reason, but a little business wouldn't hurt.

I wanted to go back to Cassandra Liltkey's house, but people kept getting my attention. It was dark before I made a beeline for the fifth fairway. I pulled the boat pulled up on the muddy shore, climbed to the nose and jumped onto dry land.

She opened the front door. "What are you doing here?"

"Came by to see how you're doing."

"I'm okay," she said, blocking the doorway, not inviting me in.

* * *

159

As the druggist let me off on the second story balcony of what was left of my house, less than a mile from the evil Stalworth property, he asked, "Harry, you going to be okay here alone?"

"I'll be all right. I just want to be home. Most of my house is upstairs anyhow and it's still dry."

"I'll check on you tomorrow."

I gave him a perfunctory thank you, waived and stepped over to my sliding glass door. I wondered how I was going to get through a keyless door guaranteed to be burglar proof, but the door was already ajar. I pulled it open, took off my muddy shoes, then stepped on my new white carpet which had tell-tale wet footprints traipsing all over the room. My hand polished, cherry wood night table sitting closest to the open door, was soaked. Who cared about a carpet that could be replaced, my coin collection could not. I quickly stepped through the master bedroom and into the adjoining office. There it was. My safe was open and at first glance everything except papers were missing. My heart dropped to my toes. My day, which had reached rock bottom, dropped further into the abyss.

I fell to my knees and looked inside the open safe. I didn't care so much for the missing stacks of gold coins saved for a rainy day. I wasn't even concerned about the thousands of missing dollars in stacks of fifties. The three one-carat diamond rings and a Rolex that was my dad's didn't hold a candle to my penny collection. The penny's including my prized 1909 S VBD were the only things that counted. There were only a few of those penny's made and that one coin cost me a months profits back in the days before the Tenican debacle when I was making a profit.

I hoped it had been overlooked. I wanted to see the thin,

blue cardboard book. With closed eyes, I visualized the book sitting on the bottom under the papers where I left it. I opened my eyes, picked the papers up and it was gone too.

All the previous night I'd thought there was little left to live for. I only wanted to even the score between the Stalworth witch for screwing up my entire life, then I could rebuild, but now that my collection was gone there was really nothing left to live for.

I had vast real estate holdings, stocks and bonds, state and national senators and congressman who owed me dearly. All that meant nothing compared to my coin collection.

Although she had been nice to me when I was freezing and I probably owed my miserable life to her, it wasn't enough.

It's time to settle old scores. It's time that chicken woman took some knocks. If there were a way, I'd have gone over there and emptied my pistol into that Stalworth woman. I'd save the last bullet for myself, of course.

Without thinking about anything other than how to bridge the ice water gap between myself and the house on the fifth fairway, I ran downstairs and into the muddy water of the Yuba. There was a space of two feet between the water and the high ceiling of my garage. The boat might still be afloat. Getting it out of the garage might be a whole different affair, but I'd deal with that problem when I got to it.

Instinct and blind rage drove me. I plunged into the murky liquid with my waterproof flashlight and ducked my head underwater to find the knob of the door between the kitchen and garage.

By the time I found the handle, opened the door and swam to the boat, my bones ached. My teeth chattered.

I burst through to the surface, clamored into the boat and looked around. Its windshield touched the rafters.

I rolled into the boat panting and lay shivering on the

floor until I caught my breath.

Once back on my feet, I shone the light around and found the windshield was digging a hole in the ceiling Sheetrock. Nothing else seemed to be holding the boat from floating freely. I flipped the flashlight beam around the triple car garage to make certain my plan could be accomplished. The only thing holding it back was the contoured windshield. It was one of the main reasons I'd bought the boat in the first place.

I reached in the inside panel along the side of the boat and pulled out the single paddle, a cautionary alternative sold with the boat but never needed. I used the handle of the paddle as a battering ram against the windshield. After a number of whacks, it gave way and shattered into a thousand pieces.

Once the windshield was gone, the boat bobbed clumsily six inches from the ceiling.

It would be tight, but I was certain the boat could fit between the two support post from the auto side of the garage with its twelve foot ceiling to the RV side and the fourteen foot ceiling and twelve foot garage door. Lucky, my RV was in the shop.

It took some time, but I maneuvered the boat at an angle and slid it between the posts to the RV side, I stood and slid the boat along the wall with ease.

All I had to do was get the door open and I'd be free to pursue my personal vendetta against the Stalworth house and its inhabitant.

I was back in the water swimming for the opener switch at the back door when I remembered the electricity was off. Mid-swim, head under water, flashlight in hand, I turned and made a freezing bee line for my tool bench, pulled open the bottom cabinet door then removed a crowbar and large pipe wrench. I bought those tools seven years ago when I was reeling from the loss of Tenican Heights and my hard gained fortune. In those days of strapped checking accounts, stock margins called in and little if any income, I thought I might just as easily fix my own plumbing as pay a plumbers. The first time I barked my knuckle when the wrench slipped, my budding plumbing career was over. With a rag wrapped around my hand, the handle of the thrown wrench sticking deeply into the sheet rock, I made a phone call to Peter's plumbing. Once the tool was extricated, it and the crowbar got placed in the bottom cabinet of my new tool bench. Those two tools and some old rags were the only implements inside the cabinet. When I opened the door it was easy to find them.

Heavy as they were, I grabbed them and pushed off the floor to the surface of the water. When I burst into open air, I gasped for air.

I lay on the floor of the boat violently shivering, gasping for one breath after another. I could have easily turned and forgotten the whole thing. I wanted to go upstairs and take a shower then sit in front of my fireplace and get warm. I longed to soak in my hot tub. I was sure it was still warm. I wanted to curl up in bed and sleep until morning, but I was on a mission.

As soon as I got my breath back, I took the pipe wrench and attacked the bolts holding the garage door motor to the opener chain. As luck would have it, the bolts loosened with ease and the door was free from its constraints within minutes. I grabbed the chain and pulled the roller door up a foot before my strength gave out. On my second try, I wrapped the chain around the crowbar and used it as a handle. Although not easily, the door slid up until it rested in a horizontal position on the ceiling. I looked out on an overcast day, started the engine, pulled my boat out of the garage, then found my way around the side of the house to the second story deck and tied the boat to a railing.

I jumped to the deck, climbed over the railing and ran for the house pulling ice-cycle soggy clothes off as I went. When I reached the spa I'd stripped to my skivvies. I pulled the lid of the tub back, leapt in and felt the warmth. It wasn't as hot as if the power was on, but certainly enough to warm my skinny old body.

I sat in the tub until I could feel my toes again.

Despondent as I was, angry at what fate had dealt me, I took my time bathing, shaving and getting dressed. I was sure it was the last time and I wasn't about to do it sloppily. Although I was planning on piloting my boat to that pesky Stilwalsky property and forced to slog across the muddy terrain of the future fifth fairway, I wasn't about to end my life without wearing my full tux one last time.

With cumber bun in place, evening dancing shoes on, I stepped in front of the mirror. I looked good. Any gruesome newspaper articles would catch me in only the best.

When I stepped onto my upper story deck and shimmied my way over the railing, I had my pistol tucked in the back of my slacks like in the movies. I had a toothpick in my mouth with spares in my pocket. When I climbed into the boat and started the engine, I was sure my personal score card would soon be balanced. When I pulled away from the house, I was positive I'd never see it again.

Once the engine was started, I steered the boat in a long, slow arc around the front of my house. When it was facing the direction of future fifth fairway, I was happy once again. My life had purpose. When the engine picked up speed and the boat panned out, I felt the biting chill of the cold morning in my face, but I didn't care.

With the speed of the boat, the wind in my ears, the hint of a drizzle dotting my stylish, but shattered windshield, I raced across the murky lake, around trees, over hidden fairways, until I spotted the property in question. Once I drew a bead on the Stilwalsky house, I slowed the engine and lub-lubed it across, what was certainly soon to be the fifth fairway.

I was a bit sad I wouldn't be around to see the Stilwalsky house bulldozed into small sticks. I'd have loved to be the driver of the tractor. I wanted to crush every little two by four, shatter every shard of glass, then spread it over every inch of Stalworth's silly little chicken farm. I wanted to pollute the soil with used motor oil. Maybe I'd bury some used tires under the remains of the house. I wanted the little piece of property turned into a garbage dump. I could only imagine the transformation from garden, to trash heap, then to the fifth fairway. I had a satisfied look on my face as I quietly steered the boat onto the property. In the next few minutes, I was going to even up my long time score with the granddaughter of Stilwalsky. I was going to finish it, finish myself too and that would be that.

* * *

I awoke with a thick head, but that wasn't unusual. When I reached up to rub my lower jaw, a sharp pain kept me from doing little more than carefully exploring its new contoured puffiness.

When I was able, I stood and wobbled into the bathroom to look in the mirror. My jaw was puffed to twice its normal size leaving me looking like a squirrel in autumn. My teeth didn't fit anymore.

"Jesus Mother of Mary, that Yamelda packs a wallop."

Sundog spoke from the living room. "What's up ol' buddy,"

"She really whacked me."

Dog Man staggered into my little bathroom and straddled the toilet. While his stream hit the toilet rim, the lid, the seat and the floor, with very little actually reaching the inside of the toilet, Sundog inspected my face. "Who got to you?"

"Yamelda."

"Ya-melt-a?"

I nodded.

"She packs a wild one?"

"It was a total surprise. She swung on me without a hint of warning. I had no idea she was even upset."

"Sounds like a woman to me."

"I thought we were doing fine and out of nowhere she cold cocked me."

"Where were you?"

"In the street."

"How'd you get here?"

"Just woke up in bed a little while ago."

"Looks like you better be staying away from that babe. Gimme' a whack at her. I'd tame a wild babe like her in no time."

"She's all yours, but first, we got some goodies to retrieve. The longer they sit where I left them, the better the odds someone will find them. I think we get our butts over to the stash pronto."

"Where'd you say it was?"

"Stalworth place."

"How do we get into Tenican Heights?"

I gave him a small grin. Anything larger and my face hurt. I reached deep in the front pocket of my jeans and pulled out a plastic card with a clip on the top edge. I held it up.

"You got Keating's press pass? How the hell you think you're going to use the most well known woman in Marysville's press pass?"

"Give me some credit, Dog. I'm able to think on my feet once in a while."

There was a long silence before Sundog spoke. "What's you got in mind?"

"Tammy."

"Tammy don't look like no Yamelda Keating."

"Sure she does. With some makeup and us as camera crew we'll waltz right in there like nobody's business. We still got that camera we boosted last summer. Those gate guards are about as aware as the sleeping sickness. All we got to do is catch 'em at the end of their shift."

"How you plan on getting Tammy to agree?"

"I know what I'm doing."

I had the phone in my hand and was dialing, when I realized there was no dial tone. I slammed the phone. "Well, shit, phone company's pulled the plug again."

"Forgot to pay the bill?"

"Fuck em', we'll use the phone at Clancy's."

I searched for enough reasonably clean clothes to wear to Clancy's. Dog wore what he slept in. Within five-minutes, we stepped out to a thick, gray, foggy morning.

I put both arms in the air. "It's is a perfect day to go get our goods. Stalworth won't even know we're there."

At seven-thirty in the morning Clancy's Bar and Grill sported six drinking men, a scraggly yellow tom cat and a Jessica who was in her mid thirties but looked fifty. It was the normal crowd.

When Dog Man and me walked in, everyone, including the cat, greeted us. Dog sat at the bar while I went to the phone at the back of the bar.

She picked up after a half-dozen rings. "Tammey, what's ya' doin'?"

"Why are you calling so early?"

"Just got up."

"What do you want, Billy Marlin?"

"Thought you'd want to spend the day together. We could go for a nice romantic boat ride or something."

"A boat ride in the fog? What, are you nuts? It's cold and even if it was sunny, I don't like riding in boats."

I had my response rehearsed. "You're always complaining we don't spend enough time together. Just thought you'd put aside your, I-don't-like-to-ride-in-boats, thing and come spend some time."

I said the magic words I knew would get her. "Just you and me?"

"Will you go slow? I don't like speeding in a boat."

"Like a snail, I promise."

"When?"

"How about an hour. We'll come by and pick you up."

After a pause, she asked, "what do you mean we? I thought it was just you and me."

"I meant me. It'll be you and me." I held my right hand up so The Dog Man could see my fingers were crossed.

Dog shook his head after I hung up. "Billy, you are a total dick."

I grabbed my crotch and gave it a yank. "A rich dick."

We laughed and bellied up to the bar.

Jessica looked at me with blurry eyes. "What happened to you?"

"Talking when I should have been listening." It was the response that kept the Billy F. Marlin myth alive in the minds of the people in Clancy's.

An hour and four Bloody Marys' later, Sundog and me sauntered outside and climbed to the top of the levee behind Clancy's.

Dog pointed across the bay. "We're going to have to get

ourselves something to get across that."

"No problem. We'll borrow Barlow's boat for the morning. He's at work. If we get back by three he'll never know it was missing. Hell, we might even put some gas in it."

We walked a half-mile along the levee to the marina then along the docks to the sleek lined ski boat of James Barlow. I pulled out a ring of keys, fingered through them until I found the right one. We stepped from the dock onto Barlow's boat. I slipped behind the steering wheel and put the key in the ignition.

Dog sat in shotgun. "How'd you get the keys?"

"Copied them last summer when Jim took us out skiing."

"You're always thinking, Billy."

"Can't help myself. It's in my blood."

The engine kicked. I backed the boat out of its moorings like a sea captain and slowly pulled it into the bay.

Far away from the marina, I pulled to shore.

"I'll drop you for a bit to get Tammy in the boat or she'll never come along."

"Sure man, I understand. Just don't leave me long, it's cold out here."

Sundog climbed out and I jetted away.

"Hey babe," I said after a short ride further down the levee. "You ready?"

"It's not exactly a great day to go on a picnic, Billy." She loaded a basket and a large purse packed to the brim, then got aboard. "Where'd you get the boat?"

"Borrowed it from a friend."

She got a worried look and tenderly touched my swollen jaw. "What happened to your face?"

"Talking when I should have been listening."

"No, Billy, what really happened?"

"Ain't nothin.'"

Once Tammy was aboard and seated, I backed the boat out into the channel then raced upstream.

"You said we were going slow."

I reluctantly pulled the throttle back a bit.

"Where are we going?"

"Upstream a ways. Hey look, there's Sundog."

"So what?"

"Can't let him stand on the shore. This is an emergency. We gotta' give him a ride."

"We don't gotta' do nothing of the sort, Billy Marlin. I don't like your friend and you know it."

As she finished the sentence, I slowed the boat, pulled it toward shore and slid up to the Dog Man.

"Damn you, Billy Marlin. This was supposed to be just you and me."

"Hey Dog Man," I yelled across the water as the boat slowed then coasted toward him. "Where you headed?"

"Thought I was going with you to Tenican Heights."

I shook my head slightly and winked.

"Tammy and I are going on a picnic. Can we drop you somewhere?"

Dog shrugged. "Suppose to go with you."

Obviously, Sundog wasn't getting the message. I winked more, shifted my position so Tammy couldn't see my face and mouthed my message.

"Well, get in and we'll take you where you want to go."

Tammy gave me the evil eye. "Billy Marlin, let me off this boat right this minute."

Unfortunately, she was speaking as Dog stepped from shore onto the boat. She stood, pulled her bags together and prepared to get off. I kicked it into reverse and gunned the engine. Sundog lost his footing and fell to the bottom of the boat. Tammy was pushed back and sat hard on her seat.

"Billy Marlin, I want out of this boat right this minute."

I backed out to the center of the river, set the jet drive into forward motion and tried to think of a way to calm Tammy down without telling her exactly what we were up to. "Tammy honey, Sundog and I got a job to do and we need your help."

"I don't care what you got to do, you asshole, I want out of this boat, and I want out right this minute. Pull over right here Billy Marlin and let me out or I'll. . ."

I smiled, pushed the throttle forward and we rocketed upstream toward the break in the levee.

Once through the break and onto calmer water, I shut the engine and coasted to a stop. Tammy hadn't so much as looked at Sundog. I hadn't looked sideways at Tammy. Sundog wasn't looking at anyone. He'd stared out toward shore. He knew what Tammy was like when she got riled up. That chicken shit Sundog wasn't coming any closer to it than he had to.

When the boat coasted to a stop in the middle of the bay, I looked over at Tammy. I didn't like trapping her, but business was business. I knew no other way to handle it.

"Tammy honey—"

"Tammy honey nothing, you sleazeball." She snorted the words out like a steam engine. "You take me back to shore right this minute or I'll scream."

It took a half-hour, with Sundog hanging off the back of the boat, before I was able to convince Tammy to help us. I lied of course; I had to. I said we were going into Tenican Heights to help Marylou Stalworth get off her island.

"I've never known you to help anyone except yourself, Billy Marlin."

"Things change, Honey Pie. I've turned over a new leaf. Getting caught in the flood has given life new meaning."

I started the engine and the boat rocketed toward Tenican. Tammy was skeptical, but if I didn't give her time to ask more questions, maybe we could pull this little caper off.

Ten minutes later, I slowed the engine and pulled the boat around the last bend leading to the front gate of Tenican Heights.

"Here," I handed her Yamelda's press badge. "Clip this to your shirt."

I gave her no time to do anything but quickly clip the badge to her blouse. Tammy gave me a grimace, "You trick me this one last time and I'll get you."

"Good morning," I said as I pulled to the flooded gate. The guard, a pimply faced kid of twenty, sat upright in a small aluminum fishing boat tied to the top of the guard shack roof a half inch under the muddy water.

"Good morning sir. You're the guest of?"

"Marylou Stalworth."

"And your name is?"

I unclipped the badge and handed it over.

The guard looked down at his paperwork and ran a finger down a list. "I don't see any Keating on Ms. Stalworth's guest list."

"She called this morning," I lifted the camera. "We came out to interview her and take some flood pictures."

The phones were out, that was a no brainer. There was no way to check if we were genuine or not.

After a long pause, the kid handed the badge back, turned the clipboard around and handed it to me. "Sign in please."

Inside Tenican Heights, I idled the boat around trees and buildings until we faced the small island.

"Okay Billy, what are you really up to?"

"Were going to the Stalworth property. Look, there it is."

"Yes, I know you're going there, but my question is, why?"

I cut the engine long before we reached the island and let the boat drift in the light current.

"Shhhh," I whispered. "Were coming to the place now."

"Billy Marlin!"

I put my finger to my lips as the boat coasted the last fifty yards toward the back of the barn and bottomed on the mud.

I took the keys, leapt out, pulled the boat closer to shore and tied it to a bush.

"You wait here," I said to Tammy. "We'll be back shortly."

With shovel in hand, me and Sundog sloshed our way through a foot of icy water.

* * *

I couldn't sleep because the same hand that slugged Billy Marlin in the jaw hurt like the dickens. Also, I worried about Billy. Did I hit him too hard? Is he still lying on the street? Why am I so obsessed by him? I had hundreds of questions and they all kept me awake.

The six o'clock buzzer went off. I got out of bed, pulled on my night robe with the fur around the collar, stumbled into my full-sized, mirrored bathroom and turned on the light, except there was no light. I went to the kitchen and found some candles. I peered in the mirror with the dim candlelight and I look like shit. How was I going to do the news?

I poked and prodded at my skin, unable to find any satisfactory resolution to a face that had not gotten enough rest.

I turned on the water and watched it spray out of my gold shower head while I waited for the water to get steaming hot. I slipped my clothes off and stepped into the glass stall.

By the time I'd finished showering, my maid had slipped into the room, laid out my underwear, then gathered up the discarded night garments. I hired her three months ago, but I never remember her name.

173

I'd half-dressed before the smell of breakfast wafted into my bedroom.

I walked into the kitchen, as I'd done every workday morning, half-clothed, half-awake and half-ready to face the world. Sandy, or was it Cynthia, had already straightened up, cooked the breakfast, cleaned the dishes and disappeared.

Except on payday, I seldom saw her. The woman was like a ghost and I liked it that way.

After breakfast, I finished dressing, stepped out of my second story apartment and waited on the landing for the WASS boat.

At work, my boss, Bob Slaterly, in his unredeemable male fashion came out of his office and looked at me. "Yamelda, you look like shit."

While the temp prepared me for the morning news, I thought about how Billy was doing. I hit him pretty hard. From my dressing room, I called. It surprised me that I knew his number from memory, though I'd never actually dialed it.

I was disappointed when I heard a recorded message. "The party you are calling has been temporarily disconnected."

All the way through makeup, the morning news and three short meetings with department heads, I couldn't get Billy out of my mind. At nine-thirty, I found myself with phone in hand dialing the memorized seven digits. When the disconnect message came on, I held my temper and quietly set the phone back on its cradle.

Just before noon, Bob called me into his office. He sat there with his stinky cigar and his dog face reading the local news. "Little distracted?"

"Didn't get much sleep last night."

He ignored my words and steamrolled into his subject. "Go over to Tenican Heights and get us an interview with Stalworth. While you're at it, see if her chickens are drowned."

174

"What kind of spin do you want?"

"Turn her into the wicked witch of the north. Maybe you can make this flood her fault."

"You really got something against this woman."

"She screwed us out of the fifth fairway and a million bucks."

"That was ten years ago and wasn't it her grandmother that took the whole thing to court?"

"I don't care. Stalworth's just like her grandmother."

"Isn't it just one small grassy area in a huge golf course?"

His face turned red as the little veins in his nose swelled. He took one draw on his cigar and snorted like a bull. "I golf there every week. Every time I have to skip the fifth, I'm pissed. Rake that Stalworth bitch over the coals."

I'd never seen Bob with that much venom. It was funny that I'd be revisiting the very sight where I spent the night with Billy. I wasn't sure how I was going to rake Stalworth over the coals, especially since she had been so nice the day before, but I was a professional. My job was to deliver and deliver I would.

I gathered Shawn, my skinny cameraman, a raincoat and three extra sweaters. Henry huddled in the pilot's seat dressed in an insulated plaid shirt and felt-lined levies that made him look like a fat, though colorful penguin. His Hemingway, windblown face grimaced as I ordered us to Tenican Heights. As Shawn was casting off, I settled in the relative warmth of the cabin cruiser then yelled up. "Can't find my press pass."

Shawn poked his head below. "Guards won't let us in without 'em."

Henry idled while I tore through the contents of my bag.

I leapt from the boat, ran across the deck and into the studio.

A half-hour later, new pass in hand, I pushed through the

double doors and stepped into the boat. "Sorry guys."

I sat hard as Henry pulled the boat fast away from shore.

Henry turned to me. "Once were in Tenican, where we going?"

"Fifth fairway."

"There ain't no fifth fairway."

"Exactly."

"Holy shit, Stalworth's?"

I nodded.

We looking for trouble?"

"We're going."

Although it wasn't raining, the day was dark. I stayed below where it was warmer. Half way to Tenican, the fog attacked my hair. It lay limp and lifeless, plastered to my head. Where was Sylvia when I needed her?

I peeked out when we pulled up to the miserable looking guard sitting in the middle of the little aluminum boat.

The guard looked at my pass. "How could you be Yamelda Keating?"

"Look at me, idiot. Who else could I be?"

"But, she passed through here an hour ago."

"I don't know who went in earlier, but I'm Yamelda Keating. I have an interview to get to. You better figure this out pronto or there'll be shit to pay."

"Do you have another form of I.D.?"

I fished in my purse while I grilled the guard.

"What's your name?"

"Sammy O'Dell."

"Well, Sammy O'Dell, you start looking for another job, because I'm calling your boss."

I found my driver's license and snapped it over to him.

He studied it, then handed it back. "I'm sorry if there was any inconvenience, Miss Keating. I'm just doing my job."

176

"Well, you little creep, better start sending out resumes', because your job is almost over."

"Thank you miss. You can pass."

Henry took off fast almost swamping the kid.

A mile later, I was looking for my phone to get that kid fired when another boat passed within twenty yards of us. It was Billy and he was driving a sleek ski boat toward the entrance with a blonde. I stared in fascinated horror as the ski boat approached to the left. I glared at Billy as he stared at my breast, not even bothering to look at my face.

I screamed as Billy passed. "Turn this boat around this instant."

Henry jammed the throttle into high and spun the wheel to the left. The boat rotated on a dime, throwing me to the deck.

I pointed at Billy and screamed, "catch that boat."

Shawn yelled, "what about the interview?"

"Fuck the interview. Can't you see this is more important."

Shawn lifted his camera. "Want me to shoot ii"

CHAPTER 8

CHASE SCENE

Sundog rotated as the boat passed. "Shit, Billy, it's Keating."
Dog grabbed my right shoulder and spun me toward the back of the boat. "Jesus fucking H. Christ, Billy, they're turning around."

"Slam it, Billy and lose them or we're in big trouble."

I jammed the throttle and the ski boat hunkered down.

* * *

I'd been sitting miserably in my little aluminum skiff since before dawn. I was freezing as I huddled in my too thin Security jacket, wiping my nose with a soggy handkerchief. My glasses had been steamed up for hours as the morning fog rolled over flooded Tenican Heights. What a mess.

My grimace turned to a, greet-the-guest smile as another in a short list of boats lumbered up to the roof of my guard shack. My shift was almost over and I was glad. Too many more shifts like that and I'd quit that stupid minimum wage

179

job without the slightest benefits.

I tucked a lock of hair under my military bib hat, pulled down on my jacket to straighten the creases and sat up with a military stiffness. I'd just finished an eighteen-month stint in the Navy. The automatic at attention stance was hard to let go. I held myself back from saluting.

Once I got out of the service, the last thing I thought I'd be doing was to stand guard on another body of water. I applied for the security job expressly because it was about as far away from water as I could get. I never liked boats. I hated open water, and despised standing watch in freezing fog.

It had been a strange shift. First, I had to sit chilled to the bone in the aluminum fishing boat, tied to the roof of our drowned guard shack. At ten, the first weird thing took place. The news crew from WASS came through with, of all people, Yamelda Keating. I'd seen Ms. Keating on TV, heard her friendly voice, and most of all, had seen her amazing breast. In person, though my glasses were so foggy I was having a hard time seeing anything, she looked just as sweet, but her breast weren't half the size they were on TV. With that one revelation, my morning burst. Maybe my entire life was shattered. While the boat pushed away from the guardhouse, my mind struck on every possibility. She must have worn falsies on TV. The camera played visual tricks to make her look bigger. Maybe she had one of those push up bras.

If Yamelda Keating didn't really have breasts as big as the camera portrayed, then what about all the rest of the women I'd seen on television. What if the cameras faked their breasts too?

My world was crumbling right before my very eyes. I'd spent the better part of the hour in introspective depression. My minds eye kept falling on the ugly truth. If the famous, Yamelda, Big-tits, Keating didn't have large breast at all, who could I trust in a world of illusion?

It was about the same time I came to that depressing conclusion that a large cabin cruiser pulled up to my little aluminum boat outpost.

I sat up straight and refrained from saluting once again. A bedraggled, washed out woman with a sneer handed me a press pass. I carefully looked at the pass. "How could you be Yamelda Keating?"

"Look at me, idiot. Who else could I be?"

"But, Ms. Keating passed through here an hour ago."

"I don't know who went in earlier, but I'm Yamelda Keating. I have an interview to get to. You better figure this out pronto or there'll be shit to pay."

"Do you have another form of identification?"

She looked in her purse while she asked my name.

"Sammy O'Dell."

She handed me her driver's license. "Well, Sammy O'Dell, you'd better start looking for another job, because I'm calling your boss."

My mind screamed as I inspected her license. If she was Yamelda Keating, then who did I let through?

I was sitting in my boat that floated much lower than the gunnel of the cabin cruiser. There was only one way to prove the real Yamelda Keating. I stood full height and peered over the top of the larger boat. Trying not to be obvious, I stared at the driver of the boat, looking at the chest of the woman in my periphery. Oh my God, it was Ya-melt-a. I'd been in Clancy's more than once in the last few months and I knew her nickname.

Bewildered, yet fundamentally reassured about all my female icons, I smiled and handed back the identifications. "I'm sorry if there was any inconvenience, Miss Keating. I'm just doing my job."

"Well, you little creep, better start sending out resumes', because your job is almost over."

She gave me a dirty look, then turned toward the front of the boat. The Cabin Cruiser kicked into high gear and almost swamped me as it left.

If she's Yamelda, then who was the woman I let through an hour ago.

While I reached for my radio, I looked out to the junction of Hummingbird Lane and Silver Fox Road under ten feet of water. I watched as the big cruiser made a lazy turn toward what would someday be the fifth fairway.

At the far edges of the fog, almost invisible, like a ghost ship, the cruiser's engines bogged then caught and the big boat whipped around. In the silence of the cold morning, the engines crank up and I watched as the nose repositioned itself pointing directly at me. Two hundred yards away, the boat was closing fast. Their wake alone was enough to swamp me and the engines weren't slowing. The cruiser was chasing a ski boat. A hundred feet between me and the ski boat, I pulled my engine starter rope. It coughed. I pulled again and it sputtered. I had seconds before I'd be mowed down. I pulled a third time. The Tweedy-Pie engine kicked into life. It pushed me out of harms way to the length of the tether I forgot to unfasten. The rope spun me around and drove me right back into the path of the two speeding boats.

* * *

Sundog looked over his shoulder. "You'd better step on it, Billy, cause you and The Dog got big trouble."

I gave a quick glance at Tammy, then jammed the throttle.

Sundog, slapped me on the back of the head. "They're gainin."

CHASE SCENE

* * *

Billy ogled the breasts of that washed out blonde leaning over the side of the cabin cruiser. I wished I were on that boat where I could get warm, instead of sitting in this stupid testosterone special.

After he got a good eye full, Billy glanced in my direction.

I was an unwilling participant in their stupid little caper. I wanted nothing to do with it, but I did use the press pass. When everything was all said and done, I'd be the one the authorities would identify.

I really didn't want to know even one silly detail of their idiotic little plan.

I'd thought about leaving Billy many times in the past six months we'd been together, but I'd never gotten the courage. But then, I'd never been kidnapped and forced to pretend to be someone else, especially Yamelda Keating. She was my icon. I wanted to be like her, not impersonate her.

The big cabin cruiser was gaining. Whatever was in those soggy pillowcases was either contraband or stolen. Either way it wasn't good.

I promised myself that if I got out of this, I would never talk to Billy or that sleaze-bag Sundog again.

My second promise was I'd personally turn Billy and Sundog in to the police. I'd walk right into the sheriff's department and fill out a report that would put both of those idiots behind bars. I made that promise to the Holy Father, The Son and The Holy Ghost. I crossed myself, then slammed Billy with the heal of my hands and screamed over the loud macho motor. "Get us out of here."

I hate men.

* * *

I lifted my eyes from those amazing hooters and saw the scowl of a jealous woman. Was it Yemelda? I'd seen that look many times.

Sundog slammed me in the back and yelled, "You'd better step on it, Billy, cause you and The Dog Man got big trouble."

I was no longer worried about police. I wasn't thinking about loosing the jewelry heist of the century. I, Billy F. Marlin, Casanova of the south side, was worried about another kind of jewels; the ones between my legs.

I jammed on the throttle. The boat leapt forward in the placid water and I prayed aloud for the first time in years.

My ol' buddy hadn't really kept the boat in top running condition because when I punched the gas the engine spit and sputtered. It continued to run and picked up speed, but it didn't have the power it once had.

Sundog gave me another whack on my head. "They're gaining."

If Yamelda's Sunday punch last night was any indication, I was in big trouble.

I glanced back at the big cruiser fifty yards behind us and gaining. When I looked forward again, sitting in the middle of the only channel between us and freedom was that stupid pimply-faced guard. I saw his terrorized look and the little aluminum boat straining against a taught rope. There was no where to go.

My only opportunity to get clear of Yamelda, screaming-maniac-fist-flying, Keating, without plastering the kid was to turn.

* * *

I'd been happy to sit comfortably and watch the misty morning float by. I loved watching calm water on a winter's day. The only thing missing was my fishing pole and a beer.

My second love was photography. It was why I liked my job so much and why Keating took me along that morning. I was famous for pulling amazing camera angles from the most mundane scenes.

Since Yamelda said nothing about why she was turning around and failed to answer my question, I assumed she was off on another newsworthy adventure.

My camera was up as the boat panned and chased the ski boat. Although things were bumpier than I wanted, I stood and leaned with the pitching of the boat to take the roll out of the camera. I clicked on the steady cam feature and got a perfect shot of the ski boat skipping like a stone over the calm, flat plane of water. It was fifty yards ahead of us.

Each frame merrily clicked away. Like a mural painter with a ten-story building to paint, I saw what lay before me. I retracted the lens to frame the tops of the drowned houses. I opened the aperture for more light. I saw it coming. The young guard grabbed his starter rope and frantically pulled the engine to life. The little aluminum boat lurch forward and suddenly stop on its red nylon rope. I slipped the zoom out and brought in very close the guards anguished face. Everything was so perfect. There was no place for the ski boat to go but plow into the kid. Some great footage was in the bag. My only problem was anticipating what the ski boat was going to do.

I pulled the zoom back until the boat was in full view. I smiled when it veered to the right. The guard's expression was excellent. I was in Shawn heaven. I could have died right there, everything was so perfect. My camera, the frame, my very life was running in slow-mo. Every second that ticked by, the camera caught another frame of an impeccable shot on another incredible chase scene, which had no other conclusion than a wild ending.

Had I been driving the boat, I would have plowed right over the guard and filmed every detail. I didn't care why the ski boat was being chased, all I wanted was the shot and it was rolling like a runaway freight train, unstoppable. I felt the shift of our boat. I readjusted my feet to rotate with it. I was still in good shape. As the big cruiser went into a deep spin, I slipped. I wasn't going to be able to stay on my feet much longer, but I wanted the shot more than I wanted anything. I guess it wasn't anything new. I wanted every shot more than I wanted anything.

I grumbled as I was forced to pan the camera across the nose of the boat at Henry and Yamelda's tangled, limp hair. I lost precious seconds scrambling to get footing, to find another camera angle and re-focus, but I slipped on the wet deck. The camera slid from my grip and shot overboard. I grabbed the rail and looked into the murky water as it sank out of sight. I looked up at the ski boat.

* * *

Lucky for Yamelda and Shawn, it was me piloting, the stable, conscious of everything going on around me, Henry Ponce. I'd moved back in the captain's seat to give the wheel room from my overly paunchy belly, pulled my right hand through wavy thinning hair and focused on the scene. I didn't care how much that witch Yamelda wanted to catch the ski boat, R.J.'s cabin cruiser was not going to get a scratch. I'd driven the boat too often. I had history with that boat. I loved boats and that classic mid-fifties Criss Craft, I loved more than any other.

As the ski boat reached the guard, I stopped the engines, cranked the wheel and veered to the left.

* * *

There was only one thing left. With so many witnesses, I wasn't going to add a murder to the list of things I was about to get caught for. Grand theft, burglary, trespassing and impersonating would lock me away for plenty of time. I'd burglarized the houses of all the local judges, Chief of Police, District Attorney and probably any other attorney working within Marysville County. I had to face the cold, hard truth.

I turned the boat away from the pimply-faced kid. I gripped the steering wheel and braced myself. The boat hit the guard shack and I expected everything to go airborne.

How was I to know that ten years ago, when Tenican Heights was first finished, the guard shack had a big wooden sign on the roof, and that three years later the wind blew the sign down on a new BMW? The sign was never replaced. Since no one ever went up there, the heavy steel brace that held the sign was ignored. Instead of using the roof as a ramp, the brace divided the boat in half.

Head over heals I sailed through the air. From certain angles during my flight, I saw Tammy, Sundog, and most importantly the seventeen pillowcases flying with me.

There was a time or two, during one of my many rotations, I could've actually grabbed and held onto one of the bags, but I was much too busy hanging onto the family jewels. I was going to hit the water and it would be hard and cold. The boat was moving too fast. When I hit the freezing water, it wouldn't be fun. I knew one thing for sure; I was getting out of the water as soon as humanly possible. The only likely way out was to accept help from that Black-Widow, cold-cocking-terror, Yamelda, fucking, Keating.

In anticipation of hitting the freezing water, I opened my mouth and let out a long, painful howl. The water was coming and I could feel its hard coldness.

When I hit butt first, the surface of the water was like polished concrete. I bounced. When the water enveloped me, one arm dipped into the murky depths. A leg followed. My head wedged into the water and I dove straight for the bottom. I didn't know which way was up.

When I stopped, I made contact with one of the famous white picket fences of Tenican Heights. Dazed and confused I grabbed a section of fence. I yanked it out of the ground. With a death grip, I held onto the wooden debris. I wanted to take a breath, but there was no breath to take.

I waited for the fence to pull me toward the surface. It didn't. I was out of time. I let go. I kicked for what I hoped was the surface.

CHAPTER 9

SHE IS A HERO

I watched in horror as the ski boat shifted direction, obviously to miss that stupid, pimply-faced guard. I found myself feeling a seldom-considered pride for a man.

I turned to Henry and pointed. "He turned to save the kid."

Henry looked at me. "What else could he do?"

From my limited, sparkley eyed vision, Billy was a hero and that was all there was to it. He could do no wrong.

I watched the boat turn into shredded wheat. A tinge of jealously pierced my heart when I saw the blonde go airborne.

I stood to keep an eye on Billy. I didn't care that our boat missed the kid in the aluminum dingy by inches. I wasn't concerned if I fell into the freezing water. I didn't even care when the five thousand dollar camera slipped from Shawn's hands. All I cared about was one thing. That thing flipped through the air and bounced on the surface of the water.

I winced and held my breath as he skipped like a stone. When Henry came around to the remaining shreds of the boat, Billy had disappeared.

I slammed Henry on his shoulder and pointed at where Billy had gone. "Get over there, you bastard, those people need help."

Had I been by myself, I would have definitely saved the bimbo last. Let the bitch sit in the water until hell froze over, the little witch deserved it.

But, I wasn't alone and there was an image to maintain.

I waited to see Billy resurface. I wanted to be there to save him. He would owe me and that was good.

Billy didn't surface.

The cabin cruiser slipped over to the closest person bobbing in the water. Shawn pulled him on board. I kept my focus on the place where Billy went down. The boat was on its way over to the blonde before I got worried. Billy should have come up for air. As Henry and Shawn pulled the blonde aboard, I lost all semblance of my precious reputation. "Forget the bitch, let's find Billy."

The second the blonde twit was in the boat, Henry leapt to the driver's seat and pulled the cruiser forward.

"Faster, you idiot. He's drowning."

The boat lurched. My eyes were glued to the very spot where Billy disappeared. He was still moving fast when he went under, so I calculated his momentum. Then, without thinking, I did something inconsistent with my nature. It was so out of the ordinary with my emotional makeup, it even surprised me. I kicked my shoes off, yanked at my three hundred dollar Cardavan skirt, ripped my hundred fifteen dollar white silk blouse down the center and dove overboard like an Olympic swimmer.

* * *

I reversed the propeller and slammed forward on the throttle. While the cruiser came to a halt, I glanced at Shawn then gapped again at the spectacle. Yamelda's sleek body cut the water and disappeared into the frozen murkiness.

Once the ripples from her flawless entry subsided, we looked at one another.

Shawn grinned. "She's got it bad."

"I've never seen her this way."

It was all I could do to keep a straight face. The sheer memory of Yamelda the-ice-queen, leaping overboard to save someone other than herself, made me want to howl with laughter. In deference to our two new passengers, I abstained.

I grabbed Shawn and pulled him closer. "Can't wait to tell the guys."

* * *

Once I entered the freezing murk, I realized that maybe I'd made a mistake. My muscles were already locking up from the cold. My breath immediately stuck in my chest.

Since I was already under water, I searched the chocolate depths and found nothing except broken sticks and shredded boat parts. Only my Olympic training as a child and my ever-vigilant laps at the pool every day allowed me to stay under much longer than even I expected. It didn't matter how long I stayed under, I couldn't find the only man I ever felt anything for other than contempt.

The cold water was clouding my thoughts and brought a deep, guttural whine from my belly which turned into a full-fledged feline howl. Lucky I was under water and no one could hear.

I wasn't giving up. I was determined to find him and bring him back from the jaws of death. Other than disgust, or rage, or spite, I couldn't believe that I, Yamelda Keating actually had feelings.

"I love him," I screamed open mouth, in the water.

There was a moment when I forgot I was freezing. I didn't seem to care. I waived my arms involuntarily, more as an extension to my inner revelation than any attempt to reach the surface. The realization that I actually cared for someone other than myself was more earth shattering than any potential life-threatening situation. I loved Billy Marlin and I had no idea why. It was apparent he was shifty and without morals. It was obvious he had an alcohol and maybe even a drug problem. He certainly had strange friends. He lived on the wrong side of town. He didn't seem to have any visible means of support. Considering all of those unsavory traits, I should have walked. Had any other man even had one of those traits, I'd have sent him packing.

Billy Marlin was different. I couldn't reason out why he was so different, I just knew he was. I was truly in love for the first time.

Eyes open in the murky water, I saw the surface coming into view. It was a good thing too, because I was running out of air.

My hand brushed up against something and it didn't feel like shattered boat parts. Was it an arm? I grabbed and felt flesh and bone. I had him. With my last bit of breath, I yanked the limp body toward me and stared into the face of my lover.

With a steel grip on his limp arm, I kicked the last few

feet to the surface and took in huge gulps of air. I yanked Billy's head up. I wrapped my arms around his waist and gave him a squeeze. A half-gallon of water expelled past his blue lips. I released, took another gasping breath, yanked hard on his waist and another purge of liquid shot from Billy's mouth. During my frantic attempts to get Billy breathing, I heard the lumping motors of the cabin cruiser.

I yanked hard on Billy's mid section one more time. The boat was close. Then I heard one exciting, relieving, life affirming cough and a sputter come up through Billy's throat. He expelled another incredible amount of water. There was a moment of silence. For a fleeting moment, I thought for sure death was what I was experiencing. Billy drew in another ragged, water-soaked, gurgling breath of air, this time on his own. My chattering teeth and blue lips screamed for joy. I expelled a yelp as the side of the big cruiser nudged the back of my head. A hand grabbed under my armpit and pulled me around to the back of the boat. My arms had no feeling. My legs had long ago disappeared. The nipples on the tips of my incredible breasts were numb. Although I could no longer feel my fingers, I had a grip on Billy and I wasn't letting go.

Someone grabbed for me, though I couldn't feel them. Voices said something I could not understand. There was only one thing I understood, Billy was coughing and hacking. Thank God he was he was alive. It was all that mattered.

I was yanked onto the platform at the back of the boat, but I couldn't let go of Billy. I was pealed away and I yelped as the life affirming contact was lost between my lover and myself. Without my Billy, I was lost. I lay on the deck with thoughts of nothing except being detached from my other half. Teeth chattering, knees knocking, I was oblivious to anything except my own thoughts of abandonment.

I looked next to me. Tears streamed down my face. It was my Billy lying beside me alive.

* * *

"Damn, she dove into the freezing water."

Henry killed the engine. "She's got it bad."

"Maybe she can get my camera at the same time. Who's this guy she's chasing, anyhow?"

Henry walked to the side of the boat and looked into the murky water. "We'll find out in a minute."

After two long minutes of staring into the water without a ripple, I said, "She's been down too long."

Henry laughed. "That woman swims like a fish."

"She's still been down a long time." I look at my watch. "We'll give it another minute then draw straws for who goes in after her."

Henry snorted. "I ain't going in that frozen soup for nobody, especially that witch."

I counted the ticking seconds. "It's three minutes. I don't care how good a swimmer she is, three minutes is too long for anyone to be under water." I pulled off my shoes, socks, pants, and shirt. My exposed skin felt the sting of the frosty morning air. In my patterned boxer shorts, goose bumps standing on top of goose bumps, I stepped on the bench seat and put a foot on the railing. I gave one last look into the water and dove overboard.

The very second I was committed, during the very last part of my leap, just before my feet left the railing and I was pointed at water that less than an hour before had been snow, I saw something rising from the surface. As I reached the frozen muck and my finger breached the surface, Yamelda's blond hair rose into the air. The last thing I saw, before my head plunged into the coldest water I'd ever experienced, was Yamelda's open mouth expelling the turbid water.

I wanted to turn the clock back a moment. What I wouldn't give to still be standing on the deck, but there was little I could do. There was nothing I could say, mostly because my head was under the surface. My shoulders went under and too soon my entire body would be floating with the debris and melted snow.

The second my chest cut the water, my lungs expelled all of my preciously saved air.

Once in the murk, I made an immediate about face.

My arms flailed. I was on top of the water all the way back until I grabbed at the boat. I missed and slid back under, spitting and sputtering as my legs and arms churned. What I saw as I came up for another gasp, left me with the certainty that I was not going to get much help. Henry's back was to me as he pulled Yamelda out of the water. In splashing exuberance, I kicked around the rear of the boat and clambered for the ski platform.

There never had been much meat on my thirty-three year old bones, so cold was something I couldn't tolerate. Why did I jump in the water? I shook violently as I pulled myself on the landing. I couldn't stand. My mind was foggy. My teeth were chattering and all I could do was huddle on the eighteen-inch platform, watching Henry unlatch Yamelda's hand from the collar of the guy.

When he succeeded, he yanked her out of the water and flopped her into the middle of the deck. The guy was much heavier and it took hank three tries to get his hacking hulk over the rail. All I could think of was my wool shirt, my flannel lined Levi's and those luxuriously thick wool socks.

Finally, Henry reached down and pulled me over the rail and carelessly flopping me on the freezing deck. All of us were shivering violently. I saw my discarded clothes, but couldn't will my arms to reach out. I couldn't slide over to reach even those wonderful socks.

As Henry cranked up the engines, I focused my will. My right hand broke its trance and made an arthritic, creaky, movement into the air and toward the pile of clothing. Once my right arm responded, the rest of me reluctantly followed.

When I reached the pile, still warm from when I removed them, I grabbed the socks and tried to slip them on. My body wasn't bending. Everything was frozen.

* * *

The moment everyone was on board, I started the engines revved them and the cruiser lurched forward. I spun a circle and raced for the Stalworth house because it was the closest. I was familiar with hypothermia and it was nothing to mess with. I wasn't about to have my passengers expire from exposure.

I pushed the boat along the main boulevard toward the center of Tenican Heights. I kept looking back at the guy Yamelda pulled from the drink, still hacking water.

Yamelda's teeth were chattering, but she was getting her color back. The most frightening person of all, sitting on the bench, huddled in his wool jacket, his skinny legs pulled up in a fetal position, was Shawn. His lips were blue. The tips of his fingers were blue. The tip of his nose was blue. The kid didn't have much circulation in the first place. Add a dip in freezing water and his blood was certain to turn to molasses. I could give a shit about the other three.

It was for Shawn that I raced to a warm bathtub. After some fast turning through the quiet neighborhood, the sight of the only house surviving the flood came into view. I'd been to the Stalworth property many times, though not for five or six years. Back then, I'd cart my buddy Shawn and whatever news anchor was popular at the time to do a story from the borders of the property. There was a time when I ran into six or eight news teams. I was pleased the run-down house was still there and though the beautiful gardens had been swamped, the house was high and dry. I was happy that, after so many years, I was going to have an excuse to go inside.

Tenican Heights was far along in the planning and running smoothly when the old Stilwalsky woman said those famous words for the second time in history. The first time was Rosa Parks sitting on the bus in Selma, Alabama as a white man stood over her, expecting her to move to the back of the bus.

The second time was when the police showed up and Grandma Stikes' front door with an eviction notice. "I ain't movin'" both women said and both women went down in history.

"I ain't movin'!" What a statement of finality. It took guts to stand alone and say such a thing in the face of overwhelming odds.

I slowed the boat as I approached the little island.

Of course, Rosa Parks sparked off an entire revolution. Ol' Grandma Stikes faced a litany of legal departments, judicial maneuvering and heavy corporate juggling. She endured negotiating, cajoling and threats. She and her granddaughter faced an army of reporters, TV crews, radio announcers, local and national media, and finally mad dog sensationalist climbing trees and laying interview traps at grocery stores and gas stations.

Yes, Rosa Parks was the first. She was the beginning of black America standing up and saying no. She was the forefront of a tidal wave of change. Ol' grandma Stikes also stood alone. She had no one except her granddaughter. But, like Rosa Parks, her little ten acres also survived.

A wellspring of people followed in her footsteps. They said no corporate takeover and many won.

I was kind of giddy about stepping onto the property that started it all.

I slipped the cruiser into a muddy shore and leapt out coaxing the shivering passengers to follow with promises of a warm house and hot shower.

CHAPTER 10

FROM A CANNON

The punchy passengers groggily climbed over the side and reluctantly jumped back into knee high water, slogging their way onto the only dry land for ten-miles.

Once I got them moving toward the house, I raced ahead and pounded on the front door. When Stalworth opened, I pointed at the line of people behind me. "Most of us took a swim. We're going to need to use your shower and some warm blankets."

She looked over my shoulder. "Oh my."

I sensed her reluctance. My Nam jungle training kicked in. Something was out of kilter, but there was no time to consider. I ignored my intuition. "Some of these people are going into hypothermic shock if they don't get warmed up soon."

She stood blocking the door. I pushed, forcing her back as the first of the shivering group stepped over the threshold.

I turned to Stalworth. "Where's your bathroom? We've got to get these people warm."

She pointed. "Back and to the left."

I grabbed a stumbling Shawn and pulled him toward the bathroom. "Can you get the rest of them to a warm room and get them some blankets?"

I got three steps into the living room and suddenly a chrome barrel the size of a jet engine loomed in my face.

"You ain't going nowhere."

I don't know why I did it, but I was frantic. My buddy was fading. There was no time to talk. A burst of rage rolled up from some deep reserve. It blasted out of me. My right hand snapped up and I slapped the chrome revolver. The gun flipped end over end and hit the wall.

I didn't care where the gun had gone. I wasn't watching. All I wanted was to get Shawn warmed up. I'd deal with the idiot later.

I rushed down the short hall and to the left. While Shawn sat on the toilet, I opened both taps in the tub and dropped the drain plug into place.

There wasn't time to undress him. There wasn't time to do much of anything except usher him over to the filling tub.

Shawn was sitting on the toilet, still shaking, teeth chattering, mumbling to himself as someone pushed open the door.

"Okay, the two of you out of here."

I pointed without looking back. "This guy is going into convulsions if he doesn't get warmed up. We'll leave him here."

"I want both of you in the living room, now!"

"Well, you're going to have to help me pick him up. I can't handle him on my own."

"Pick him up!"

I heard the crazed tension in the gunman's voice. I sensed he was on the edge of sanity, but I didn't care. Shawn was staying in the tub until he stopped shivering.

"I'm going to need some help."

The gunman turned and faced up the hall. "You, Blondie, get in here."

The assailant turned his face, allowing me a profile as heavy footsteps clunked down the hall.

"Trunk, what the fuck are you doing here?"

Harry spun, as if stung by a bee and glared at me.

"Henry?"

"What's with the gun?"

"I got my reasons. All you gotta' do is get the skinny little bastard out of the tub." He pulled back and a tall, thin guy stepped into the bathroom.

He put out his hand to shake. "I'm Sam."

I shook hands for as long as possible. I'll stall until the cows come in.

"Where'd you come from?"

He pointed toward the front door. "Volkswagen."

"The car floats?"

"Stop your gabbing and pull skinny out of the tub."

"Gees Harry, can't you give the kid a little more time. He needs to get warmed up."

Trunk pointed the gun menacingly at my face and casually pulled the hammer back. The report of the huge gun in such a small room blew my ears out. The feel of the bullet passing inches from my ear got my attention.

"You going to get him out of there or am I going to have to aim this thing more carefully?"

My heart was playing jump rope in my chest. I was more than enraged.

"Harry, you're acting like a fucking lunatic."

Trunk raised the gun and pointed at me.

"Gees Harry, have you thought this thing out?"

"I've done enough thinking about Stalworth for ten men. I'm tired of this crap and I'm putting an end to it today."

"Put an end to what? Because if you're going to put an end to what I think you're going to do, then your life is going to be a mess from here on out."

"I don't need any lectures from you."

"Just some obvious facts." I raised one hand and counted off my fingers. "Number one; if you harm anyone here, you'll have more law suits than you can handle. Number two; You're already in big trouble for kidnapping and assault with a deadly weapon. Do you want to add murder to the list?"

Harry scrunched up his face. I thought he was going to pull the trigger. I actually saw Harry's finger squeeze and I talked faster.

"Harry, we play poker every Thursday night. You do this, there's no more poker games, at least not outside of prison. Hell man, you aren't going to shoot one of your fellow poker players are you?"

Harry's index finger relaxed and I sighed with relief.

Trunk spun, pointed the gun into the living room and yelled, "It's not you, it's that Stalworth bitch."

Before I could even think of the next word, another blinding flash of light burnt my retinas. Another deafening explosion blew out my ears.

People screamed in the other room. After the sound of the blast subsided, I heard a chorus of whimpering and moans.

Harry was not playing with a full deck. He was a few bottles short of a six-pack. Harry was coming up short across the board and I wasn't sure what to do. If I continued to engage him, I might get shot. If I backed off, everyone might get shot.

Trunk had always been more than a little weird when we played poker. Who knows what deep end he went off of?

Harry's toothpick twirled, glass eye glared. His ever dressed-to-the-hilt attire always worried me, but I'd pegged Harry suicidal rather than homicidal. I'd always thought Harry would implode alone somewhere with a razor. Harry's cool attitude was a bit contrived. There was a frightening edge to Harry's jousting at the poker table.

Facing the business end of Harry's cannon, all the times he acted weird made some kind of odd sense.

Harry S. Trunk was such an important player in our little town, I passed off his eccentric behavior as quirky and never considered that it might turn dangerous.

"Harry," I shouted. It was the only thing I could think to do. I might again be the recipient of Harry's rage and find myself with a neat little hole in my chest, but I had to do something.

"Harry, god-damnit," I screamed, as the chrome pistol swung back toward the bathroom. "What do you think you're doing?"

Harry brought the big pistol back around to bear on my chest and I immediately regretted every word. But, the big gun swung carelessly and hung loose in his hand. It was not a shooter stance.

"Harry." I spoke more softly, though the report of the gun still rang my ears. "Gees, man, what's happening? Why are you doing this?"

"She's ruined me," he said with a catch in his voice. His chin quivered. "She ruined me."

"How has she ruined you?"

"She forced me into bankruptcy. I've never re-cooped."

"Harry, you're still the main player in this county. You still are Mr. Right when it comes to the who's who around here. How could you say you're ruined?"

"Trust me, I'm ruined, and it's all because of that bitch."

Harry's gun hand stiffened, he turned toward the living room and his eyes searched the building.

"Harry." I screamed. Harry's attention returned to the bathroom. "What will this accomplish? What will shooting her do but land you in jail?"

"It'll even the score."

"You looking to go to prison?"

Harry S. Trunk looked up with his single pool-shooter eye and directly into mine. "I don't care anymore. It's one prison or another. It doesn't matter."

The guy really didn't care. He'd shoot Marylou Stalworth, then probably finish with the rest of us.

"There must be some other way out of this."

"I don't think so."

As if he'd made up his mind, Harry turned and stomped toward the living room.

"Harry." I yelled as I leapt out of the bathroom and looked at the backside of him stomping along the hall. "Where are you going?"

"Get that Stalworth bitch!"

Several whimpering voices came from the living room.

Not being a man prone to violence, I wasn't prepared for the next few seconds, nor was I ready to do what I had to do. I wasn't expecting to do what I did, but I did it, and that was a surprise in itself.

I took three quick steps to close the gap. I laid myself out, sliding into the backs of Harry's knees and knocked him down like a bowling pin.

Harry flipped over me and onto his back as the third ear shattering blast filled the room.

With a speed surprising even me, I rolled out and stood. The barrel was pointing at my face.

Harry's index finger turn from tan-pink to pressure white.

The muzzle flashed. I recited a quick prayer.

Help me
To find my way
in this darkness.

Help me
to make my day
safe from those
who would harm me.

I hadn't said the prayer since I was a kid. The explosion tore at my already shattered eardrums and another bullet flew past me. A jingle ran through my mind. "Faster than a speeding bullet."

Instead of running, I leapt at Harry and grabbed for his gun.

* * *

I own eleven completely restored Volkswagens. Last night I saved Bunny Ollinski and I'd been talking the madman down for an hour. That alone rates me as a hero. When the guy burst into the house with Yamelda Keating he turned our calm discussion into pandemonium.

When the first bullet left the gun, I let loose with an involuntary screech and jumped behind the couch. Marylou and Marie followed. We'd have left the building, but the hall faced the front door and the gunman had it covered.

When the crazy man sent another screaming bullet into the ceiling above my head, I took Bunny's hand. "We got to get out of here."

Marylou grabbed my arm. "Take me with you."

I nodded at her and peeked over the top of the couch. The crazy man was yelling and swinging his gun at the guy in the bathroom. I didn't think anyone in the bathroom had much of a chance at the rate he was going.

"Let's go!"

I stood and sprinted across the room for the front door. I had no idea what I was going to do once outside, I just wanted out.

Little bunny, the Flamenco dancer and myself were half way across the room, ducking in and out of table lamps, dining room chairs, tripping over throw rugs, when the crazy man turned.

Before the gun exploded for the third time, I looked around. When it went off, I was positive the bullet had my name on it.

The bathroom guy body blocked the back of the gunman's knees. I watched in horror as the muzzle flashed a fourth time. I was sure the bullet was closing in on my face, but not until a dusting of sheet rock powdered my head did I realize the bullet had punched a hole in the ceiling.

I wasn't exactly a coward. Hell, I'd done the Baja One Thousand more than a few times, and a person can't be a coward to pit himself against that kind of nature, but I surprised myself by pulling Bunny down behind me to protect her.

"You've been shot," Marie shouted.

I couldn't answer. My mouth wouldn't move. My thoughts were jelly. My limbs wouldn't obey. All I knew was I was much less of a target laying on the floor and it felt good to have Bunny in my arms.

She asked a second time. "Are you hurt?"

I shook my head and opened my mouth, but no words came out.

I watched in horror as the guy from the bathroom made his move at the madman, grabbing and missing the gun hand.

The barrel pointed in my direction a dozen times in the struggle as the two men wrestled. I couldn't run. I was mesmerized. For the fifth time, in as many minutes, the gun went off. This time no one knew where the bullet went. There was a halt in the struggle of the two men. Had one of them been shot?

* * *

Sam put himself in harms way to protect me. It was a first. I'd never met a man who didn't have a what's-in-it-for-me, agenda. I was seeing Sam Kitridge in a different light. Instead of the goofy-looking, puppy-dog-faced, I'll-do-anything-for-a-scrap-of-your-attention, male, I saw a strong, self-reliant man. In a few seconds he'd turned into my hero.

The forth explosion of the gun sent the bullet nowhere close to me, but I was sure if it had, Sam would have blocked the bullet with his body. My eyes softened. The horrible lines in my face relaxed. There was a tingling in my belly. I wanted to kiss him. I wanted to do other things with Sam Kitridge that I hadn't felt in a few years, since Frank raped me and sex became a nasty three-letter word.

Something about throwing his body in front of me lit my love fire.

The two men were still struggling. Sam tugged again, this time yanking me to my feet. We were half way to the door when the gun exploded and the fifth bullet slammed into the door directly in front of us.

"Hold it right there," the voice of unreason demanded. The madman wasn't going to let us go.

I turned, looked back and saw the husky guy lying flat.

Baldy's gun was pointed in our direction. "Come back here and sit down."

I continued to hold Sam's hand as we turned and slowly retraced our steps to the couch. I pulled Sam down on the couch next to me. Ms. Stalworth sat on the far side of Sam.

Baldy grinned. "You don't want to go, the party's just beginning."

Mr. Husky, lay on the floor moaning, a trickle of blood running from his right temple.

Baldy stepped back and sat at the far end of the living room on the satee', leaning comfortably on its one arm.

I slid close to Sam and squeezed his hand. I wanted to take him to the back room and squeeze something else.

* * *

I didn't know what to do with the sudden turn of events. I hadn't done anything different, but for no reason I could fathom, Bunny Ollinski was holding my hand.

Her body was close. Her warmth passed through her wrinkled waitress dress. One breast snuggled against my arm. In the midst of that madman Trunk holding us hostage at gunpoint and bullets flying every which way, me, the man with the smallest dick in the world found myself rising to the occasion.

CHAPTER 11

SARAN WRAP WRAP

Other than the sound of that damn gun going off in the other room, I was paying no attention to the goings on. I had my hands full. When I came into the house, of all people, Harry Trunk was pointing a gun directly at me. I was so frazzled I shot him a glare. "Harry, get out of my way."

"Sit down Yemelda."

I walked past his pointing gun as if it was not there and pulled Billy through the living room toward the kitchen. I'd been dogging Harry for years. I was always sniffing around his sleazy deals.

"Yamelda!"

"Fuck you Harry," I said and disappeared into the kitchen.

Although I was freezing myself, I gave no quarry to my own needs. I was concentrating on my man. Caring for someone before myself was a first for me. It felt good. I lit the oven and fired all four burners on the gas stove. In the few minutes it took me to remove Billy's soaked clothes, find a kitchen towel and dry him, the gun fired twice. Knowing how strange Harry Trunk was, even in the best of times, I wasn't about to return to the living room. But, there was nothing in the kitchen to cover my Billy. There were no blankets, no extra dry clothes, nothing except food and the warming oven. In the pantry I found the only thing that might help. At least I hoped it would help. A number of years ago, one of my sexual playthings covered me in plastic wrap. It was fun, but he had to remove the wrap almost immediately because I got too hot. It was a long shot, but Billy was freezing and he didn't look like he was going to warm up any time soon, so I had to try it. Just the thought of him surprised me with a tingle that spread from my solar plexus.

The room was warmer, but not enough. I tried to help Billy stand, but all he could do was hack up more of that damn River.

I shook him. "Get up you lug, so I can get you warm."

He coughed up another mouthful of liquid and spit it onto the floor.

"You have to get up, Billy or you'll freeze."

He couldn't stand.

Out of sheer frustration, I screamed in his ear, "Get your ass up Marlin, right this second! That's an order."

He leapt to his feet and saluted.

I knew it wouldn't last, so I quickly spun my web of life around him, unrolling the Saran Wrap with each pass. In seconds I had him wrapped in the first layer. He fought the constraining layer, but had little strength. He tried to get his hands up, but I was too quick. I had a second, then third layer on him before he could push his way free. I swirled around him, spinning my cocoon. As the roll emptied, a third bullet made me jump when it crashed through the ceiling. I helped the cocooned and hacking Billy back to the chair. Almost instantly, his shivering subsided. He continued to hack and spit river water, but the Saran Wrap idea was a winner.

As I stepped over to the ancient stove to warm myself, the forth bullet sounded, snapped through the wall behind me, ricocheted off of a cabinet door knob and disappeared through the wallboard above the sink. I dove for the floor, pulling Billy with me.

Although bullet number five came nowhere close to the kitchen, I hid behind the refrigerator.

Bullet number six took another five minutes. When it came, I jumped to my feet, sprung for the swinging door and dove for that idiot Trunk.

* * *

I wished I was back in the attic of my drug store with Cassandra. Please, anywhere would be fine as long as it was safe. I'd been sitting on the sofa, where Mr. Trunk told me to sit. I wasn't about to move, unless, of course, Mr. Trunk wanted me to. I'm a practical man. Wrestling the gun away from the madman wasn't a job for an old guy like me. It really wasn't a job for anyone other than maybe Humphrey Bogart or Sam Spade.

When someone knocked on the front door, Mr. Trunk looked at Cassandra. Up to the moment before Yamelda Keating and her entourage showed up, though Mr. Trunk held the gun, things had been pretty calm. He was relaxed. I had time to compose myself. The couple that came to shore in the Volkswagen were sitting next to me. The only person who wasn't so calm was Cassandra, but she had a right to be nervous. The gun was pointed at her. The crazy man's angry threats were directed toward her and her dead grandmother.

I wished I could have been Bogart for one minute. Just once in my pathetic life I could save the damsel.

Mr. Trunk waived his gun hand toward the door. "Get rid of 'em."

I leapt from the couch toward the door. "Not you." Mr. Trunk pointed his pistol directly at Cassandra. "Bitch woman, you get the door."

She slowly got up.

"Do it now," Mr. Trunk growled.

Cassandra stepped across the room and opened the door. The stocky fellow shoved the door inward, pulling the little skinny guy with him.

When the stocky guy slammed the gun out of Mr. Trunk's hand, I could have sprinted for the door, but I didn't. The first shot scared the piss out of me. A moment later, when the second report zinged over the top of my head, I was ready to sprint for safety, but all I'd managed to do was huddle on the couch.

The third and forth shots confirmed my foolishness in not making an escape, but the fifth bullet was the clincher. It was all I could take.

With the ear shattering fifth report from that giant gun, while the two men wrestled on the floor in front of me, I, William Dickerman, druggist, Mickey Spalane want-to-be, Humphrey Bogart look alike, leapt to my feet and ran for the door. Without turning, without even wanting to know whether the next bullet was destined to plow through my back, without taking Cassandra with me, I grabbed the door handle and yanked it open. I sprinted through the door and pulled it closed behind me. I was free. As fast as my old frame could carry me, I ambled for the boat.

I was half way along the carefully manicured, rose-bush-bordered path, when bullet number six left the gun. The report startled me. We looked later and found that the bullet pierced the center of the heavy wooden front door like it was cotton candy and made a streak right down the very path I was running.

* * *

Sundog's teeth were chattering as we rode in the boat across Tenican Heights Bay. Dog was thinking about nothing else except for them pillowcases filled with booty.

Dog Man turned to Billy and whispered, "How will Dog and Billy retrieve the goods?"

Billy shrugged. He said something, but to The Dog, it didn't make sense.

Was Sundog suffering from hypothermia? Dog had read about the symptoms in Guns and Ammo last fall. Dog Man might not survive, but in his mind he'd already cashed in the goods and was in Peru with more blow than any one person could snort.

Dog had been led by Tammy out of the boat, into the house and under a warm cover before the first shot was fired. Dog was sure it was a three-fifty-seven. The Dog Man had shot a three-fifty-seven many times. The report had a sound of authority.

Once the gun went off, Dog Man was on duty. He was back on track, ready at a split second to spring for the door or a window. Dog would crawl up the chimney to get away from the business end of a three-fifty-seven. Sundog wasn't nobody's fool. The first chance Dog got, he was headed for the door.

The problem was, the famous Sundog Anderson, maker-of-men, lover-of-woman, man-among-men, the pinnacle of the male species had been hobbled out the gate. The second bullet flew right between Dog's legs and split his gold anklet. He'd hid it on the inside of a sock for ten years and never even shown it to Billy, you're-a-fag-if-you-wear-jewelry, Marlin.

Dog Man had been given the anklet by a Sandra with a promise that she'd return before it fell off. Ten years later, her name couldn't be mentioned without The Dog choking. The Dog Man had waited all that time for it to fall off. When the bullet broke the anklet, Dog look to the front door expecting Sandra to saunter in. She didn't.

The Dog Man was about to leap for the door when that cheapskate Harry Trunk stomped down the hall toward him. Sundog was certain Trunk blamed him for breaking into Harry's house and cleaning him out. Dog Man pointed toward the kitchen. "It was Billy."

Lucky for the Dog, the stocky dude tackled Trunk at that moment. As they tumbled to the ground, the gun went off for the third time. The Dog Man leapt to his feet and took a run for the door. When Dog's right foot hit the floor, his ankle gave way. Dog found himself face down screaming with pain on the floor in front of Trunk.

Dog looked at Tammy. "Dog's shot."

* * *

"He's shot," I screamed. "Sundog is shot."

At that moment, for the first time in my life, I found something inside me that would have made Mother Teresa proud. The nurses at Mercy General, where I worked as a receptionist, would have also been proud. Heck, maybe even my mother, had my mother ever given a shit, might have given me a point or two.

I leapt on Sundog, knocking him to his side.

He screamed in agony. While he flailed on the carpet, I sat on top of his butt facing the injured foot. It wasn't bleeding and that was good.

He screamed again as I lifted the foot and felt it crunch. My nursing instructor's voice kept telling me what to do. "If it's broken, then protect it from further injury with a splint."

Sundog screamed, "dog's foot."

There was something so satisfying about the biggest blow hard on the south side screaming with pain. I hated him, but it was no reason to not care for him.

I looked for an object to splint Sundog's foot and found the TV remote.

Explosion number four hurt my eardrums. I'd been so intent on getting Sundog's leg splinted I failed to notice the two men wrestling three feet from me. I shook my ringing head a slid the remote next to Sundog's ankle.

"Get me some tape or something to bind this," I yelled. No one moved. When bullet five left the gun and drilled a hole in the kitchen wall, I screamed the words again.

Ms. Stalworth leapt off of the couch and sprinted through the door in the kitchen. A moment later she handed me a roll of duct tape.

The men were still wrestling.

"Pull a strip and wrap it around where my hand is."

Ms. Stalworth pulled a long section of gray tape from the roll and ripped it with her teeth. The wrap was neat and clean. The ankle was bound. Sundog had passed out.

Bullet six left the gun. Ms. Stalworth and I jumped when the great Yamelda Keating slammed through the kitchen door. She slugged Nutcase in the side of his head. As he crumpled and she shook her hand in pain, the gun fell to the floor.

* * *

Long ago I'd come to the end of my rope around that Stalworth bitch. I wasn't going to shoot her. I was just going

215

to even the score by terrorizing the living daylights out of her. I wanted to scare her out of her ramshackle home on my fifth fairway. I wanted her to take her fucking chickens and move out of my neighborhood.

The gun going off the first and second time was simply another tactic, but Henry hadn't exactly respond like I wanted him to and I was forced to wrestle with him. Jesus, I was Fifty-seven for god sakes. My wrestling days had long since past, but there I was, man-about-town, Mr. Shaker-and-Mover, tux and all, being wrestled to the ground. The third bullet was accidental. While I was fighting for my life and my tux was being torn to shreds, the gun went off.

The fourth bullet I let loose on purpose. I was getting tired and Henry was winning. I wanted it to stop. I pointed the gun at Henry's arm and fired to stop the nonsense, but I missed.

Every explosion after number four happened on their own. God, I was running out of steam. I got an upper hand for a moment and clobbered Henry with the butt of the pistol.

I couldn't believe things got so crazy so fast, but there I was swinging the pistol around and getting all of my little ducks back in a row when a freight train hit me from the side. As I lost consciousness, I realized I'd lost everything. I'd lost my house and my business. My wife left years ago when Tenican Heights took a dump. The flood took the last of my fortune. My biggest loss was the opportunity to even the score with Stilwalsky.

CHAPTER 12

TURNING TIDE

"You knocked him out," the tall, skinny guy said.

Dirty Waitress Suit pointed. "Somebody get the gun."

Henry, who'd wrestled that idiot Trunk to the ground, sat on the floor moaning and holding his bleeding head.

Since Billy was in good shape in the kitchen, it was time to check on my cameraman in the bathtub.

I stepped over Harry and snatched the chrome cannon from the carpet. It was the biggest gun I'd ever seen.

I looked at Blonde Twit tending the Sun Deck, or Sun Duck, or was it Sun Dick. I'd seen him with Billy. "Your boyfriend going to be okay?"

The girl sneered. "This one's not my boyfriend." She pointed at Billy still wrapped in Saran Wrap, who'd just opened the kitchen door. "He was my boyfriend, but he's an asshole."

Billy said, "will someone cut me out of this cocoon."

I could see why Billy dumped her, but I was curious. "Why's that?"

"He's a liar."

I looked at Billy and his face was scrunched.

I turn to Twit. "I don't get it, you're dumping him?"

"In the six months we've been together, he was never once straight with me."

Billy scrunched his face. "That's not true."

Marylou Stalworth came in with a length of clothesline.

I pointed the gun at Harry. "Tie him up, then we'd better get to the bottom of this mess before the cops show up."

Stalworth flipped Harry on his face with her foot and wrapped the rope around Harry's wrists behind his back. "No one's called the police. Phones are out."

Billy yelled, "someone cut me out of this."

I hand the gun to Henry. "It's out of bullets. If Harry acts up, whack him."

"Galdly."

I walked down the hall and looked in the bathroom. Shawn was still shaking, so I turned the water on to finish filling the half-empty tub.

A moment later, Stalworth yelled, "he's getting up."

I raced back into the living room as Harry was lifting onto one foot. I came in low and gave him a body slam forcing him hard against the wall. He released a gasp of air and slumped to the floor.

I dusted myself off. "That ought to keep him."

Henry was passed out.

My lover, my man, my future husband, the father of my children, yelled, "will someone get me out of this wrap, I'm burning up."

* * *

218

I came out of a dream, sitting on an uncomfortable chair in a strange kitchen feeling like a popcycle wrapped in plastic. "What the fuck is going on?" I growled as Yamelda bolted from the kitchen. What kind of weird sexual stuff was she up to?

I remembered the boat splitting in half and me landing in the freezing water, but I had no memory after that. I struggled to get loose, but the binding was too well wrapped.

I couldn't figure out the commotion in the next room, so I tipped forward and finally got to my feet. The wrap was so tight, I could barely stay standing much less waddled toward the swinging door. In the few minutes it took me to get to the door, I quickly went from cold to being overly heated. Sweat was pouring from my face.

When I pushed through the kitchen door, stumbling and almost landing flat on my face, I said, "Will someone cut me out of this cocoon."

I scanned the scene and Tammy was talking to Ya-melt-a.

"He's a liar."

She turned to Tammy. "I don't get it, you're dumping him?"

"In the six months we've been together, he was never once straight with me."

I moaned, "that's not true."

I should have kept my mouth shut. Yamelda thinking I was a liar could just work.

Harry Trunk lay in the floor with his hands tied. A trickle of blood dried on the back of his bald head.

I pointed at him. "What's going on?"

Yamelda, pain-in-the-ass, Keating was looking at me with glassy, I-love-you-Billy-Marlin, eyes. Oh God, I hate that look. She leapt to her feet and pushed me into the kitchen.

"What the fuck is going on?"

She grabbed a butcher knife and pointed it at me. Is it some kind of cult ritual thing? They already did Trunk, now it was my turn?

I backed up. "Hold on one second."

She smiled. "Hold still."

I gave a resigned sigh and sat in the chair. She had me. There wasn't much I could do.

What happened to our great plans and the seventeen pillowcases I'd worked so hard for. It was more booty then I'd ever seen. How close had Dog and me come to some paradise in Peru with all the coke we could snort?

Yamelda brought the knife in close. "Stop squirming."

She carefully slid the knife between my arm and chest splitting the plastic wrap enough for my arms to be free. I wriggled out of the rest. I pulled on my wet shorts and soaked levies.

Not giving her a second glance, I walked through the door into the living room and stared at Harry looking at me from the floor. "What are you doing here, boss?"

Stalworth spoke. "He tried to shoot me."

Last night I took Harry's coin collection, his three gold watches, some jewelry the three banded bundles of ten thousand dollars. I was glad he didn't have the gun.

"Anyone get hurt?" I asked, keeping an eye on Harry.

Yamelda came through the door. "Amazingly not."

Dog Man spoke from his place on the floor. "The Dog is hurt."

Yamelda rolled her eyes. "No bullet holes, I mean."

I looked around the room at the holes in the walls and ceiling. "All those bullets and no one got hurt?"

Harry rolled to get to his knees.

Yamelda pointed the butt of the gun at him. "Harry."

It was too bad Yamelda and me hadn't hit it off. She and I could do some real damage in this town. Her with the mike and me with, well, all those things I know how to do.

I looked from Harry to Yamelda and felt something else in her longing gaze. It was a different look, but I couldn't read it.

* * *

Billy Marlin was the sexiest man I'd ever met. While I pointed the gun at Harry, I didn't know if I could keep my hands off Billy.

I handed the empty gun to the tall skinny guy. "You keep an eye on Harry. We got to get some warm clothes." I grabbed Billy by the elbow, but he yanked his arm free and glared at me. "I'll get my own clothes." He stomped off toward the bedroom.

I turned to Marylou. "You got anything dry for him?"

"My cousins clothes were left from last winter. They're in the spare bedroom. I'll get them."

"I'll get them. Anything I shouldn't use."

"Well, no, I guess not."

I heard the reluctance in Marylou's voice, but I didn't care. I wanted to be alone with Billy, pronto.

"I'll pay for anything he messes up."

"They were throwaways. I hadn't gotten around to taking them to the thrift store."

"We'll get some for my cameraman too."

"Sure."

I tugged at Henry's shoulder on the carpet. "You okay enough to get some clothes for Shawn?"

He groaned, touched the lump on his head and got to his feet. Dippy Blonde put her hand up. "I'm still cold."

Dog Face nursed his ankle. "Dog Man too."

Stalworth stood. "I'll see what I can do."

I glared at her. "I'll be back in ten minutes. You come get the rest of the clothes when I'm done.

She shrank back into her chair.

I followed my Billy down the hall and turned left past the bathroom. I swung the closet door open and picked out a pair of sweats and a plaid shirt. In the dresser I found sox.

Billy was in Marylou's bedroom, the one we'd trashed the night before. He was sitting on the bed when I walked in with the clothes.

"Get the fuck out of here," he murmured.

I said, "just thought you wanted something warm to wear." I held out the folded clothes.

"Thanks." His voice was softer. He accepted the clothes, stripped his wet pants and began to climb into them.

I was beside myself. I wanted to take him. It was all I could do to not leap on his naked body.

"Why don't you like me?" I asked the question for the first time in my life. I didn't want the catch in my voice, but it was there.

He pulled on his left sock without looking at me. "I like you okay, I guess. I have other things on my mind."

"What could you possibly have on your mind?"

"You wouldn't understand."

"Give me a try, I might surprise you."

He finished pulling the sock up his ankle and looked at me. "Sorry, it's personal."

Sorry it's personal. What a dick. Sorry it's personal. I pulled him out of the drink, brought him back from hells gate and it was too personal to tell me. The little twerp.

I wanted to tell him what I was thinking, but for some ungodly reason, I didn't. For the first time in my life, I cowed to a man. "I understand."

It seemed to work, because Billy looked at me with his little boy face. "You do?"

"There are things that are too personal. I have a bunch of them myself."

* * *

"You do?" I said. This was a first for me. I had never in my life had a female come close to saying she understood. Yamelda was the last person in the world who I thought would understand anything. What she said added to narrowly escaping certain death, left me vulnerable.

Although I didn't let loose and cry, because any man worth his salt would never cry, especially in front of a woman, I did however pucker, my chin quivered, and my eyes got glassy. I couldn't help it.

"Are you okay, Billy?"

There was another first. A female asked if I was okay. Not even my drunken mother ever asked if I was okay.

I was experiencing a number of firsts. I'd found my pot of gold. Sundog and me were about to live in the lap of luxury for the rest of our lives, and this woman was. . .

I looked into Yamelda's melt-your-heart, sky-blue eyes as her chin quivered.

"I get the feeling you don't like me, Billy."

"Your okay," I said. There it was, all of the guilt crap. I saved your life, Billy and it was so good the other night, why don't you like me?

I was preparing myself for the worst. I got my guard up

and was ready for the onslaught, but it didn't come.

Instead, she said, "you're probably the first guy I ever really liked."

Where was the lecture about truth and honesty? Where was the, you-owe-me discussion? Where was the, I love you Billy, crap, I'd heard so many times from so many females.

Instead, she said, "I have a hard time with men. I guess you all scare me."

"Women scare me." I'd just reveled more about myself to her than any other woman I've ever been with.

Yamelda reached out her hand to shake. "Maybe we can be friends."

Something unexpected happened to me. Some kind of shift took place while reveling myself. It was my first time trusting a woman with anything. I reached out to shake hands, to be friends, but something overcame me. I had never thought about it, nor had I ever wanted to think about it. Yamelda, blue-eyed, Keating was the sexual fantasy of every man in Clancy's Bar and Grill, probably half the state for that matter. She was the woman with tits to die for, though I knew her real secret. The woman who, only two nights ago, had worn me ragged, suddenly looked desirable again.

The next second after I shook Yamelda's hand, I yanked her onto the bed on top of me and she let out a muffled yelp.

I pulled her close. I felt her womanly body and reached for her lips with mine.

I felt cold hands search down from my bare chest. There was a pressing, a tongue searching, but then Yamelda turned her head and grabbed my neck with her teeth. Not a tender grabbing either. She was trying to draw blood and it drove me on. I grabbed her blouse and ripped every button in one pull. I tore the clips and released her breasts from their restraining bra. When I saw her for the second time, though I knew they were fake, I buried myself between her tits.

She giggled, then rubbed herself back and forth across my scratchy beard.

CHAPTER 13

HEADS TOGETHER

I heard a familiar squeal, though I don't think I'd ever let out such a sound. It was the noise of mating and not gentle mating either.

Sam stood. "Someone's is in trouble.

I grabbed his shirtsleeve and pulled him down. "They'll be okay."

I hadn't thought about those sounds until a few minutes ago when I wanted to kiss Sam. It had been a long time since I'd considered having those kinds of feelings. The noisy couple in the back didn't help matters. All I knew was my libido had been reactivated for the first time in years and it wasn't going back where it came from. One thing for sure, I would not be acting like that embarrassing couple in the bedroom. I'd wait until I had Sam alone. I'd hold my urge at bay until the right circumstances, though there was a secret part of me who wanted to thump on the floor, scream and yell like Keating and that weird guy.

I felt more like a bunny than ever. With another libido

warming scream, I reached out and snaked my fingers into the large hand of Sam. He turned to me, his hand a little shaky and whispered, "Maybe I better see if someone's getting hurt."

Ms. Stalworth spoke. "They spent the other night in there and the room was a disaster. Let's leave those two to their nasty little business and try to decide what we're going to do with Trunk here."

I'd almost forgotten about the bald guy who sat at table seven. He was a good customer. He always left a generous tip.

"I'm okay now." Table Seven pulled a toothpick out of his vest pocket and started to get up.

Sam pulled the gun back like a hammer. "Stay right where you are."

"The gun's empty."

"I'll brain you with it."

Table Seven grimaced, put the toothpick in his mouth and slumped back to the floor.

I looked at Sam. "What do you have in mind?"

"I don't know, but I wish those two in the bedroom would quiet down. The noise is getting on my nerves."

The guy who wrestled Table Seven to the floor walked the little skinny guy into the living room. He pointed toward the bedroom. "Maybe someone ought to go in there and calm those two down."

The skinny guy spoke for the first time. "Once Yamelda gets wound up, nothing'll stop her."

Ms. Stalworth walked over to the ancient stereo. "I'll put on some music."

I hated Johnny Mathis. It reminded me of that asshole Frank. After the first song was half over, I couldn't help myself. "How about something more current?"

Ms. Stalworth walked back to the stereo. "Other than a lot of Flamenco music, I don't have much of a collection." The Mathis sound died and a fast paced guitar filled the room.

Ms. Stalworth's face lit up maybe for the first time since I'd known her. She came into the restaurant at least once a week.

Stalworth grabbed something from the side table and turned to face us. "Sorry, I can't help myself." She began what would prove to be a dance I had never thought existed. With snapping castanets and stomping feet, she put on a show that was exotic and sexy. It sure didn't help the tingles I'd been trying to hold at bay.

* * *

I ran along the flagstone path toward the boat when the last explosion happened. A freight train rushed past me, piercing the air next to my right ear. My eardrum almost exploded under the pressure. In front of me, the branch of a small leafless tree sheared and fell to the ground with spatters of blood.

I reached to the side of my head and pulled back a greasy handful of blood. I stumbled on the cobblestone walk. I'd been shot. That fucking Harry Trunk shot me.

I caught my fall as I slumped to the ground, skinning my right knee.

Being shot was the last thing I remembered before my world went black.

It might have been a few minutes or a few hours, but when I opened my eyes, the life I'd known for all those years was still there.

I reached to check the side of my cheek as I heard the

familiar Flamenco music in the house.

I pulled my hand away from the side of my face and the gobs of blood I saw on my way to the flagstone, seemed only a trickle, like a nosebleed.

I'd been shot, but I survived.

I made my first moves to see if everything was still working. My right knee pained me, but in general, I was okay.

The music drew my attention. The sound took me back to my store before the flood when I watched Cassandra. The music calmed my frayed nerves.

The situation must be under control or they wouldn't be playing music, and wasn't that stomping and the clicking of castanets? The thought of Cassandra dancing drew me and I turned away from safety of the boat and walked back to the house. A ragged hole the size of a quarter had pierced the exact middle of the door. Drawn in by the flowing music of the guitar, I opened the door. My heart jumped as Cassandra spun and twirled, leaping and stomping, snapping her castanets. The music flashed and flared, then came to a dramatic finish. Cassandra did a few last stomps with her heals and ended her performance.

My hands came together in automatic response and my applause filled the silent room. It spurred the others to join in.

Cassandra glanced at me, took a long bow and ran into the kitchen.

The applause was dying when Cassandra came back with a wet towel and a bottle of rubbing alcohol. "You've been hurt."

"It's just a scratch."

She pointed at the bench against the west wall. "Sit here and let me clean you up."

I sat.

"It's your ear."

"What about my ear."

"The lob is missing."

"The lobe. Is that all?"

She dabbed at my ear. "It seems to be, but it's bleeding a lot. We're going to have to put pressure on it to stop the bleeding. It might hurt."

I smile. "It's only my ear. I thought the whole side of my head was missing. Ouch, what are you doing?"

"Applying pressure."

CHAPTER 14

STALWORTHS REVENGE

"I wouldn't try to get up," said the tall guy, pointing the gun at that crazy man.

When I started into my dance, I'd completely forgotten Harry was lying on the floor. I was so shaken from the turn of events, dancing was my only way to release tension.

"I'm shifting positions," Harry said, then turned his gaze in my direction. "That was an amazing performance. Where did you learn to dance like that?"

"Thank you."

He sat up. "I'm serious, that was wonderful. Who is your teacher?"

"A friend."

"She give private lessons?"

What was Harry pulling?

"You'll have to find out for yourself, now won't you."

He slumped back in position. "No reason to get testy."

"No reason to get testy? You come in here with a gun the size of Alaska and you say there's no reason to get testy."

"I didn't mean to shoot it."

I point at him. "Don't you get it, Mr. Trunk, guns are never meant to be fired."

"Nobody got hurt."

"By the skin of your teeth, no one got hurt. My nerves are ruined. I don't know if you've looked around, but there are six large holes in my house, one of them right through my grandmother's front door. She brought that door from the old house in Chicago. That door's been in my family for five generations."

Harry shrugged. "I'll replace the door."

My voice level rose higher than it had since grandma Stikes died. "That door can't be replaced. It's a family heirloom." Ten years of holding in every sleazy little trick pulled on me. Ten years of calling the police and not getting a response. They all wanted me out. I had a lot of built up frustration. What was coming to the surface was only the tip of the iceberg. "I can't believe you, you sanctimonious bastard. You act like you're innocent."

Harry shrugged again, which enraged me more. My voice rose. "I know who you are. Your dirty tricks have been hurting me for years. I know who poisoned my well and who tried to burn my house to the ground, twice."

I grabbed the gun from the tall guy, flipped it around holding it by the barrel, "I ought to stove your head in right here and we might call it even."

I pulled my arm back to give him a whack. It would have felt good, but I came to my senses, looked around and tossed the gun back to the tall guy.

"What, do you get some kind of kick out of messing with a single woman trying to live her life in peace. Don't you know the court battle was not my battle? It killed my grandmother. It was her battle."

Harry got an odd look. "But, you're still living here on the fifth fairway."

"You're God damn rights I'm still living on the fifth fairway. You and your little development buddies killed my grandmother. If that's not reason enough to continue living here, then I don't know a better one."

After a long silence, I looked around the livingroom and everyone was staring.

He spoke in a quiet, sheepish tone. "I only wanted to know who teaches that kind of dancing."

It was the last thing I would have guessed. Harry S. Trunk was interested in Flamenco dancing. Of all the men I knew, William Dickerman excluded, not one was even the slightest bit interested in the Flamenco.

Harry asked quietly, "who's your teacher?"

"It'll be a cold day in hell before I'd be dancing in same room with you, Harry Trunk. If you come around me while I'm dancing, I'll have a restraining order on you faster than you can think."

"I'm sorry you feel that way, Miss Stalworth. I never meant to harm you."

"Well you've harmed me and you've harassed me for the last time. When the police get here you'll be put away for a long time."

* * *

I was sitting in that stupid little aluminum skiff guarding what was left of the front gate, trying to place a call to my boss, when the big cabin cruiser turned at the last second and threw a wake the size of a city bus over me. Lucky I had my rain jacket and pants on, because the water was freezing.

Instead of going back to town, the big cruiser turned around and blasted to the only property not ten feet under water; that ever troublesome Stalworth property. While I bailed water with frozen fingers, I tried to call home base on my water soaked walkie-talkie. I'd been trying for twenty minutes with no answer.

I jumped when I heard the familiar crack of muffled gunfire. A minute later, the second shot echoed across the silent water.

"Hello, Stan, this is Sammy at the gate. Come in Stan. We've got a problem, over."

Last week I'd gotten in big trouble for leaving my post for the twenty seconds it took to step across the alley and get a coke from the vending machine. I almost got fired and I needed that shitty-assed job, so I wasn't leaving the gate no matter what.

"Hello, Stan. Come in Stan, Over."

I was tired of calling, and there was still two hours left of my shift, but I wasn't sure I was going to make it before I turned into a solid block of ice.

The third report rolled across the water from the Stalworth property, then the fourth and fifth. When the sixth pop of the gun sounded, I found out later that it plowed through Stalworth's front door, nicked the earlobe of the druggist William Dickerman and bridged the gap across the water to my little aluminum skiff. It pierced a hole, first in one side, then the other, slightly under the water line, missing my foot by inches. I was so intent on trying to get my boss on the walkie-talkie, I failed to notice until the craft was three inches deep in water and beyond bailing. I was going down. I called in a mayday, but got no response. I was six inches deep in water when I saw the only solution to my predicament. With some fast thinking,

I paddled to the roof of the security shack. As the boat made its last gurgling effort to stay afloat, with my soggy walkie-talkie in hand, I deftly stepped from the doomed craft, balanced on the steel plate bolted to the top edge of the roof and started more frantic calls for help.

* * *

I pointed the pistol at Harry Trunk while Stalworth yelled at him for five minutes. I was getting concerned that maybe she might start hitting or kicking him, so I interjected with the only sentence I could come up with. "I thought the police were coming, Ms. Stalworth."

She turned away from Trunk and looked at me with a sarcastic grimace. "I couldn't tell you, Mr. whatever your name is."

"Kitridge. Sam Kitridge."

"Look, Sam Kitridge, if they haven't gotten here by now, I'd say they weren't coming. The phones are down and I'm sure they have their hands full."

It worked. The momentary distraction calmed her.

She turned to Trunk, but before she started in, I said, "This gun's getting heavy. Maybe you could take it for a while?"

She turned back to me with a sneer. "I hate guns. Give it to someone else."

I looked around the room, but no one volunteered, so I just let it fall to my side. I could still bring it up and club Trunk if necessary.

Stalworth turned back to Trunk who was still sitting on the floor and started naming each circumstance where the guy had harassed her, but the intensity of her speech was lessened, so I relaxed and sat back in the couch next to the ever so lovely Bunny Ollinski.

Stalworth was working her way back the entire ten years with a pile of complaints and she was naming Trunk in every one.

Trunk pulled another toothpick from his pocket and though he calmly stayed on the floor, he winced with every new accusation.

It had been a while since the last bullet was fired and the police still hadn't arrived. Stalworth was going strong. She had a lot of grievances and Harry was being forced to listen to every one. Unfortunately, except the couple romping in the bedroom, so was everyone else.

Every time things looked dangerous, I asked another of my stupid questions. She'd turn to me and toss some snide remark, then return to Trunk, but she would also be calmer. I felt like a fool, but it worked.

All I really wanted was to put the gun down, grab Bunny and get the hell out of there. If I hadn't thought the police would be arriving and that my report would be important, I would have left long ago. Fed up with the yelling, I did something completely out of character; I stood and screamed, "Stop!"

Both Stalworth and Trunk looked at me.

"Stop this insane bitching. Okay, the guy has made your life impossible and he's shot up your house. Now we all have some decision's to make."

"What do you have in mind," she spit sarcastically.

"I don't really know, but I do know you've been yelling at him for a long time. It and that insane mating in the bedroom is getting on my nerves. We need to decide what we want to do with this guy?"

The same moment I finished my sentence, the banging and moaning from the bedroom reached a crescendo and then came to an abrupt halt.

I pointed at the bedroom. "Let's get everyone out here and make some decisions."

* * *

I held pressure on my missing earlobe while the tall guy got up and handed the pistol to the waitress.

She held it by the barrel with her fingertips like it was a greasy car part. "What am I going to do with this?"

With his back to us walking down the hall, the tall guy said, "brain him with it if he moves."

He banged on the bedroom door. "Hey, we need you out here."

Although it was muffled, Ms. Keating said in a much more husky voice than I'd ever heard. "We'll be out when we're damn good and ready."

The tall guy knocked on the door again. "We got some talking to do before the police get here and we need you to be part of it."

"I don't have anything to say," the dopey surfer guy's voice echoed down the hall.

The tall guy said, "Were deciding what to do with Trunk?"

There was a silence, then rustling.

Both the surfer guy and Yamelda spoke at the same time. "We'll be right out."

The tall guy stomped up the hall and sat close to the waitress. When he spoke, it was with a voice of authority.

"Considering no one got hurt, we're left with a lot of choices." He put one finger up. "We turn Trunk over to the police, if they ever get here."

He put a second finger up. "We figure a way to forget

this whole episode ever happened."

"Ever happened?" Cassandra shouted. "This total nut-case comes into my house and blast it to pieces and you want to act like nothing happened."

"You really want to go through another court battle?"

She put a hand on her hip. "So?"

"We charge this guy and we're all going to court right along with him and get up on the witness stand. All of our personal quirks are going to be public as the lawyers try to destroy our credibility. It's the way the system works."

She got a worried look. "You've got a point."

Harry Trunk grinned.

I turned to Trunk. "I wouldn't smile so quickly. You got a lot to make up for."

Trunk looked at me. "I'm not smiling, I'm nervous."

Harry slipped his hand into his coat pocket, pulled out a toothpick and placed it in his mouth.

Yamelda Keating walked in. "This guy is a nutcase. I say we lock him up and throw away the key."

Harry grumbled, "you would say that."

The tall guy pointed at Trunk. "If we're going to get through this, you'd better keep out of it."

Harry shrugged.

Cassandra turned to the tall guy. "I think Mr. . . . What is your name again?"

"Sam Kitridge."

"I think Mr. Kitridge has a point. If we charge him with anything we're also going to have to sit in the courtroom with him."

Yamelda pulled out her compact and looked in the mirror. "What do you have to hide?"

Kitridge stood, walked to the window and looked out. "So, since it was you he was after, and it was your house he shot up, what do you want to do?"

"Certainly, he pays for repairs."

The waitress spoke for the first time. "What about your front door?"

Cassandra walked over to the door and put her finger though the hole. She turned and faced us. "A bullet hole will add to the history. I may not even have it repaired."

Kitridge turned from the window. "He pays for repairs. It's a good start."

The ugly guy spoke up. "He pays medical expenses for my ankle. I'm not going to be able to work with my ankle like this, so he pays disability too."

I touched the side of my face. "How does he pay for my missing earlobe?"

Yamelda spoke in her commanding tone. "Through the nose."

We all looked at Yamelda, then down at Trunk.

Harry whispered. "It's only fair."

Kitridge swept his right hand. "Compensation for each of us for the trauma.

Surfer guy takes a deep breath and exhales. "We ought to let bygones be bygones. I vote to let the poor bastard go."

Yamelda looked at him with cow-eyes and reached for his hand. He pulled away and took a step to the right. "Hell, nothing really happened. What's the big deal?"

For a split second Yamelda got a hurt expression, then looked at us. "The big deal is, Trunk is a certifiable nut case. We let him go and we'd be liable if he goes off the deep end again."

Kitridge looked at her. "Good point."

The waitress blurted. "We make sure Mr. Harry Trunk doesn't go off the deep end again by having him commit himself for a given period of time.

Harry grimaced. "I'm not going to a nut farm."

Kitridge turned to Trunk. "I'd keep out of this."

Yamelda laughed. "Why not, Trunk? You'd fit right in."

Kitridge grimaced. "No need to get personal."

She spun and glared at Kitridge. "He almost killed us. It's as personal as it gets."

Silence permeated the room. The spell was broken when I spoke. "Let's look at this as a business deal. If Mr. Trunk agrees to all our terms, then he gets to stay out of prison. If he doesn't then we turn him over."

CHAPTER 15

EPILOGUE

And so, they forced me to commit myself to one year inside the protective walls of Sunvale Sanitarium, fifty miles south of Phoenix. From within those walls, through my lawyers, I negotiated a long protracted settlement with the affected parties. To pay the settlements, I was forced to sell off more properties for less money than I'd ever considered or admitted.

I'd been inside the fluffy walls of the hospital more than six months before I began to compose my letter. I worked hard to find a place of peace and understanding about myself. I was becoming a new man. I no longer carried those old feelings of desperation. I had daily therapy session with Conrad Ilrad, the one person who truly was able to help. I had come to terms with my dysfunctional childhood, with my parent's single-minded focus on money who didn't want me around. I'd delved into the deep-seated feelings that no one liked me. I realized that living my entire life in Marysville perpetuated my feeling of self-loathing.

It took the next six months, longer than it had ever taken to write a simple two paged note to my nemesis. I'd rewritten it more times than I cared to remember. In some way the letter was my revival, though I never told Conrad I was writing it, nor Margaret Flader, the woman I met a few weeks after my forced incarceration. Margaret had come from Hollywood where she attempted suicide every time she didn't get a movie roll. I knew her by her more famous stage name. Over the years, I'd seen her many times in many rolls. She was older, but then so was I. She didn't seem to mind my one wandering glass eye, my que ball head, nor my ever-nervous, toothpick-chewing habit.

Once I dropped the letter in the mailbox, I felt lighter. The next part of my life could unfold. I hoped it would include Margaret Flader.

* * *

Sundog and me, though we were due a shitload of money from Harry, once free of the Stalworth house, went straight to Fred's sport shop, in the darkness of night of course. With my new set of pick locks, Dog Man jimmied the back door and we borrowed two full sets of scuba gear. Fred, who lived upstairs in his bachelor apartment, didn't hear a thing. At dawn, we slipped into the freezing water and dredged every inch of the area in front of Tenican Heights gate. We'd retrieved eleven of the seventeen bags by the time we ran out of oxygen.

We surfaced a few hundred yards from the submerged guard shack and The Dog Man, the maniac that he is, spit out his mouthpiece and looked at me. "Tonight the Dog and Billy go back to Fred's and trade these tanks in. Dog Man wants those other six bags."

I grinned. "Six more bags means that much longer we get

to stay in Peru with all that blow."

Fred lay in wait for us with his twelve gauge. He had two rounds of rock salt.

The salt stung for days. The little punctures took weeks to heal.

While recuperating, we watched while news did endless reports about the manhunt for the two suspects who'd cleaned out Tenican Heights during the flood. Both Sundog and me were forced to hide out at a friend's house in the hills.

Once we could sit again, we drove to San Francisco and fenced three hundred thousand worth of slightly questionable goods. For our services, we negotiated a total sum of thirty-two thousand and change. It wasn't exactly the best deal we could have made, but for obvious reasons we were in a bit of a hurry to get south of the border. We had Trunks cash too.

We abandoned Sundog's weather worn Honda Civic at the airport and booked the next flight to Lima, Peru.

When the plane landed, there was an entire platoon of Peruvian military waiting at the bottom of the ramp.

Our undeclared sixty-two thousand dollars in cash found wrapped in two towels, was confiscated. By the end of the first year, Sundog and me had not once seen the outside of Lima federal lockup. One might say we were snared in an old Peruvian catch twenty-two. We had been charged with transportation of undeclared money exceeding ten thousand dollars and were awaiting trial. A trial could not continue without evidence, which had somehow gotten misplaced. Until it was found —and every official involved was sure that someday it would be found— the trial would have to wait. Whatever happened to constitutional rights?

* * *

Without the constant harassment of Harry S. Trunk ripping up my garden, poisoning my well and otherwise making a total nuisance of himself, I was able to concentrate more freely on Flamenco dancing.

A month after the flood, because the owner and his wife just happened to be my first audience in the window of Dickerman's drug that rainy night, I was booked to do a one hour set at the Knights Landing Bar and Grill. It wasn't exactly Albert's Hall, but it was a start.

* * *

One afternoon, while driving north on business first to bo-hunk Woodland, California then on to Ashland, Oregon, I not only got lost on one of a maze of back roads, but I blew a tire close to the town of Knights Landing. I hobbled into that minuscule river town looking for an open service station, ruining a two hundred dollar tire in the process. Since only the bar was open, I was forced to stay the night in the meager accommodations of the local hotel.

Later, when I came down for dinner, I witnessed the most amazing sight. The Flamenco dancer, Cassandra Liltkey spun and twirled, snapped her castanets and stomped her feet in a display of gypsy dancing.

When she took a break, I stepped outside and called Frank, a twenty-three year veteran L.A. talent scout.

"Frank."

"Sol, what the hell do you want?"

"You're not going to believe what I've found."

"You're supposed to be in Ashland getting that rap group signed on." His voice came through a scratchy phone. Not much reception in Knight's Landing.

"I blew a tire. I'll be in Ashland tomorrow."

"I don't give a shit, Sol. Rent a car and get to Ashland."

I ignored his demand. "She's a Flamenco dancer."

"What the fuck do we know about Flamenco?"

"Nothing, Frank, but she's great."

"Get your ass to Ashland and sign these guys—"

I interrupted. "I'll be in Ashland tomorrow noon, but I'm sure we could get her for peanuts. I'm flying her back to make a demo."

As usual, a long series of shouts came through the line.

"I'll pay out of my pocket if you don't like her."

I hung up the phone half way through a long series of angry threats and abusive language, but I was used to Frank.

When she finished her set, I took her aside and talked her into meeting me in our Los Angeles studios two weeks later.

Of course, Frank liked her and by the end of the first afternoon, Cassandra Liltkey had a signed contract and I gave her a check for nine hundred, seventy-three dollars. Her twelve best dances had been recorded on video and we owned the rights. I love working with green horns.

By the end of the first year, after a successful nationwide distribution campaign, T.V.A. had netted three hundred fifty-seven thousand dollars from that single video of which I got eight percent. Not bad for one video. I wished all of them were that easy.

* * *

A few weeks after the release, when the flamenco video reached San Francisco, I found my first booking agent. Maybe I should say he found me.

It wasn't long after, when a New York agent ran across my tape, and I was on my way. He set up a private performance with me in a small theater off-Broadway. He and six of his co-investors sat while I danced and twirled to the music of my first live Flamenco guitarist.

From that single performance that afternoon, I took a short, almost vertical rise to Flamenco stardom.

* * *

By the end of the next year, I'd received enough money from Trunk's estate to reopen my drug store. In January, I flew to New York to meet Cassandra and see her first Broadway performance. The thwarted night in my secret sex den had not been repeated, though I would have given anything for one more chance. But, through it all we had become friends. In itself, our friendship was a cherished miracle.

In an Italian restaurant a few blocks away from Broadway, we sat at a table behind a frosted front window overlooking the shoppers and street hustlers traipsing in a light snow.

Cassandra smiled. "I've eaten here often. It's very good and best of all, it's close to the theaters."

I held my glass in the air. "Here's to a great performance."

We clicked glasses. She nervously swirled her wine and took sips while I watched the liquid slosh in my glass. It had been ten months since she'd spirited off to New York. Although we talked on the phone, I hadn't seen her since she'd left. I was always a little nervous when she was around. Wished I was twenty years younger.

I broke the awkward silence. "I saw Marie Ollinski the other day."

"Oh, really. Was she still working in the restaurant?"

"Yes, but it doesn't look like she'll be there much longer."

"No kidding?" She continued to swish the glass absently. "Where's she going?"

"Eventually to the hospital."

She got a worried look. "What happened? Is she sick?"

"She's going to have Sam Kitridge's baby."

"Sam Kitridge? Should I know him?"

"The tall German guy at the house that day."

A grin spread across Cassandra's face. "There's symmetry to that union, don't you think?"

"I do. They got married a few months ago, but she looks eight months pregnant."

"A perfect end to the story."

We both giggled.

An awkward minute went by before she broached another subject. "Whatever happened to those two sleaze balls who ripped off half of Marysville? You know, that weird guy, Sunwolf and his surfer buddy Bobbie."

"Sundog Anderson and Billy Marlin. They made it to Peru and that's the last we'd heard of 'em."

"What happened?"

"I don't know the particulars, but they're buried in some Peruvian jail awaiting a trial that may never come. Something about smuggling money into the country."

She lifted her glass and took a sip. "There is a God after all."

Another awkward minute went by. The rotund waiter with a long handlebar mustache and a booming voice delivered our dinner. He told a short Italian joke, then, while we were giggling, turned on his heals and sauntered away from our table.

She sprinkled Parmesan cheese on her pasta. "You know that lunatic Harry Trunk sent me a letter the other day."

"Does he send you letters often?"

"No, no, just the one. It was very sweet though. He said that going to the funny farm was the best thing that ever happened to him. He told me about his emotional progress and thanked me for my part in forcing him to get help."

"What was your part?"

"I don't know exactly, except maybe providing a house into which he could shoot holes. But, here's another piece. He sent me a heartfelt apology for all the dirty tricks he'd pulled over the years. He asked if there was any way he could make it up to me."

"Wow, what a turnabout."

She grinned. "The best part of all is, of all people, he's learned to dance the Flamenco."

We sat through another awkward moment then Cassandra asked, "How's your new drug store?"

"It's great. I wasn't sure if I was going to have the energy to rebuild after the flood. With Harry's settlement and the minuscule amount of insurance I got, I was able to lease a storefront out by the new mall.

"The day I decided to open another store, an energetic young man sent me a letter saying he'd just graduated from Sacramento pharmaceutical collage and he wanted to work with me. I agreed to make him a full partner if he would set the store up. It's been open four months. With my experience and his business school savvy, we're giving the big discount guys a run for their money."

A long silence passed while we ate pasta and garlic bread. I asked, "heard anything about Billy's young girlfriend?"

"I got a letter from Tammy last summer. She took Harry's money and went to nursing school. She'll graduate at the end of this year."

"Another symmetric ending. She's a natural as a nurse."

A minute went by as we ate and finished our wine. My eyes perked up. "The other day I heard about the cameraman and his sidekick."

"Oh sure, Henry and Shawn, I remember."

"Last week they chucked their jobs, went to San Francisco and got married. They'd been lovers for six years and no one knew."

She smiled. "You know, the way Henry protected Shawn during those tense moments, it makes sense."

When lunch was cleared, Cassandra asked, "I haven't heard about Yamelda Keating since our little incident."

I finished my bite of pasta. "Yamelda is the only sad story. Apparently, she'd never been in love before she met Billy. Once she fell for him and he disappeared, her whole life crumbled. When she heard that Billy and Sundog had left the country, she tossed her job and took a plane to Peru. The first time she went, she couldn't find him."

"Wasn't he in jail?"

"Yes, but it took a few months for the information get back to the states. During that time, she searched every little town and village. When she returned, the town was just getting wind of the duo."

"The day she found out, she booked a second flight for Peru. It was the last Marysville's seen of Yamelda Keating."

Cassandra lifted her wineglass in salute. "Ah yes, a woman in love is unstoppable."

THE END

Other Books in Print by Nik C. Colyer

"This compelling adventure series teaches solid ways men and women can be together and enrich their lives."

Bill Kauth Author and co-founder of New Warrior Training

Channeling Biker Bob 4 part series
Nik C. Colyer's

Avaliable through

Singing Reed Press

www.NikColyer.com

Nik's Favorite Story

"... a very interesting metaphysical science fiction novel structured around the soft science of psychology, sociology and futurism. The plot is fast paced and shoots off in unexpected directions." Bob Spears Grit Lit

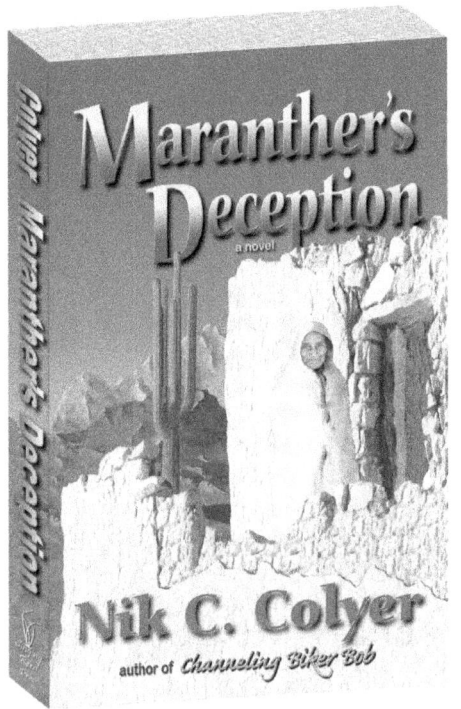

"Nik Colyer's poetry is so emotionally honest it shoots directly into one's own heart. His raw, naked truths touch that hidden place we all share. Never a dull moment, his poems are evidence of a life fully lived."

Will Staple - Author of I *Hate The Men You Sleep With*

**Available through
Singing Reed Press**

www.NikColyer.com

Trillian Rising

Jason Oakley's Jungle vacation turns to a nightmare when his buddy smuggles a gold medallion out of the Amazon.
The cursed medallion is both the cause of a world wide pandemic and the only hope for life saving vaccine.
Time is of the essence, and for Jason time is running out.

Available through
Singing Reed Press
www.NikColyer.com

Books to be published by
Nik C. Colyer

Flamenco Flood Discusion Guide

1. Billy Marlin represented who?
2. Why was Sundog Billy's hero?
3. Why couldn't Billy "score" with older women?
4. Why were Billy and Yamelda a perfect match?
5. Harry Trunk represented who?
6. Why was Marylou bitter and why did dance help?
7. Why did she raise chickens?
8. Why did Marie and Sam seem so ill matched?
9. How did Sam finally win her over?
10. The flood represented what?
11. Why the name Sundog?
12. Why was Tammy finished with Billy?
13. Why did Yamelda fit in at Clancy's?
14. Why did Billy pull away from Yamelda?
15. What caused Harry to go off the deep end?
16. Why blame Stallworth?
17. Why Flamenco dancing?
18. How many chickens?
19. Why Billy and Yamelda's sexual violence?
20. Why not jail for Harry Trunk?
21. What was Dickerman's big embarrasment?
22. Who finally took the gun from Harry?
23. Why did Harry send his letter of appology?
24. What helped Cassandra leap into stardom?
25. How does this story apply to your life?